STARDUST IN THE TIDES

STARDUST IN THE TIDES

ALYS MYKELS

PART ONE: ECHOES AND WAVES

1

CHAPTER ONE: THE SALTWATER SIREN

The rain in Ashcliffe-on-Sea wasn't a gentle weep, it was a full-blown, theatrical outpouring that seemed to echo the vibe of the grey and mournful sky. It smeared the cobblestones of the High Street, reflecting the faded charm of the buildings – pastel coloured shopfronts clinging precariously to life, a church with a sadly drooping spire, and a general air of remembering past glories rather than bustling with fresh, new life. The wind whipped across the harbour, carrying the scent of salt and something vaguely ancient, like damp seaweed infused with forgotten dreams.

Stella Sinclair hadn't intended on ending up in Ashcliffe-on-Sea, but, really, what could go wrong in a small Kentish seaside town, handily placed on the London trainline? A desperate need to escape the suffocating shadow of her past had forced her with her two huge and battered suitcases (one full of clothes, the other packed with boots and vintage musical paraphernalia) and her trusty guitar on her back to take the train away from London, her home of fifteen years. As it pulled into the station, the train had seemed to sigh with the weight of the journey, a weary rumble accompanying the relentless drizzle.

Dragging her life with her across from the station to the dilapidated venue she'd pushed her life savings into, Stella realised she was running significantly late. The rain had caused delays to her travel, with wet leaves clogging up the track and causing many sucked-in breaths and mutterings from her fellow passengers. She was still used to holding her keys so they peeked out from her fingers, ready to defend herself should the need arise. Somehow, she didn't think that would be an issue in Ashcliffe-on-Sea, and she smiled to herself as she opened the door to her new life. The Saltwater Siren, it was called, she hoped it would drive both the local community as well as those from further afield to step in and soak up the atmosphere that she knew she could create.

After dumping her cases and locking the door behind her, Stella was back out in the rain, her eyes scanning the streets ahead for the small-business-owners' walking group that she'd discovered online. By all accounts, it was run by a colourful yet delicate looking woman called Krissy. Stella spotted what she hoped was the group in question, the Ashcliffe Afternooners, huddled beneath the protection of a bus shelter. Krissy, looking quietly intense, spotted the somewhat nervous-looking Stella approaching with care. "Stella, you made it!" Krissy loudly welcomed the new arrival, voice pitched to carry despite the weather's best efforts to the contrary. "Come on, don't dawdle, the path to the cliffs is rather steep and we want to get back before it really starts to rain!"

Stella raised an eyebrow, as if to point out that the weather might already have other ideas. Instead of giving voice to her concerns, she fell in with the other walkers and they started to wend their way towards the seafront. With some alarm, Stella realised that Afternooners had been waiting for her arrival. She fell into step beside a rather bedraggled looking woman of about her own age, who, by way of greeting, muttered, "A Leo Moon, perhaps, with a strong Sagittarius influence. A heart full of fire, certainly, but also a tendency to wander. A passionate soul, but not without its wounds."

Shifting the weight and timing of her steps, Stella looked around for another person to walk beside. This woman, with her bright expression and dreamy eyes, seemed to have gleaned a lot about her from... what? A first glance? "You're reading a bit deeply, aren't you? You don't even know me!" she said, trying to laugh off the deep feeling of unease that was settling in her stomach. "How rude of me," the bedraggled, dreamy-eyed woman said, "I'm Eloise and I'm afraid that you'll have to get used to me chatting about planets, signs, houses, and aspects as if they're my old friends!" Conspiratorially she added, "And maybe they are!" Stella looked unconvinced, so Eloise continued, "It wouldn't surprise me if you were running with a reckoning at your heels, looking for a fresh start only because you feel you've exhausted all other opportunities. You have a very distinct energy, you know. Something of a magnetic quality, like a lighthouse struggling to shine its beam."

Before Stella could respond to Eloise's strange pronouncements, Krissy was beside her. "Are you enjoying the walk so far?" Krissy asked, her voice gently laced with layers of concern.

"It's lovely, thank you." Stella replied, trying to project an air of relaxed enjoyment, "A bit blustery though, perhaps?"

"That's what we call character-building!" Krissy chuckled, "It's part of the charm of Ashcliffe, really. Although, saying that, Eve's been grumbling about the wind almost snatching her postbag this morning, whilst Albert here -" Krissy gestured at the lone man in the group, walking next to who Stella presumed must be Eve, "has just finished fixing the wiring for the lights on the harbour. Essential work, that."

Just then, Eve – a woman with a perpetually amused expression paired with a surprisingly sharp gaze – came into step with Stella. Clad in a bright yellow raincoat that even this continuous drizzle couldn't disguise, Eve said "Don't listen to her, Stella. Krissy has a penchant for exaggeration." She dropped her voice and continued, "And Albert's electrical work is... well, let's just say that he has a unique approach to the sanctity of safety regulations!" Recognising what must be some kind of insider knowledge being shared, Stella smiled as warmly as she could. They'd reached the cliff path, a wide and winding walkway that must be well-used by dogwalkers and hikers alike if the flattened earth was anything to go by, and were able to walk together in such a way that the five of them – Stella, Eloise, Krissy, Eve, and Albert – could chat to their hearts' content.

Albert, his face looking weathered in a way that had nothing to do with the immersive rain, chimed in with a small and self-conscious smile, "I'm just ensuring that the town's not going to blow over in the next storm, you know?" When Stella nodded, he carried on, "It's a gorgeous view, this. But you know about that, don't you? You see what this place was, what it could be again, or you wouldn't have bought the Siren!" This time it was Eloise's turn to nod along.

"A tragic loss for the community, by all accounts, when it shut down. We though it would be gone forever!"

"But here you are!" Eve said, her raw and honest gaze enveloping Stella into its thrall, "And here we all are ready to tell you about your new home!"

The conversations continued in a loose, easy flow of local gossip and weather observations, under the watchful gaze of the waves. Stella found herself drawn to Eloise's oddly comforting tones, as she realised that this was a town steeped in stories. With a creeping sense of dread, she wondered if she'd made another lightning-fast mistake in spending almost everything she had on The Saltwater Siren. This was the biggest move of her life, a change of direction that splintered from the past she didn't want to ever face again and the future that she was knew she could force into being by her own grit and determination. The thought felt hollow, a well-practised deflection within her own mind. Before too long, the small group had walked their allotted route and were back at the bus-stop, promising to see each other again at the same time next week.

Stella found her mind wandering as she walked back to the place she now called home. She'd spent the last fifteen years constructing a life of quiet anonymity in London, a performance of normalcy that had become increasingly exhausting. The cosy flat, the record-store job and carefully-crafted collection of records that she just had to buy, bring home, and add to her shelves – they had all been shields to buffer her from that one moment that had wrecked her life. That one song that she would never sing again. The Saltwater Siren, the idea of what she wanted it to become, threatened to batter down some of her walls – it would let music back into her heart in a way that it hadn't for the last decade and a half. Stella hoped that she was ready.

Buying The Saltwater Siren had been on the impulsive side of reckless, a desperate gamble fuelled by a yearning to reclaim something. Was it the pushed-down memory of music filling and fulfilling her, or merely a sense of purpose that she'd so long kept an empty spot for in her head? Stella wasn't sure. She'd sold everything she'd collected, loved, and held dear, records included, to buy the building she now stood, dripping, inside. It wasn't just a business venture, it was a symbolic act – a defiant rejection of the ghosts that clung to her. Stella envisioned the place as a sanctuary, a place where she could not only open the floodgates of her soul and being to write music again, but where she could showcase the best of the local scene that she hoped to create. If it ended up that she could truly feel like herself again by the time it opened, then so much the better!

Now, though, after meeting some of the community that she'd thrust herself into, a seed of doubt had been planted. Eloise's pronouncements about her character, teamed with Krissy's overly-concerned attitude, were clearly not just random chatter. There was a current running beneath the surface of this small seaside town, ancient and unsettling and somehow linked to the feeling she had now as she forced sodden suede trainers off her aching feet. She remembered the last thing that Eloise had said to her before the group went their separate ways. "You're carrying a lot, you know. More than you let on," she had said, speaking low and yet somehow as clear as a gull's screech. Stella had instinctively recoiled, a wave of defensive anger threatening to burst out, "I'm perfectly fine," she'd snapped, sharper than intended, "I'm just starting over."

The lie had tasted all kinds of bitter on her tongue, leaving an aftertaste that still lingered. She glanced down at her hands, tracing the lines etched into her soggy palms, and sighed at the thought of her life mapped out in those shadowy creases. Stella knew better than anyone that the past wasn't something a person could simply run away from to start over, it followed you: a persistent echo thundering its opinions until they were all you could hear reverberating. She raised her eyes to the window, noting the continued rain, and was struck by a new and devastating thought – maybe The Saltwater Siren wasn't a sanctuary. Maybe it was a trap. A flash of lightning illuminated the harbour and, with it, Stella felt a jolt of something primal – a recognition, a resonance, that her arrival in Ashcliffe-on-Sea might be more to do with running away than with starting afresh.

The following morning dawned grey and hesitant, as though the previous night's rain hadn't quite relinquished its grip on the sky. Stella awoke in the living quarters above The Saltwater Siren, not with the smug satisfaction of a successful arrival, but instead with a sense of bruised anticipation. The building was still damp from its time spent empty of life, the air thick with the scent of salt and wood, a low hum of electricity buzzed from the exposed wiring. It felt expectant, a place waiting for something to happen.

Determined to shake off that particular brand of unsettling feeling, Stella started the practical task of assessing what exactly needed doing and in what order. There was the leaky roof and the tangled mass of wires that seemed to be a watchful part of every room to be contended with. With any luck, Albert might be willing to help her get the place up to code. Whatever problems she faced, she was hoping to face them with a focused energy that couldn't help but bring results. Around midday, she left to grab a much-needed cup of something warm, wet, and intense.

The Chiron Cafe was Eloise's domain. Sat in the window, sketching, the light from a prism shedding rainbows that scattered across the cafe and Eloise both, she was lost in thought when Stella opened the door. "Hello," Stella said, with Eloise starting in response. The cafe itself was, Stella could see, a comforting space filled with the aromas of various blends of tea, coffee, and chocolate. "I thought I'd pop in and see if the coffee is as good as it smells," she said, as Eloise walked from the window to the counter where she stowed her sketchbook firmly out of the way. A genuine smile spread across Eloise's face as she replied, "Well, hello yourself! The weather's been doing its best to discourage everyone from enjoying the outdoors, I guess you're included in that!" Pouring them both drinks without waiting for a distinct order from Stella, Eloise continued, "This blend is surprisingly effective against damp souls."

Stella accepted the proffered drink gratefully, tapping her phone against the card-reader before following Eloise back to the seating near the window. "This is all a bit overwhelming, if I'm being honest," she admitted, gesturing around the well-appointed but empty cafe, "I'm still trying to get my head around the extent of the work waiting for me in the Siren."

"It's a great old building," Eloise said, "with so much character and warmth." She paused, waiting for Stella's input, but realising that the new woman in town was taking deep gulps of her drink rather than replying, she continued, "You're so calm about it all. We don't get a lot of newcomers, but the ones who do appear are generally somewhat taken aback by the mix of odd weather, endless gossip, and strict council regulations that this town enjoys." Stella wasn't sure exactly how enjoyable that sounded, and when she remarked as much, Eloise let loose a throaty and earthy laugh.

"Would you like me to read your chart, see if we can't work out exactly how your new life in the Siren is going to turn out?" she offered. Stella was quick to respond with "No, that won't be necessary." When Eloise couldn't hide the hurt in her eyes, Stella continued, "I'm just trying to start over, no need to bring all that weird destiny stuff into it. Besides," she shrugged, "all I know is that I'm a Sagittarius." Eloise's smile beamed at that, "I knew it!". She pulled a business card out of her floral dungarees and handed it to Stella. "Pop your date, time, and place of birth on that and I'll do the rest!". Stella did as she was told, hoping that this strangely captivating woman would stop talking about the stars if she just acquiesced.

"Leaving the past is a difficult thing to do," Eloise continued quietly, as she stowed the newly-informative card back in her pocket, "because it tends to resurface whether you want it to or not until you learn its lessons. It's like a current, pulling you ever back into its depths despite you trying your best to swim away." She tapped her pocket and continued, "I just run this cafe to pay the bills, my true calling is astrology." Stella couldn't help rolling her eyes, causing Eloise to continue with more gusto, "I don't see charts as mere predictions, though, I feel as if they're a map of a person's potential which highlight your challenges, pursuits, and hidden truths. I believe that everyone carries a story within them that's just waiting to be unearthed. What, I wonder, will your story be?"

As if on cue, the bell above The Chiron Cafe's door jingled, announcing the arrival of Krissy, with Albert and Eve hot on her heels. A sense of quiet anticipation settled over the cafe, a palpable shift in atmosphere that suggested to Stella that her arrival in Ashcliffe-on-Sea was about to become a lot more complicated than even she had planned for. Eloise met Krissy's eyes and all but flew to stand behind the counter and serve her regulars with what she knew they needed, rather than what they themselves might think they wanted! In The Chiron Cafe, there were no menus – Eloise decided what was served and to whom, and the residents of Ashcliffe-on-Sea happily accepted her guidance – both in beverage choices and the stars!

Stella continued to drink her strong cup of coffee in the window seat next to the one that Eloise had just vacated. She watched the rain, and would have tried harder not to eavesdrop on the conversation at the counter if they hadn't all – except for Eloise – been carrying on quite so dramatically. This cosy place, with its mingling scent of spices, coffee beans, sweet treats, and tarot decks, seemed at odds with the scene that Stella could hear unfolding. Eve kept telling Krissy to calm down, to breathe, whilst Albert got Eloise up to speed. "You were right, obviously, about him feeling connected to someone else. He's married," Albert paused here as the words clattered across the counter in a sudden silence, "and he's hoping to introduce Krissy to his wife! I kid you not!" Immediately, Stella heard the click and tap of fingers on a laptop's keyboard.

"How you made head or tail of all of these colours and symbols, I'll never know," Stella heard Krissy say to Eloise, who had apparently brought up Krissy's natal chart on her laptop ready for an impromptu reading on the current situation, "but however you manage it – I'd be grateful for any of your advice and insight."

A wave of silence buffeted into Stella as it felt like the whole cafe held its breath. Eventually, after the passage of two seemingly never-ending minutes, Eloise began to speak, "Venus in Scorpio is a huge key player here – it's not that you want to be with someone, it's more like you want to be completely submerged in their tidal pull. You crave connection, deep emotional currents."

Stella heard the blush in Krissy's voice as she slowly replied, "I just... I like feeling seen, you know? Like there's a whole world of understanding between us."

"Exactly! Now, the Scorpio Venus could be being amplified by your Sagittarius Ascendant – you might be feeling drawn to adventure and new experiences in relationships... perhaps a willingness to try anything once?" Eloise drummed her fingers on the counter. "It suggests a real willingness to challenge traditional ideas about love." Stella, still nestled in the window seat, took a slow sip of her coffee with quiet amusement. The rain intensified, a steady rhythm against the glass. "See!" Eloise exclaimed triumphantly. "Don't sleep on your Jupiter in Pisces, it could be wonderful for this dynamic as it can highlight a love that's huge – expansive, in fact – and steeped in compassionate depths."

"Those compassionate depths are telling me that I might just be destined to have a boyfriend and his wife as well as a rescue dog, if I'm hearing you correctly?"

"Possibly!" Eloise gently responded. "It depends on whether you're willing to let go of control and trust the flow."

"Don't get too attached to the rescue dog. In my experience, they tend to run off as soon as the front gate is opened," Eve darkly observed.

Stella, finishing her coffee, rose gracefully from her comfily-faded chair. It seems – she thought, a slight smile playing on her lips – that the universe is already setting someone up for something quite lovely. She paused at the door, turning back briefly to capture the image of the three friends surrounding Eloise's dark blue laptop on the counter of The Chiron Cafe. Lovely, although perhaps just a little bit complicated.

As Stella squelched back to The Saltwater Siren, back "home" as she was desperately trying to reframe the place, she ruminated on just how peculiar a town this was. It was nowhere like she'd experienced before, and in her music career she'd played gigs across the world in two-bit venues and sold-out arenas alike. Despite that, she'd never played in a venue quite like The Saltwater Siren, nor had she ever stepped off the train in a town quite like Ashcliffe-on-Sea. Is this the kind of thing that normal people do, Stella wondered, when they start afresh? Abandon the life they knew entirely and rock up to a constantly raining seaside town that is, quite frankly, more seaside than town? She hurried her steps, nearly slipped on the soggy cobblestones and audibly thanked her love of heavy walking boots that kept her from falling flat on her face. Relieved, she pushed her key into the door, locked it tightly behind her, and sighed. This was going to be a lot, she could tell. Luckily, she'd dealt with a hell of a lot before.

Freeing her feet from their solid boots, Stella shook her head at the puddles of water she'd tramped in. "Although, I don't know how much more water I could drag in than what's leaking through already," she mumbled to herself, as if in answer to the building's unspoken judgement. She'd spent most of her adult life trying not to be noticed, yet here she was trying to build something designed to be seen. Heard. Felt. A sound from upstairs startled her. Not the usual creak of settling floors or the sigh of coastal wind through loose panes. No, this was deliberate. Measured. A footstep?

Quickly, quietly, she began to walk in her socked feet up the winding stairs that led to the living space above the sprawling venue. Nothing. But she couldn't shake the feeling that caused the hair on her arms to be standing to attention, that sang to the low coil of adrenaline unspooling in her belly. She took a deep breath, shrugged it off with more bravado than she felt, and said aloud to the empty building, "I'm here now, and there's nothing to be jumpy about. This is a fresh start for you, Saltwater Siren, as much as for myself." She perched on the corner of the old, metal-framed bed that had been here when she arrived, and unzipped her two suitcases. Everything that she'd decided she could bring from her old life into this one was there looking back out at her. Conspicuously absent from her suitcases was her guitar, which had it's own battered and sticker-laden case laid behind her on the bed. Stella turned and reached for her instrument now, almost without realising it she unfastened it and ran her fingers over the strings. It had been years since she'd properly played. She hadn't expected it to ache so much.

She strummed once. The note rang out, flat at first, then true. Outside, the rain eased slightly, the sky lightening to a steely blue. For the first time since her arrival, Stella let the sound of the chord hang in the air without rushing to fill the silence after it. Maybe, she thought, The Saltwater Siren wasn't a trap. Maybe it was an invitation.

2

CHAPTER TWO: A TANGLE OF WIRES

Albert arrived with a spring in his step and a canvas toolbag that looked as though it had been through two world wars and a house fire at the very least. His glasses were fogged from the sea mist, and his well-worn boots squeaked on the tiled hallway floor as he stepped in. "God's teeth, this place," he breathed, reverently. "Look at the brickwork. Look at that cornicing. You don't see detail like that any more. Absolute joy." Stella smiled, a little unsure, and found herself nodding along before sheepishly offering, "Well, it needs a lot of work."

Albert gave her a long and shred look over his glasses, already unrolling a coil of wire like a priest preparing for a ritual. "That's what makes it real. Buildings like this have stories in their walls. You don't just rewire it—you talk to it." Stella wasn't entirely sure how to respond to that, so she showed him what she hoped was the breaker box instead. Albert set about his work with gentle reverence. He didn't talk much at first, which suited her just fine because she had a lot to do – addresses to change on bills, mainly, and all sorts of related paperwork to complete. Still, she kept looking up to watch him navigate the old wiring, whistling occasionally, murmuring the names of components like they were old friends: "Bakelite junction box... oh, you cheeky thing... textile-covered... crumbling, but proud."

After a while, Stella remembered her manners and invited Albert to stop for some tea. Albert leaned on the kitchen counter, warming his hands on the mug. "You know," he said, glancing at her, "Ashcliffe-on-Sea's not just a charming little backwater. Place has layers. You feel it yet?" Stella shook her head and answered honestly, telling him that "It still feels like I've landed on another planet, to be completely honest with you." Albert grinned. "Then let me give you the tour. Not the streets, we began that already with the Afternooners, but instead let me give you a cheat sheet on the soul of the place." He sipped deeply and swallowed, eyes going distant. "There's an old story, long before the Victorians came and tarted everything up. This whole town was once a place where the sea spoke louder than the church bells. They say there were people here who could read the tide like scripture. Knew when it would rise, when it would turn black with grief, when it would offer something back."

Stella leaned in. "Offer what back, exactly?"

"Well, that's the surprising part! You know the story that this place is named after, right? The Saltwater Siren herself?" Stella shook her head. Alarmed at the apparent holes in the newest member of the community's knowledge, Albert took it upon himself to explain fully.

"It's about resonance," he began, "about longing given form. You'll know about that, being a musician." Stella bit back an incredulous snort, oh yes – she did know more about that particular thing than Albert knew. She wouldn't have ran away from the life where she was treading water in the record shop for a decade and a half had that not been the case.

"You see," Albert continued, "Ashcliffe-on-Sea has always been a place that listens. The sea itself, the wind... they carry stories." He leaned forward, gesturing with his hands as if conducting an orchestra. "It all started, you know, with the storm – the Storm of Echoes, they called it."

"And the siren?" Stella prompted, intrigued.

"The Saltwater Siren," Albert corrected, a small smile playing on his lips. "That's what gave us this venue, you see. The name itself is tied to it. For years, it was just whispered – a memory like sea foam clinging to the rocks. But then it became a schoolyard rhyme - 'Listen for her song in the thunder...' And from that came the folksongs." He paused, letting the rain and his words settle. "It's said that during that storm, everyone – every single soul in Ashcliffe – heard the song. Not just a rumble, not just a crash of thunder that rolled on and on... but actual words. Like a siren, calling out, clear as day. 'Come back to me!' it cried. 'My love! My heart!'"

Stella shivered slightly, despite her cup of piping hot tea. "And?"

"And," Albert continued, his voice deepening with the story's weight, "that song... that longing... it didn't just vanish. It lingered in the air, woven into the fabric of the town. And ever since, whenever we have a truly massive storm – one of those squalls that threaten to swallow you whole – there's a peak. Nine months later. A surge. The people say it's her yearning for her lover, that drowned sailor. They believe she cries out across the waves, and her song is so intrinsically sensual, so full of heartbroken desire... it unlocks something in everyone. It's primal, you see? A need to connect," he winked, "to create, if you get my drift."

"Nine months later... oh! You mean there's a spike in the birth-rate after a big storm? Because people don't have anything better to do when the weather's playing up?"

"Not quite," Albert corrected gently, "it's more like the storm's echoes triggers them. It ignites a certain... fervour. The storm's echo reminds everyone of the beauty and intensity of love itself. And when that happens, when you're caught in the thunder and feeling her longing in your bones – well, desire becomes almost unbearable." He grinned, a flash of something more than just fondness in his eyes. "It's quite remarkable, really, especially how now it's all linked to Eloise," he added, as if he couldn't help bringing her name to his lips rather than as an afterthought. "Eloise knows when the big storms are coming. She reads the sky like a book. She says she can feel her influence – that siren song – building before we even see the clouds."

Stella considered this. "So, it's not just a coincidence – everyone's suddenly fertile when there's a storm? You think it's… literal?"

"I believe so," Albert said, his gaze meandering from Stella's incredulous eyes to the window behind her where he could see the grey horizon looming. "I think her longing is so powerful, so beautifully tragic, that it has shaped our town for centuries. It's beautiful and terrifying all at once – a reminder that even in the face of loss, there can be creation." Stella felt a chill crawl up her spine, though the kitchen was warm. Albert smiled at her reaction. " Of course, most people in most places will tell you that folklore is all stories. But here, stories leave marks. This place, for instance, has got a peculiar energy. Not bad. But alert. Like it's waiting for something."
"You mean like an electrical fire?"

Albert winced, "No, lass. Like it's listening."

Stella hesitated. "You believe all that?"

"I believe places remember," Albert said softly. "People forget. Bricks don't."
They returned to their tasks – him to the wiring and her to completing the endless barrage of paperwork that somehow didn't feel less like work just because it was part of this fresh start. Something had shifted in Stella's perception, though. The creaks of the old floorboards sounded more deliberate. The wind through the flue seemed almost like a breath. The Saltwater Siren was no longer just a project for Stella, it was a character in her story – a note in her own song. "How did that schoolyard rhyme go, Albert? Do you remember?"

"Remember? Why, I've made a bit of a hobby out of collecting the scraps that tell the tale of the Storm of Echoes. If you're interested, I can bring some bits and bobs over to The Chiron Cafe and show you?"

"That would be great! Maybe I can use some of your insights in renovating this place – and I don't just mean the wiring. I want to create an authentic venue that speaks to the community in a language they'll understand and warm to, and now I have a feeling that The Saltwater Siren and the Storm of Echoes should face the world hand in hand." Stella got up, stretched, and walked over to admire Albert's notes, "Thank you, you've given me a lot to think about."

Recognising a dismissal when he heard one, no matter how politely it was offered, Albert nodded and promised, "I'll type these up into something legible to give you an idea of the scale – and price-range – of the work that needs doing, and in what order." His eyes, dark as a stormcloud, settled on Stella's face so long that she blushed hurriedly. "Shall we reconvene tomorrow? At The Chiron Cafe?" Before Stella could respond, he continued, "I'll bring those rhymes, folksongs, and anything else I can carry along with the plan of action for this gorgeous place." His notebook stowed in his bag that had definitely seen better days, Albert bid Stella goodbye.

The shadows lengthened as the day turned to evening, and Stella felt accomplished with the amount she had managed to complete: from banks and direct debits, to changes of address in every imaginable place she'd ever touched in with – she truly felt as if the move was complete. Her life, what little she'd carried forward from London anyway, was now fully oriented in this folklore-rich town. She went back upstairs and looked at her guitar. It was almost the oldest guitar she'd ever owned – not quite as far back as the one she'd learned to play on, but instead the first real instrument that she'd painstakingly searched out, chosen, saved up for, and cherished. Even though her fingers hadn't been called to rattle across its strings properly in years, she still found that she couldn't sell it like she did with the rest of the things that tied her to London, to Alanna. Alanna Brooke – her name sounded like a foghorn in her mind, ricocheting over her thoughts until she was back there, back reading that awful article in The Quill for the first time. Now, of course, she could just about quote it word for word – she'd read it so many times that it almost felt like an intrinsic part of her being at this point.

If not for Alanna's article – her damning dissection of not only Stella's music and musical ability but also her emotional vulnerability – then Stella wouldn't be sitting on her bed and holding back tears as she stroked the back of her guitar's long neck lovingly. Stella also wouldn't be remembering the feel of Alanna's breath on her own neck as she cried in her arms. Alanna had been the only person that twenty-year-old Stella had ever fully opened herself up to. That Alanna's article had forced a song out of her – the only song that had ever made an impact in the charts – broke Stella's heart anew every time she heard it. It's why she'd nestled herself into a job at a vintage music store for so long, her one-hit-wonder was too recent to stock the shelves, and the speakers, of that particular shop. It's why she came to such a sleepy backwater of a place, more than because the venue on the auction website had spoken to her, at least.

I should have sold it along with the rest, Stella thought as she dug her way through the wires and old recording equipment that she'd brought with her in her second suitcase – the one she hadn't stuffed full of her favourite clothes. From within a zipped pocket at the very bottom of the case, Stella pulled a well-thumbed magazine: The Quill, March 2007 edition. She didn't need to find the page, as soon as her hands tugged that particular edition of the arts and culture magazine unceremoniously from where she'd stowed it days ago, it fell open to a large black and white portrait of Stella herself.

Alanna had taken it from backstage when Stella had been young and hungry enough to have still been finding her voice in bars and clubs across London. So eager to share her music with the world, so ready... or at least that's what she'd thought. In this photo, Alanna had been standing behind Stella, whose brown cascade of hair fell as a waterfall down her back. Stella herself was out of focus, instead Alanna had trained her lens on the captivated faces of the audience members. Sure, the place looked cosy rather than boisterous, but the faces of the listeners made it clear that something special was going on.

The Quill, March 2007: 'Art may be worth firing up the kiln for, but comfort never is' – *Alanna Brooke on life, the lacklustre, and how the firing process fuels both art and love.*

It's a truth as familiar as the grit under your fingernails after a long day at the wheel, really: comfortable love is hardly worth firing. It's just... glazed over, isn't it? Like settling for a pale slip when you could have rich, vibrant stoneware. You need to see that spark – that insistent pull – before you even think about throwing something beautiful into the kiln.

Consider the clay. It sits there, in its riverbed glory, plump with sediment and content. Nice, isn't it? Perfect for a sturdy pitcher. But does that contentment translate to potential? Does it hold the memory of water rushing past, the whisper of ancient stone? Of course it does! And it waits, patiently, for the right hand – for the right pressure, the right heat – to coax out something completely new.

Same with love. The quiet evenings, the gentle hand-holding... lovely for a while, perhaps, if you like that sort of thing to begin with. But is there a true oxidation? Is there that searing heat building, shaping something bold and unexpected? Or just an ember, content to smoulder in the shadows of predictability? I've seen it before – like a piece left too long on the shelf, losing its lustre, becoming simply... serviceable.

Take the bright young Stella, for instance. Her music – all soft edges and predictable resolutions – is like a low-fire earthenware: pleasant enough, but lacking the depth to hold a serious burn. She's offering comfort, sure, but where's the tension? Where's that necessary shrinkage, that beautiful warping of form under pressure? It doesn't serve her, or any artist for that matter, if they're yearning to be pulled, not pushed.

I spent a few weeks orbiting Stella, warming my hands at her hearth - a hearth built on a steady temperature but not a raging one. Her songs are lovely; easy to digest, like a well-worn bowl. But you don't want to settle for just *easy*, do you? You want something that feels like it was forged in the heart of a storm. She's comfortable with her comfort. She wants to sing what feels good, say what's obvious and not shake things up too much. Where's that feeling you need to hurry your hand up to protect it from the heat, but are drawn irrevocably to the flame nevertheless? I cut ties.

Stella drew in her breath sharply, holding back the tears that were battering at her eyelashes from the very first glance at that photograph. The article itself had added weight to those tears, of course. But that photograph? It sang so loudly in her mind that it was difficult to focus on anything else. She picked up her guitar almost unconsciously, it looked the same as it did in that photograph... could probably use new strings, though, to be fair. Perhaps getting this old friend back to looking her best would be good practise for getting The Saltwater Siren, and Stella's own life, back on track. It was, Stella decided, worth a try.

CHAPTER THREE: FLOODED FOLKLORE

"Right, so a vintage venue needs... vintage dust?" Stella muttered to herself as the bell above the door to The Saltwater Siren jingled, a dancing tune over the thunk of persistent drizzle that drummed against the large windows of the venue. She looked up from wrestling with mismatched furniture and slightly damp linens, a task that she felt was – at this point – never-ending. Still, she'd been at it for hours and the entry of her visitor, whoever they were, was a welcome distraction from trying to put some sort of neat and tidy order to the chaos surrounding her.

Stepping through the door with a flurry of raindrops in his wake, Albert arrived. As remarkable as his soggy arrival was his bag, bulging with all sorts of huge, coiled wires and various tools which Stella didn't dare ask about... in case he told her that each pair of pliers held the soul of the person who'd wielded it before him. Or something equally fantastic and steeped in local lore like a teabag left too long to brew in a cup, staining it with its memories. "Well don't you look like a particularly dramatic vision this afternoon?" Stella asked Albert playfully, gesturing to his dripping visage with a grin. "Oh, 'particularly dramatic' is it?" Albert quoted Stella back at herself, took a long and considered breath, then continued, "I'll take that. I can work with 'particularly dramatic' for now."

Not knowing exactly where to look – should her gaze linger on the sodden hair that had settled into dark curls that seemed to beg out to be ceremoniously dried? – Stella busied her hands with folding the curtains that she'd unearthed in the basement of The Saltwater Siren earlier that day. They seemed to have a repeating pattern of musical notes, cliff edges, and dark swirling waves, picked out in various tones of blue, green, purple, and grey. Albert made his way from the doorway to the stage and dropped his tool-bag beside him as he perched on the edge. He tapped his shoulders and said, "Don't worry, everything in my backpack is safe and waterproof – it's just these fellows," and here he rattled his weather-worn bag of tools and wires, "that can take a shower or two!"

"They've seen worse than this, is what you're saying?" Stella countered.

"Oh yes, they've seen me through many a storm, they have," Albert agreed readily.

Stella set down the curtains she'd been surveying for holes, burns, or ungodly stains and, finding them mercifully free of all three, meant to keep them that way. "I bet they have! Did they help you with the quotation for the work here?" Stella gestured around her at the ancient and no doubt temperamental wiring that was already visible in various places around the room in which they now stood. "Oh yes, though it didn't take me as long as you might imagine to come up with a price," Albert looked hard at Stella, she raised an eyebrow in confusion, "I've had my eye on this place ever since the last owner... well, I can already tell that you care more about the place than she ever did... but that's neither here nor there. What I mean to say is that I've had my eye on this place since long before I ever finished my apprenticeship. To think that I'm actually going to get my hands on it is something special indeed!"

It was becoming obvious to Stella that Albert had some real history with The Saltwater Siren, and that perhaps he wasn't the only one. She'd bought the place in a blind, online auction, unaware of its history of ownership as much as she had been unaware of the folklore surrounding its very name. Perhaps he's the key to my feeling part of this place, Stella pondered, before shrugging the thought off. Stella Sinclair was not one to pin her hopes of anything on the whims of a man, even a darkly attractive man who was sat on her stage looking like a storm-drenched sailor from some shanty or other.

Pulling herself together, Stella asked Albert, "Is the quotation discussion one we're going to have right now, or...?" she left her sentence lingering in the damp air. "I don't think so," Albert replied, "I'd prefer to warm up in The Chiron Cafe, get you up to speed with the folksongs and things that we talked about yesterday!" His voice lowered, conspiratorially, "It's something of a passion project for me, the folklore of this place. Of Ashcliffe, the siren, the way that the song travelled through the storm and keeps echoing even today? It's enough to send shivers down my spine!" Silently, Stella agreed. This place really did seem steeped in something more than met the eye. Pulling on the her waterproof jacket, Stella told Albert to "Lead the way!".

"Before I do, let me be the first to properly welcome you to Ashcliffe-on-Sea," here, Albert pulled a small chapbook from his inside jacket pocket, "It's only haiku – and it's only sold in The Chiron Cafe – but I thought a fellow artist might appreciate some poetry about the place you've come to live in." He pushed the humble book into her hand, his own palm warm and solid, if a little damp from the unrelenting drizzle outside. Stella, not realising exactly what was going on, said, "Thank you, Albert, what a lovely gesture," and stowed the book on a nearby table, one that she'd spent the better part of an hour scrubbing and shining up that morning.

Albert watched Stella, a smile playfully skirting his lips and warming his eyes to a fiery glow. He could see that she hadn't read the name of the author, hadn't twigged that it was his own words that he offered her. Shaking off a shrug before it took shape in his shoulders, he took her arm in a gentlemanly way and strolled into the damp street. Did he just come here to parade me across town? Stella wondered, a little unfairly she soon realised. No, Albert was a professional who had brought not only a quotation for the work ahead, but also a collector of fascinating folklore that he was willing to share with her. Albert was, perhaps, exactly the gentlemanly fellow he appeared to be. How very unusual, Stella thought, little knowing that the book she'd received from him held the keys to more than just the town's character.

Albert didn't waste a second with idle chitchat. Instead, he navigated the narrow streets of Ashcliffe with an easy confidence. The rain hadn't let up – a persistent, drizzling grey that seemed to cling to everything – but it felt somehow softer now. The Chiron Cafe was exactly as Stella remembered: a haven of mismatched tables, worn leather armchairs, and the comforting aroma of woodsmoke tinged with something faintly floral. Eloise, her rusty-blonde hair pulled back in a loose bun, was already behind the counter, meticulously polishing an ornate teacup with a practised hand.

"Ah, Stella, what a treat it is to see you again so soon! And with Albert on your arm already," she greeted them, a knowing smile playing on her lips. "Taking your muse with you, I see." Stella raised an eyebrow at Albert, who simply offered a polite nod. They settled into a table by the window, the rain drumming a gentle rhythm against the glass. "It's like it remembers everything," Albert murmured, "this building. It's... almost as if it *feels*."

"Are you always so eloquent about the buildings of this town of yours, or am I getting special treatment?" Stella asked, a cheeky barb sneaking into her tone.

"He makes it his business to be eloquent," Eloise appeared with two steaming hot cups of... something that neither of them had ordered. Albert tapped his phone to the proffered machine as he blushed, accepting that Eloise had a handle on both of their fated orders. "Electricians don't tend to be so well-spoken, or they didn't in my neck of the woods in London anyway," Stella began, but Eloise cut her off – smiling, but somehow still firm – with, "Not his electrical business, his poetry!" Stella's head turned sharply to meet Albert's eyes, the resonance of the chapbook he had gifted her barely fifteen minutes before suddenly coming into focus, "It was yours? By you, I mean? That chapbook of haiku about Ashcliffe?"

"Guilty," Albert agreed, not knowing whose eyes – Eloise's or Stella's – to meet as his blush deepened, despite his weather-worn complexion. "But enough about me, let's talk about the Storm of Echoes and the songs that have been sung about it. So far, I mean," he added with a knowing twinkle in his stormy grey eyes, as if he was daring Stella not to add her own song to those that already existed. Stella scoffed good-naturedly. "You mean to tell me that a violent tempest actually influenced music in a big enough way that there's multiple songs about it?"

Albert chuckled. "Precisely! The ferocity of the wind, the wildness of the rain – they all find their way into a song. It's about capturing the mood." He took a sip of his beverage. "The locals here have been telling me tales for years, I've got tapes and tapes of recorded living history at home that I really should take the time to back up," a look of mild alarm passed quickly over Stella's face – how could he only have one copy of such precious material? – before Albert continued, "Suffice to say, storm lore is a big deal in Ashcliffe."

"Right," Stella said, a little more intrigued. Across the room, Eloise could be heard talking to a local fisherman called Steve (so Stella gleaned from a little bit of eavesdropping), "I understand, Steve, I do... but perhaps this time the tide isn't rising so frantically because of weeping mermaids. You should know, better than most, that the tide always rises after the rain."

"Not like this! Not in years. I'm telling you, Eloise, something's different this year. Something's brewing."

"You don't need to tell me, Steve. I've been plotting the changes in the sky for years, as you well know."

"What I 'well know' is that you've got a set of uncanny abilities that somehow make sense of this town," Steve began, his deep voice grumbling with what sounded like practised ease, before Eloise cut him off. "You know as well as I do that astrology is not an 'uncanny' ability, but rather a set of lessons to be learned. A framework for understanding the language of the sky."

"That's nice and poetic, I suppose," Stella said in hushed tones, trying to hide her scepticism. Albert pretended not to hear, and changed the subject as he unzipped his backpack and rifled through its contents. As if he couldn't help himself, he started talking about his surroundings: "It's remarkable architecture, really," he said, gesturing around the room. "The way the light catches on those weathered beams... you can feel the history in it." He paused, a little lost in thought. "It's like it remembers everything."

Suddenly, he straightened up, his eyes gleaming with excitement. "I've been doing a bit of research," he said, pulling out a worn notebook from his bag, "about the previous owners of The Saltwater Siren... starting with the previous owner, one Alanna Brooke."

"Alanna Brooke?" Stella echoed, frowning. "The potter?" Albert consulted his notes and nodded slowly, "She was quite... eccentric, from what little I can gather about her, so perhaps? She bought the place as an investment – quite a savvy move, actually. A bit of a recluse, though. Neglected it terribly. Just let it fall into disrepair. Became more of a tax write-off than a venue." He flipped through the pages.

"And what else did she do?" Stella asked, leaning forward, trying to focus on Albert and his furrowed brow, instead of on the clawing that began in the pit of her stomach and threatened to climb up out of her throat. "What she did do is much less important than what she didn't do," Eloise chimed in. Stella had been so focused on Albert and the growing horror of hearing Alanna's name on his lips, that she hadn't even noticed the conclusion of Eloise's chat with Steve, let alone realised that Eloise had come to sit with Albert and herself clutching a piece of paper. "She didn't ever even visit, as far as I remember, let alone take care of The Saltwater Siren. She was indeed a potter, how did you know? I seem to remember her beginning to use seaside motifs in her pottery and an article that made a lot of her connection to the tides. We all thought that was fairly hilarious, as you can imagine – or at least a bit cheeky for someone who's never even stepped inside their property to use the local landscape to their own advantage like that."

Stella drew in a long, deep breath, forcing down the devastation that had made its way into her throat and threatened to spill out in her words. How could it be that Alanna was the previous owner of the very place that Stella had come for a fresh start, a new life that was only necessary because of Alanna Brooke herself. "I knew Alanna quite well, once upon a time. Or I thought I did, at least," Stella began, "but I had no idea that she was connected to Ashcliffe in any way, let alone The Saltwater Siren!" I would never have bought the place if I'd known, Stella thought decisively. Knowing what she'd already ploughed into the place, money-wise, just to buy it in the first place, let alone what she planned on putting into it to get it to really shine now felt tarnished by the clay-gritted fingers of Alanna. The short, sturdy fingers that used to delight in traipsing around Stella's own body. The same Alanna who had "cut ties" with Stella, as Alanna had so starkly put it in that bloody article over a decade ago.

Albert and Eloise, Stella realised too late, had been staring at her for some time whilst she'd been lost in the spiralling mess of her thoughts. Albert had placed piles of sheet music with notebooks of careful handwriting on the table in front of the three of them, but before he could begin to get back on the subject of The Saltwater Siren and Ashcliffe-on-Sea's specific brand of folklore, Eloise triumphantly placed on top of them all the piece of paper she had been holding tight against her chest up until that point. "It's all here, Stella!" Eloise said, looking the emotional Stella square in the eyes. "Look," Eloise motioned frantically to Stella's natal chart, "your Sun in Sagittarius is bold and adventurous, it loves a good journey – but that journey has taken you back to the sea. Do you feel a pull of the ocean current beneath your skin?" Stella took a tentative sip of her tea. "I... I do feel drawn to the sea here. Like there's something familiar about it."

"It's not just familiarity," Eloise explained, her eyes bright with intuition. "It's a resonance. The sea is a powerful mirror, reflecting our deepest desires and fears. And you, Stella, have possibly been grappling with feeling like you're not 'doing enough' for a long time. Like you've settled for something comfortable when you were meant to be creating a storm." Albert cleared his throat. "Well, yes, but the tidal patterns here have been remarkably consistent throughout history..."

"Don't worry, Albert," Eloise chuckled, waving a somewhat dismissive hand at him. "We're getting to the heart of it! That 'comfortable' feeling – that's your Capricorn Ascendant fighting for expression! It's saying 'I need to *prove* myself!'" Stella shifted in her seat, uncomfortable under this firework of an astrologer's scrutiny. Eloise, beaming at Stella, continued. "The Scorpio Venus in your chart is yearning for depth and recognition. It's seeking to be taken seriously, but it can also be critical, as if you deeply feel the pressure to show off, to impress." Stella, still shook from Albert's revelation about Alanna and reeling even further with Eloise's insights, met Eloise's gaze but remained quiet. Unperturbed, Eloise continued. "And your Venus is feeling that pressure. It's reacting to the world around it – to the expectations placed on creative souls. It's seeking authentic expression, but also a receptive audience."

Albert, who had been patiently waiting for his turn, interjected gently. "But the folklore of this place points to an interesting interplay between location, presence, and resonance, that music can express so accurately..."

"Excellent point!" Eloise said quickly, turning her attention back to Stella. "But it's more than just location, isn't it? It's about connection.

You're here because your Sagittarius Sun needs new landscapes to explore, and hat landscape is being shaped both by the sea and by your own need to be seen as something more than 'comfortable.'" Stella looked out the window at the rain-swept sea, a thoughtful expression on her face. "So... I'm not just here because of the music?" she said, almost despite herself. "Not exactly," Eloise confirmed with a knowing smile, "I'd say you're here to find your rhythm."

The bell above the door of The Chiron Cafe sounded as a small crowd of windswept customers entered, stealing Eloise's attention from their conversation. "I'll leave you both to it," Eloise said as she got up and made her way back to behind the counter. "So," Stella said, swirling the remaining tea in her mug, "you've got tapes? Tapes of actual people telling you stories about a siren?" She was still trying to process it all – Alanna Brooke, her own astrological chart, the unsettling feeling that she'd stepped into something older and wilder than herself.

Albert beamed, pulling a small, battered cassette player from his backpack along with him. "Indeed! A wonderful collection, gathered over decades. Local historians, fishermen, even old Mrs. Higgins who swore she saw the Siren herself – though she did add a touch of seaweed to her description." He popped in a cassette and pressed play. The sound was surprisingly rich – a scratchy recording of a man's voice, accompanied by the gentle strumming of an acoustic guitar. "It's 'The Siren's Lament,' recorded in 2008 by old Abraham Jones," Albert explained. "'Abe was a fisherman – born and bred in Ashcliffe. Said he heard the song himself one night during a particularly fierce storm, back when they were still using square sails. Here..." He paused, letting the recording fill the air. "'The sea she sheds another tear, for your return, my lover dear...'" Old Abe's voice boomed with a mournful resonance. "Abe always said it was about a sailor lost at sea – a young man named Thomas who'd promised his sweetheart he'd return. He'd been fishing the Ashcliffe shoals for years, and then... nothing. Just the storm and the song."

"And what did this Abraham think of the song?" Stella asked, intrigued.

"He believed it was a warning," Albert replied, nodding thoughtfully. "Said you had to listen out when the wind picked up, especially if you were heading out on the water. 'Nine months beyond his shallow death...' – that was referring to the baby that Thomas fathered on the siren herself!" Albert fast-forwarded with ease before stopping to play a significantly more upbeat recording. This time, a frantic sea shanty echoed out. "This is 'Rise Above The Siren's Snare!' – recorded by the Ashcliffe Fishermen's Choir in 2012. They called it their 'storming song'."

The chorus began, punctuated by enthusiastic clapping and the rhythmic thump of boots: "'Storm's comin' fast to shore, listen out! Hear her singin' round about! Ashcliffe's song will fill the air, and rise above the Siren's snare!'" Despite herself, Stella joined in with the clapping before the song was finished. "It's quite catchy," she agreed, a little sheepishly, embarrassed by her enthusiasm. "Indeed!" Albert agreed, grinning. "They used to sing it before every trip out – to ward off the siren and ensure a good catch. Said you had to 'harry strong past Ashcliffe's plight' in order to make it through the night safely." He fast-forwarded to a spot near the end of the tape, where an almost lullaby-like rhyme, perfect for children, began to take shape. "'Ashcliffe's Siren, Ashcliffe's Song, listen well and listen long: she calls to you, she calls to me, "Come to me now and set him free!"'"

Stella frowned slightly. "And what about that one? The 'Ashcliffe's Siren, Ashcliffe's Song?'"

"That's a classic," Albert said, pulling a small card from his pocket with the words written on it. "That was recorded by Eloise herself."

"Eloise?!" Stella exclaimed, listening harder to the rich alto that she now knew belonged to the mysterious and exuberant Eloise. Albert paused, listening too, tapping his fingers gently on the side of the cassette player. "It's remarkable how consistent the themes are, isn't it? Love, loss, the sea... and always, always a sense of urgency. As if something is trying to be remembered." He sighed before continuing. "It's curious, isn't it? How that little tune has survived all these years – echoing through the storms and the tides. Perhaps," he added with a smile, "it's not just a song. Perhaps it's a calling."

PART TWO: RISING TIDES

4

CHAPTER FOUR: DUST
AND DECIBELS

Another day and still, the rain hadn't truly ceased in Ashcliffe-on-Sea. Not entirely. It was more like it had settled into a persistent, damp grey blanket that clung to everything – the cobblestones, the weathered paint on the windowsills of The Saltwater Siren, even Stella's own mood. She'd spent most of the morning wrestling with the building's interior, a chaotic mix of peeling wallpaper depicting faded scenes of Victorian seaside resorts, mismatched floorboards that grumbled and groaned underfoot, and a surprising amount of dust – as if decades of forgotten dreams hadn't already coated every surface in a fine layer of melancholy. The air smelled of damp wood, salt spray, and something faintly floral, like dried lavender mixed with beeswax – a scent that seemed to cling to the very timbers.

It was while she was attempting to tame the chaos in what would be the venue's main hall – a surprisingly generous space with high ceilings and large windows overlooking the harbour – that she found it. Tucked away in a drawer of an old writing desk, amongst a tangle of faded receipts for fish and chips, half-empty bottles of ink stained with rust, and brittle photographs of stern-faced men in tweed jackets, was a scribbled sequence of guitar chords. It lay crumpled and slightly damp, as if it had been forgotten for decades, abandoned mid-tune. Stella pulled it out, brushing away the dust with her thumb in a quick, practised motion. The paper was thick and yellowed, smelling faintly of sea air and beeswax – the same scent that seemed to cling to the whole building. The title, scrawled in elegant cursive on the front, read simply: "M." Below that, a handwritten lyric, barely legible: "The sea she sheds another tear...".

A prickle of recognition brushed against her skin – a fleeting echo of something she couldn't quite grasp. She smoothed out the sheet of paper as best she could, her fingers instinctively tracing the names of the chords. It was a hauntingly beautiful melody – melancholic and evocative, with a distinct sense of longing, like a lone ship returning to port after a long voyage. It felt familiar, sure, but not something that she had played before. A shiver traced its way down her spine, despite the warmth of the room. She started to play it tentatively on her own guitar, letting the chords hang in the air, experimenting with the rhythm and dynamics. The melody seemed to shift and change slightly depending on how she played it, as if it were responding to her touch – a little brighter here, a little darker there. She felt a strange connection to whoever had written it, a sense that they were still present somehow, lingering in the room like a half-remembered dream.

Just as she was about to give up and put her guitar back in its place, wondering if she'd simply imagined the whole thing, there was a knock on the door. It was Albert, his face flushed with exertion and a smile playing at the corner of his lips. He'd been surveying the wiring from the outside in, muttering to himself about "ancient Romanesque installations" and "a veritable jungle of cables."

"Find anything interesting?" he asked, stepping into the hall and taking in the scene – Stella surrounded by dust motes dancing in the shafts of grey light, sheet music spread out on a table. Stella showed Albert the musical notation. "I don't know who wrote this," she said, her voice quiet, "but it's beautiful." Albert took the sheet music, examining it with his keen eyes. He turned it over and over in his hands, tapping a finger thoughtfully against the notes. "Do you know anything about 'M'?" Stella asked, intrigued.

"Perhaps," Albert replied, a little mysteriously. "There are a few theories. Some say 'M' was the previous owner – Miles Thornton. A rather eccentric gentleman who bought The Saltwater Siren back in 1928. He was an artist and a musician himself."

"And?" Stella prompted, feeling a knot tighten in her stomach.

"And," Albert continued, "and he disappeared without a trace. One morning he simply vanished from his room – leaving behind only his music. Nobody ever found out what happened to him, but I thought all of his work had been discovered and catalogued in the local archive already. This reminds me of one of the folksongs we listened to, do you remember these?" he asked, pointing to the scrawled lyrics, "They're definitely part of 'The Siren's Lament'. Old Abe was the most senior person I could find who knew that tune, but even he didn't know who wrote it and why. Perhaps 'M' fills in the gap!"

Stella shivered slightly, her gaze fixed on the crumpled sheet music. The rain outside intensified for a moment, drumming against the windowpanes. "That's... unsettling," she said, more to herself than Albert. "Like he's still waiting."

"Indeed," Albert agreed, his eyes scanning the room. "It's like he was swallowed by the sea itself." He paused, looking around as if trying to hear something. "You know," he said quietly, "places have a way of remembering things. Of holding onto echoes."

"So you've mentioned," Stella remarked dryly, feeling as if Albert's pronouncements on memories and buildings were the tip of some incomparably massive iceberg. Just then, Eloise appeared in the doorway, carrying a steaming mug. "I thought you might need this," she said, offering it to Stella. "It's Earl Grey – with a touch of lavender. Good for soothing troubled souls and attracting creative energy." Stella took a sip, gratefully accepting the warmth. The tea was warm and fragrant. "And what's your take on 'M'?" she asked Eloise, gesturing at the music as if it was all the explanation Eloise could possibly require.

Eloise tilted her head, studying Stella with her bright eyes. "He was a romantic," she said, her voice low and thoughtful. "A soul deeply connected to the sea – to longing and loss. I think he's still here, in a way." She reached into her bag and pulled out a tarot card – The Moon. "The Moon often represents illusion and echoes," Eloise explained, laying the card on a nearby table. "But it can also speak to hidden truths waiting to be uncovered. It suggests that there are secrets connected to this place, to 'M', and perhaps even to you." Stella felt a prickle of unease, as if something was watching her. "What do you mean, 'to me'?"

"Well," Eloise said with a knowing smile, "you've arrived at The Saltwater Siren seeking a fresh start, haven't you? Yearning to escape the shadows of your past." As Eloise spoke, Stella felt something shift within her – a subtle but undeniable resonance. It was as if the room itself had spun slightly on its axis, as if it were acknowledging something she hadn't yet fully recognized. The melody from the sheet music seemed to swell for a moment, then fade again. Then, Albert spoke up, his eyes gleaming with a sudden insight. "You know," he said, "I've noticed that this place seems to react to music. It's almost as if it remembers the songs that were played here – and longs to hear them again."

"You think so?" Stella asked, intrigued, her gaze fixed on the Moon card.

"Absolutely!" Albert replied. "It's like there's a current running through the walls – a resonance of emotion. I felt it myself when I was looking at the wiring. It's as if the building is waiting for something to ignite it." Stella looked up at Eloise, who was smiling knowingly at her.

"It's like," Eloise said, "this place has a soul – and it's waiting for you to help it sing again." Stella felt a surge of something – not quite confidence, but perhaps possibility, mingled with a growing sense that she wasn't just here to fix up a building. She was here to answer a call.

She looked down at the sheet music in her hand, and suddenly, almost without thinking, she began to play again, this time more deliberately, letting the melody fill the room. As she played, she felt as if the rain outside wasn't just falling – it was weeping.

"Your arrival," Eloise said slowly, "it's...significant. It's like the tides are pulling you in. And that song... it feels familiar, doesn't it? Like a half-remembered dream."

Albert nodded vigorously in agreement. "The building has been humming ever since you got here. I felt it with the wiring, old and full of stories. Almost like it was waiting for someone to play them." Eloise continued, "You have that same quality as the Siren, Stella – a little lost, a little struggling, but with this undeniable magnetic pull."

Stella frowned, "I just want to get The Saltwater Siren back on its feet."

"It's more than that," Eloise insisted. "This town, it remembers. And it seems like you're part of that living, singing, memory now."

As they talked, the rain had intensified, with a low rumble of thunder now echoing across Ashcliffe-on-Sea. A gust of wind rattled the windows, the lights flickered. Albert hurried over to the fuse box, muttering about "old wiring" and "a touch of magic.". "It's always like this around here," he observed, as he tightened a loose connection. "Like the past is trying to get in." He pointed to a small, faded photograph tucked behind the fuse box – a black and white image of a young man with kind eyes and a wistful smile, holding a guitar. "Miles Thornton," Albert announced. "The Siren's original owner."

Stella felt a jolt, a sharper pang this time. "He was very," she searched for the right word, "beautiful," she whispered.

"He was that, it seems," Albert continued wryly, "and by all accounts a talented musician. Loved to play on the beach at night, when the storms rolled in."

"And you say... he disappeared?" Stella asked, turning to Albert, her gaze fixed on the photograph of Miles.

"Vanished without a trace," Albert confirmed. "They said it was during the Great Storm of 1938." "That's just folklore," Stella stated, though even she sounded less certain than she'd intended.

"Is it?" Eloise intervened. "The birth rate spikes every nine months after a major storm. So this town, it needs its siren song to survive and grow." Outside, the storm was gathering momentum. The wind howled, and rain lashed against the windows. Suddenly, the lights flickered again, casting dancing shadows across the room. Albert rushed over to check the wiring, muttering about "grounding" and "ancient spirits." As he worked, Stella felt another prickle of recognition – a faint but distinct melody drifting into her mind. It was a simple tune, played on a guitar... and it sounded remarkably like *his* song.

Stella closed her eyes, letting the music wash over her. This time, she didn't just hear the longing and sadness; she heard something else too – a hint of joy, a touch of hope. And as she listened, she realized that maybe, just maybe, she hadn't come to Ashcliffe-on-Sea to escape her past, but to finally sing it. "Do you hear that?" Stella asked, opening her eyes and turning to Eloise.

"Hear what?"

Stella looked at the photograph of Miles again. "The echoes in the storm. I think I'm going to be able to write music again," she paused, "but only here." The rain hammered against the windows with renewed ferocity, as if trying to drown out some unspoken truth. Stella felt a strange pull, not just towards the music, but towards the whole room – towards the dust motes dancing in the shafts of light, towards the scent of lavender and beeswax, towards the memory of Miles Thornton himself.

"It's all so familiar," she said, almost to herself. "Like I've heard it before, somewhere deep down." Albert, having wrestled with the fuse box, emerged triumphantly. "Just a loose connection," he announced, wiping his brow. "Old wiring. But this place has character, that's for sure. And a healthy dose of stubbornness." He glanced at Stella and the sheet music in her hand. "You seem to be connecting with it well."

"It feels... urgent," Stella admitted. "Like I need to understand. Not just about Miles, but about *it* – about this place, about the songs that pull like a turbulent undercurrent." Eloise, who had been silently observing them, nodded slowly. "The Moon always has a way of revealing things when you'd rather they remained hidden," she said, gesturing towards the card on the table. "And today, it feels like it's trying to tell you that your future isn't just in Ashcliffe-on-Sea – it's part of it." Suddenly, a gust of wind rattled the shutters violently, and a single shaft of light pierced through, illuminating a small, almost hidden alcove in the corner of the room. Stella hadn't noticed it before, obscured as it was by a pile of dusty furniture. As she looked, she realized it housed an old, battered sea chest. "What's that?" Albert asked, stepping closer.

Stella approached the chest and, with a little effort, lifted its heavy lid. Inside, nestled amongst layers of faded velvet, were more musical scores – handwritten arrangements, snippets of lyrics, and a small, leather-bound diary. And beneath it all, resting on top of everything, was a single, perfectly preserved seashell – pearly white and iridescent. "More of Miles's music," Albert breathed reverently, reaching for the diary. "And his journal!" Stella carefully took the book, turning it over in her hands. The cover was worn and cracked, but she could just make out the name embossed in elegant script: "M. Thornton." She opened it to a random page and began to read, her voice barely above a whisper as she deciphered the faded ink. "'The sea holds its secrets close, but sometimes, if you listen carefully enough, it will reveal them to you. I feel like I'm trapped here, caught between the land and the water. Like I'm waiting for something... or someone...'"

She flipped through a few more pages, reading snippets of Miles's thoughts – his love for the sea, his loneliness, his obsession with capturing the siren's song in music. And then, she came to an entry dated just days before he disappeared: "'The storm is coming, and I think it's calling me. I feel drawn to the beach, as if there's something I need to do, something... important. Perhaps I'll finally hear her song in its entirety.'" A shiver ran down Stella's spine. "He knew," she said, looking up at Eloise and Albert. "He knew the storm was coming."

"And he went out to the beach to face it," Albert added, a note of sadness in his voice. "They found his guitar on the sand that night – broken in two. And no sign of him." As Stella continued reading, she noticed something else – a recurring symbol within Miles's writing: a stylized depiction of a seashell, with three distinct ridges. It was identical to the shell she had found in the chest.

Suddenly, a sharp crackle of thunder echoed through the room, and the lights flickered once more. As they did, Stella noticed something new – a faint melody, almost imperceptible at first, weaving its way into the storm's roar. It was the same tune she'd been playing on her guitar, but it sounded richer, fuller, as if layered with other voices. "Do you hear that?" she asked, tilting her head. "It's like the song." Albert rushed over to the window and peered out into the storm. "Look!" he shouted, pointing towards the sea. "There's a light on the beach." As they all looked, a single beam of light cut through the rain and mist, dancing across the waves. It seemed to be coming from a point just beyond the rocks, as if someone – or something – was beckoning them towards it.

Stella felt another tug, stronger this time, pulling her in a direction she couldn't quite explain. She glanced back at the sea chest, then at the photograph of Miles, and finally, at her own hands, still clutching his journal. "I think," she said, a sense of certainty growing within her, "I think I know what I need to do." She looked at Eloise and Albert, a small smile playing on her lips. "Let's find out where that light is coming from." Eloise looked genuinely sad for a moment, but had her features back to their usual friendly shape by the time she said, "I'm so sorry, I only meant to step out of The Chiron Cafe for a moment to deliver this tea – I must get back!"

"That's a shame," Stella replied, pre-emptively feeling the lack of Eloise's company.

"You'll have to make do with me, then." Albert grinned, "Don't worry, Eloise, I won't let the sea take her to its bed." Eloise gave Albert a long, somewhat calculating, look, before she responded with lusty warmth. "Don't make promises about not taking Stella to bed, Albert, you might not be able to keep them!"

Eloise left at the same time that Stella and Albert did, her feet turned to The Chiron Cafe whilst theirs retraced the same walk that they'd undertaken with the Ashcliffe Afternooners together. The rain hadn't let up, but it felt different now – heavier, laden with a saltiness that clung to their skin. They hurried along the clifftop path, Stella instinctively matching Albert's dogged pace. The air thrummed with an energy she couldn't quite place, a blend of anticipation and something older, deeper. "It was just there," Albert said, gesturing vaguely towards the sea. "A quick flash. Like someone – or something – was trying to signal." Stella nodded, her gaze fixed on the churning grey water. The melody from before had strengthened, becoming clearer, less like a single voice and more like a chorus, layered with the crash of waves and the cries of gulls. It felt familiar, achingly so, as if she'd heard it in a dream, long ago.

Together, they rounded a bend in the path and there it was – a small, rocky cove, almost hidden from view. And in the centre of the cove, bobbing gently on the waves, was a single, weathered buoy. As they stepped closer, the melody intensified, wrapping around Stella like a warm blanket. She felt that tug again, stronger than before, pulling her towards the buoy. "It's calling to you," Albert observed, his voice soft. With just those few words, Stella felt understood. It wasn't just her past that was being called back; it was the town itself, and perhaps even the siren herself. The fleeting light, the gathering intensity of the song, the weathered buoy that continued to bob despite its clear age – they were all threads connecting her to Ashcliffe, to Miles, and to something far older than either of them.

As Stella took a step towards the buoy, Albert's hand brushed against hers. It was a fleeting touch, almost accidental, but it sent a jolt through her. They stood there for a moment, suspended between the rain and the sea, their faces close enough that Stella could feel the warmth radiating from his cheek. The rain continued, plastering strands of hair to his forehead and glistening on her eyelashes. He didn't pull away. In fact, he seemed to lean in slightly, as if mirroring her unspoken question. Just as she was about to break the spell, a gust of wind whipped through the cove, carrying with it a spray of cold seawater. Stella instinctively stepped back, breaking the connection. "Right," Albert said, his voice a little breathless. "Let's not get carried away. It's just a buoy."

But Stella was convinced it was more than that. Somewhere deep inside of her, she recognised the moment that she'd just been led to share. Preoccupied with her thoughts, her foot slipped on the slick rocks. For a moment, she felt herself falling, tumbling towards the sea. Before she could fully register what was happening, Albert's hand shot out and caught her arm. They were close now, their faces inches apart. The rain continued to fall, mingling with droplets from her hair as he pulled her gently back onto solid ground. Their eyes met for a moment – hers filled with surprise, his with something that looked remarkably like concern. And then, just as quickly as it had arrived, their connection was broken again.

He stepped back, brushing a stray drop of water from his face. "Are you alright?"

"Yes," Stella said, her voice a little shaky. "Thank you." As they continued along the path, the rain began to ease, and a sliver of sunlight broke through the clouds, illuminating the buoy in the cove below them. Stella glanced back at Albert, wondering if he'd felt it too – that brief brush of warmth, that almost-kiss under the storm. "You know," she said, turning to him with a small smile, "I think I'm starting to like this town."

Albert grinned, his eyes twinkling in the growing light. "It's been a while, but me too," he replied.

5

CHAPTER FIVE: PLASTER AND POLITICS

The local town council chamber smelled of damp wool and beeswax, a scent Stella usually found comforting about Ashcliffe, but that felt cloying and suffocatingly formal today. Dust motes danced in the shafts of grey light filtering through the leaded windows, illuminating the faces gathered around the large oak table – faces etched with a mixture of polite boredom and outright suspicion. "So," Mayor Harding began, his voice a measured rumble like distant waves, "Ms. Sinclair, you're proposing some rather extreme renovations?" He said 'renovations' as if it were a particularly exotic beast.

Stella smoothed down the skirt of her slightly rumpled dress – the only one that she'd brought with her to Ashcliffe from London – feeling a familiar prickle of defensiveness. "More than just renovations, Mayor, to be sure. The Siren needs a full restoration. It's falling apart. And it has potential – real potential – which is something that should be celebrated and enhanced." She gestured vaguely at the faded grandeur of the room, at the portraits of stern-faced Ashcliffe worthies that lined the walls. "Potential for what, exactly?" asked Councillor Davies, a man whose eyebrows seemed permanently poised to declare war on something. "More noise? More music?" The word 'music' drew a collective sigh from several of the council members. It was, apparently, a contentious topic to some of the more elderly members of the Ashcliffe community.

"It needs to play again," Stella said simply. "Not just any music, but its music."

"And how do you propose to achieve this," Councillor Peterson inquired, adjusting his spectacles, "without disrupting the established aesthetic of Ashcliffe?" He looked around the room as if judging The Saltwater Siren's worthiness against the grandeur of the town council chambers themselves. That was always the crux of it, wasn't it? Not about the building itself, not about the music, but about fitting in. About adhering to Ashcliffe's particular brand of understated melancholy. "I have a plan," Stella said, her voice gaining a little force. "A detailed plan. I want to open it up – brighten it, of course – bring in some new wiring, but retain the original character. I envision a small stage, comfortable seating, a decent bar... It'll be a venue, Mayor, for locals and visitors alike."

"And what about the view?" Councillor Bellweather asked, his gaze drifting out towards the rain-streaked windows. "The Siren has always been appreciated for its location – overlooking the harbour. Too much plastering, too many additions, might block the view." It was a predictable objection. Stella took a deep breath. "I'll ensure it doesn't. It will be subtle. Elegant. And I plan to keep the large windows clear."

Before Stella could elaborate, Krissy burst through the doors, a whirlwind accessorised in a bold crimson scarf and even more chaos. She carried a stack of books precariously balanced in one hand and a half-eaten apple in the other. "Right!" she announced, surveying the scene with a critical eye. "Council! You're missing all the fun! Mr. Thornton's ghost is trying to steal my teapot again!"

"Krissy," Mayor Harding sighed, pinching the bridge of his nose.

"Don't you 'Krissy' me!" she retorted, dropping the books with a satisfying thud. "I was just about to tell Stella that Mrs. Higgins thinks the council is made up entirely of grumpy seals." The council members exchanged weary glances. Krissy was, undeniably, a force of nature. "Thank you, Krissy," Stella said, offering her a grateful – if somewhat perplexed – smile. "Perhaps you could explain to them why a teapot is important?"

"It was Miles Thornton's favourite," Krissy explained, gesturing dramatically towards the table. "He always used to drink Earl Grey in it. And he was terrified of ghosts stealing his tea. Hence, the ghost." While Krissy distracted the council with tales of spectral tea theft, Stella seized the opportunity to add the props that she hoped would fully solidify her case. She pulled out her portfolio and began to lay out her plans – sketches of the stage, diagrams of the wiring, a rough estimate of the costs. Without Albert's help, none of these things would have existed, she thought. As if drawn to the room by Stella's errant thoughts, Albert himself arrived. He stood in the doorway, leaning casually against the frame, his expression unreadable as always. The rain outside had intensified, drumming a steady rhythm on the roof.

"Looking good," he said simply when she'd finished explaining her vision for the lighting, nodding towards the sketches. "You're actually thinking about making it bright."

"It needs to be," Stella replied. "Ashcliffe can handle a little light." Albert stepped fully into the chamber and examined the plans more closely. "Just in case," he murmured almost to himself, tapping one of the drawings with his finger. That was it. That small, perfectly rendered sketch of the stage redone – bathed in warm, inviting light. It wasn't a grand vision; it was understated, elegant, and utterly perfect. Suddenly, it wasn't just about bricks and mortar for Stella, it was about knowing that Albert saw the space as more than just wood and wire.

"What guarantee do we have that this 'musical venue' will actually be successful?" Councillor Davies said, breaking the unspoken tension between Stella and Albert swiftly. "I've done my research," Stella said, her voice firm. "There's demand in Ashcliffe and the surrounding villages for live music. I plan to start small – local bands, open mic nights – and gradually build up." Just then, Eloise appeared, carrying a tray laden with tea and biscuits. "I sensed a bit of a debate," she said, placing the tray on the table. "The Moon is full in Aries tonight, which pulls action along with a solid dash of stubbornness." She carefully poured Stella a cup of Earl Grey.

"Well, that's apt," Stella muttered, taking a thankful sip. As the council continued to grill her – about the noise levels, the potential traffic, and the aesthetic impact on Ashcliffe – Stella found herself thinking back to Alanna Brooke. The memory was still sharp, almost painful: the scathing review in The Quill – the article dissecting her career. "It's funny," she said quietly, surprising even herself. "They always remember the failures here. Alanna Brooke's failures, too. As if that defined her."

Councillor Peterson nodded approvingly. "Indeed. The previous owner of The Siren had a certain flair for the unusual. She never stood before us with plans to make the venue sing again, mind you."

Stella felt a small smile play on her lips. "We're very different people, Alanna and I." Before too long, although to Stella it felt like several years had passed, the council had finally – grudgingly – granted her a provisional permit.

Stella found Albert waiting for her outside the chamber, watching the rain fall. "How'd it go?" he asked, his voice low.

"Adequate," she replied. "They approved it, but with conditions. And a lot of grumbling." He nodded. "They always do." He paused for a moment, then said, almost shyly, "I... I once considered buying The Siren."

Stella turned to face him, surprised. "You did? What happened?"

"A long time ago now, it feels like," he said, kicking at a loose pebble. "Before Alanna, before you. Just thought it needed someone who knew how to make it sing again." He gestured with his hand towards the building. "It just felt right." He reached into his pocket and pulled out a small, folded piece of paper. He handed it to her. It was the sketch – the one he'd pointed out during the council meeting. The stage bathed in light. Beneath it, in his neat, precise handwriting, were three words: "Just in case."

Stella took the sketch, her fingers brushing against his. "Thank you," she said softly. He looked at her then, a hint of something – vulnerability? – flickering in his eyes. "Don't thank me yet. There's still plenty of plaster to be applied." They started towards The Chiron Cafe, the rain now a steady drizzle, but Stella felt a little deflated. She'd been so excited about the permit, but now? "You're pretty quiet," she commented as they crossed the harbour square.

Albert shrugged. "Just thinking," he began, but was cut off when his phone rapidly buzzed in his pocket. He pulled it out, glanced at the screen, and answered quickly. "Hello?... Yes, that's right... Right, let me see..." He listened intently for a moment, his brow furrowing. "Okay, okay. I'm on my way."

"Another job?" Stella asked, a touch of annoyance in her voice. He ended the call and turned to face her. "Yeah. A bit of an electrical emergency." He offered a small smile. "Don't worry, I'll be back before you can say 'spectral teapot.'"

"Right," Stella groaned, letting herself lean against the wall of The Chiron Cafe for a moment. "Just my luck."

Albert turned and walked away, leaving Stella to enter The Chiron Cafe alone. Eloise, perched on a stool at the counter with a book and a cup of tea, took one look at Stella's expression and chuckled. "Sounds like you're missing your electrical wizard," she said, smiling knowingly. "He's always off doing something," Stella moaned to Eloise as they settled into a corner table. "And now he's leaving me here." Eloise took a sip of her tea and leaned forward conspiratorially. "Well, you know about Albert, don't you? He wasn't exactly born with a silver wrench in his hand."

"What do you mean?" Stella asked, intrigued.

"Way back, not long after he'd finished his apprenticeship, he was secretly dating a wealthy girl," Eloise explained, lowering her voice.

"Her family were... well, they weren't thrilled with the prospect of him joining their ranks. They considered him a bit rough around the edges, you see. So he agreed to do electrical work for an incredibly low price – the father of the wealthy family was very cheap, he hoarded his wealth – but that meant that he had to use old components in the job." "And?" Stella prompted.

"And it caused an electrical fire at Christmas," Eloise finished with a dramatic flourish. "His girlfriend was burned." At Stella's alarmed look, Eloise clarified, "Oh, nothing serious, just some sore hands. But the damage was, as they say, done. The family moved away from Ash-cliffe, never to be seen again."

Stella stared at her, momentarily speechless. "Seriously?"

"Seriously," Eloise confirmed, nodding. "It's part of why he's so... meticulous. He wants everything to be perfect, doesn't he? He doesn't want another Christmas fire."

"Seriously?" Stella repeated, still a little stunned. "A fire? Because of old parts? That's... intense." Eloise took another sip of her tea and leaned in closer. "Well, it wasn't just because of the old parts. He'd promised her a new chandelier – something with a really intricate crystal pattern. So she was expecting something special. That added to the pressure, you see. And it wasn't just the family moving away that really caused him harm. The local paper ran a story about it for weeks – 'Bright Spark Electrician Causes Festive Fire!' It really stuck with him."

Eloise paused thoughtfully, tapping her finger on the table. "You know, looking at his chart... Albert is a Cancer Sun... Cancers are incredibly sensitive and nurturing, naturally drawn to creating beauty and comfort. But they can also hold onto things – especially if they feel undervalued or like something precious could be lost. He has his Venus in Leo, too, which means he loves to impress and wants to shine. He needs that validation, that feeling of being appreciated. And with a Cancer Sun, he wants to create a beautiful home for himself and those around him." Eloise gestured with her book. "He's got a strong need for security and stability, both emotionally and physically. Oh, and of course, his Moon is in Sagittarius!"

"Sagittarius?" Stella tilted her head. "What does that do?"

"It gives him a huge appetite for adventure, for knowledge, but also a restless energy. He needs to keep moving, exploring, learning. But with that Cancer Sun trying to hold everything together, it can create tension! It's like he wants to rush off and conquer the world while simultaneously building a cosy little nest." Eloise smiled knowingly. "It explains why he's always off doing something – he's looking for his next adventure, but also needing to come home to that stable Cancer core."

"So, the 'just in case' sketch wasn't just about lighting," Stella said quietly, remembering Albert's meticulous drawing earlier. "It was about avoiding a repeat of the Christmas disaster and keeping that Sagittarius energy from sending him spiralling into chaos."

"Precisely!" Eloise confirmed. "And it's not just about the past, either. You can see his Mercury in Gemini – he needs to be constantly communicating, connecting with people and ideas. It's why he's a little bit, what shall we call it, distracted sometimes."

"So, what kind of electrical emergencies does he usually handle?" Stella asked, curious.

"Well," Eloise chuckled, "he tends towards the dramatic ones. Anything involving a lot of sparks or potential for a sudden surge in power. He's always on guard, you know? Always wanting to make sure everything is perfectly grounded and secure." She glanced over at the door, as if compelling Albert himself to walk in and lay claim to this astrological portrait she was painting. "He's definitely a man haunted by his past."

"Well," Stella said, smiling, "at least he's meticulous about it."

"You're very perceptive," Eloise said warmly. "It suits you." A blush bloomed across Stella's face and neck, bringing heat to the glance that Eloise was giving her. "If I am, it's only down to your insights," Stella murmured to Eloise, looking at her through her long, dark eyelashes.

"Oh, you can come back here with your compliments any time!" Eloise grinned. "Fancy a coffee?" she asked, somewhat impishly adding, "I can fully recommend this place." If Stella had been blushing before, the heat in her face intensified tenfold.

"You can serve me whatever you like," Stella told Eloise, "any time you like."

"I may just take you up on that one day soon." Eloise answered, "I get the feeling that our paths will keep crossing. And that's something I'm definitely more than okay with." The late afternoon sun slanted through the large windows of the cafe, painting stripes of gold across Stella's hair – a cascade of rich, curls that framed a face sprinkled with freckles. She was dressed simply but effectively; a cream-coloured linen shirt and well-worn jeans that hinted at an active life, but tonight she'd chosen a delicate silver necklace that caught the light beautifully. Her blush hadn't quite faded, clinging to her cheeks like a shy secret.

Eloise, perched on the edge of a plush velvet armchair, was a study in effortless chic. She had a lean, almost athletic build beneath a flowing, charcoal grey dress that skimmed her knees. Her dark hair, pulled back loosely from a face with high cheekbones and sharp angles, framed eyes the colour of moss – a deep, intriguing green. Right now, they were sparkling with amusement as they watched Stella. "So," Stella said, "'our paths will keep crossing,' you say? That's rather ominous, don't you think?" Stella shifted slightly, tucking a stray strand behind her ear. "Is that a good thing or a bad thing?" she asked, trying for a lightness she wasn't entirely feeling.

"Definitely a good thing," Eloise replied, a playful glint in her eyes. "It usually means someone interesting has decided to make an appearance. Like you."

"Well, I try," Stella said, offering a small smile. "You certainly seem to be good at noticing things."

"That's what friends do," Eloise countered, taking a sip of her coffee. "Or soon-to-be friends, perhaps?" She leaned forward slightly, bringing the scent of vanilla and dark roast closer.

"It depends on how you define 'friends'," Stella murmured, her gaze meeting Eloise's briefly before darting down to her own hands. "Let's go with 'friends who enjoy each other's company,' shall we?" Eloise suggested, a smile playing on her lips. "I find you rather... engaging."

"Engaging," Stella repeated, letting the word hang in the air for a moment. "Is that a compliment or an observation?"

"A little of both," Eloise admitted, and Stella felt a blush creep back up her neck.

6

CHAPTER SIX: BITS OF BROKEN CLAY

The rain was insistent by mid-morning, a persistent, clinging dampness that seemed to seep into everything – the wood of the Siren's stage, Stella's fingers as she tried to coax music from her guitar, even Albert's perpetually slightly-rumpled hair. She'd been at it for hours, since dawn really, fuelled by lukewarm tea and a stubborn refusal to let the melody defeat her. It was there, just out of reach, like trying to grasp smoke – a haunting tune that resonated deep within her, both familiar and utterly strange. Miles Thornton's sheet music had proven more elusive than she'd hoped. The pencil markings were faint, almost ghost-like, as if the hand that wrote it had been hurried or distracted. Miles's chords clung to the notes like seaweed to a rock, beautiful but tangled in layers of history. She'd tried everything: different keys, tempos, even layering her own music over it, hoping for a spark, a recognition. Nothing. It just came out wrong. Each attempt felt like adding another layer of frustration to a souffle already threatening to collapse under its own weight.

"It's resisting," she muttered to herself, running a hand through her damp hair. The room smelled of salt and dust, a comforting combination that usually soothed her, but today it just amplified the feeling of being adrift. The front door, habitually left unlocked, creaked open and Eloise entered, carrying a tray laden with steaming mugs and a small plate of shortbread biscuits. "Thought you might need fortification," she said, placing the tray on the table. "And a little bit of perspective."

"I'm starting to think 'perspective' is just another word for 'lost,'" Stella admitted, gesturing vaguely at her instrument. Eloise chuckled and poured herself a mug. "Don't be so dramatic. You're chasing a ghost. And sometimes, the best way to catch a ghost is to let it float a little." After a moment or two, she selected a card from a small deck of tarot cards – The Tower – its image stark against the muted colours of the room. "The Tower. Change, upheaval – things falling apart."

Stella grimaced. "Wonderful."

"It's not necessarily bad," Eloise countered, reading Stella's expression. "Just unexpected. A necessary demolition to make way for something new. Think of it like firing pottery. You have to let the clay be broken, shattered even, before you can shape it into something beautiful."

"So, I need to break myself," Stella said dryly. "That's comforting."

"No, you need to break *your music*," Eloise corrected gently. "You've been so focused on making it sound perfect. Likeable. Safe. But maybe that's the problem." Stella frowned, considering this. She had always striven for perfection in her music, a reflection of her desire to be accepted, to recapture the glittering sheen of her early success. It was a performance, carefully constructed and polished, designed to impress but rarely to truly move anyone. "I just don't want it to be awful," she said, almost defensively.

"Awful is good sometimes!" Eloise exclaimed, grinning. "It's honest. It's real. You were so afraid of failing that you forgot to actually feel." Just then, Albert entered, carrying a stack of blueprints and a small, well-worn sketchbook. He looked tired, his dark hair slightly damp, but there was a quiet intensity about him that always drew Stella in. "Progress on the structural supports," he announced, placing the blueprints on the table. "The council is still in need of persuasion alongside the constant reassurance, but I think we're making headway. They're starting to see it as an investment for the community as a whole, not just a vanity project for you." He glanced at the sheet music and the guitar. "Still battling that melody?"

"It's fighting back," Stella said, gesturing with her hands. Albert leaned closer, studying the sheet music for a moment. "Have you tried letting it breathe?" he suggested, his voice thoughtful "Sometimes, when you force it, it just resists. Maybe it needs space to be dissonant."

"Dissonant?" Stella repeated, raising an eyebrow. "You think my music needs to sound wrong?"

He nodded, a small smile playing on his lips. "Not wrong, necessarily. Just layered. More complex. Like life." He opened his sketchbook and flipped through the pages, revealing intricate drawings of the Siren – detailed renderings of the stage, the lighting, the interior. "I was just sketching out a few more ideas for the stage lighting," he said, pointing to a particularly evocative drawing of spotlights bathing the stage in a warm glow. "It's funny, isn't it? How a place can 'hum' with memory."

Stella looked around the room as if noticing it for the first time – the way the sunlight caught on the dust motes dancing in the air, the faint scent of wood and sea, the feeling that the very walls held stories. "You think so?"

"Absolutely," Albert replied confidently. "It's not just wood and wire, Stella. It's a vessel for sound, for emotion. For echoes." He paused, then added, almost shyly, "I always thought it needed something more." Stella felt her cheeks flush. She hadn't realized how much she'd noticed his attention, the way he looked at the Siren as if it were more than just a project – as if he saw its potential, just like her. Suddenly, his phone buzzed – another work call. He glanced at the screen and let out a small groan. "This fellow will want to know about the progress on the electrical upgrades." He spoke in a measured tone, efficiently navigating the details of his work, but Stella noticed a slight distraction in his eyes, a hint of something more than just professional obligation.

As he talked, Stella felt a familiar pang of frustration with herself and her music. She picked up the sheet music again, trying to recapture the feeling she'd been searching for. This time, instead of forcing it, she let her fingers wander across the notes, allowing herself to feel the melody, not just hear it. Then, something shifted. A single note, slightly off-key, resonated with a surprising clarity. She played it again, and another note followed, equally imperfect. Suddenly, the melody began to unfold, not as a polished performance, but as a raw, vulnerable expression of emotion. It wasn't beautiful in the traditional sense – it was a little rough around the edges, a little discordant – but it felt real in a way that she hadn't felt about her own music for a long time. "That's it!" she exclaimed, her fingers flying across the strings. "I think I've got it!" Albert's phone call ended abruptly. He turned to Stella, his eyes wide with surprise. "What? What is it?"

"It," she said, still playing, "is Miles Thornton's unfinished melody."

He listened intently as she played the piece again, a thoughtful expression on his face. When she finished, he nodded slowly. "That's remarkable. It's like you've unlocked something." He reached for her hand, his touch sending a surprising jolt through her. "It needs to be broken," he said softly, mirroring Eloise's words, "in order to really shine." Stella looked down at their hands, then back up at him. "Maybe," she whispered, a small smile playing on her lips, "it just needed someone to break it with me." The rain continued its gentle insistence as Stella and Albert stood, a little closer now than they'd been before. The storm forecast hadn't materialized into anything dramatic – just a steady drizzle that clung to their skin and blurred the edges of Ashcliffe's familiar silhouette against the grey sky. It was the kind of rain that invited introspection, that seemed to wash away the dust and reveal the deeper colours beneath.

"So," Albert said, breaking the comfortable silence, "do you think it needs to be broken?" He gestured vaguely towards the Siren with a hand still slightly damp from the sea spray. "I think it needs to be allowed to feel," Stella replied, her gaze fixed on the water. "For years, it feels like people have been either completely neglecting it or attempting to control it, to shape it into something that others would like. But maybe it just wants to be itself." Albert stepped a little closer, closing the small distance between them. "And what if 'itself' is a bit messy?" he asked, his voice low and laced with a hint of amusement. Stella turned to face him then, meeting his gaze directly. "Then it's messy," she said, a genuine smile finally reaching her eyes. "And maybe that's not such a bad thing."

There was a long lull in their conversation, filled only by the sound of the rain and the distant cry of a seagull. It wasn't a tense silence, or an awkward one – just a quiet acknowledgment of something shifting between them. "I used to think everything needed to be perfect," Stella confessed quietly, "like my music. Everything, really, though."

"And did it make you happy?" Albert asked, tilting his head slightly. Stella hesitated for a moment, considering the question. "Not always," she admitted. "It made me successful, I suppose. But success isn't always happiness." Albert reached out and gently brushed a strand of damp hair from her cheek. "Sometimes," he said, his thumb lightly stroking her skin, "the most beautiful things are born from imperfection."

Eloise cleared her throat, "Shortbread, anyone?"

"You're like a walking barometer of good mood," Stella said, smiling at her.

Eloise chuckled. "Just observant. I noticed you were staring at the sea. It's always good to listen to what it has to say." She took a sip of her tea and then turned her attention to Albert. "He's been thinking about that lighting sketch, hasn't he? Said it felt like it needed something more."

"It did," Albert confirmed, a faint blush rising on his cheeks. "I just don't usually say things like that." As they settled back into the Siren, mugs in hand, Stella couldn't help but feel a sense of lightness she hadn't experienced in months. The rain continued to fall, but it no longer felt oppressive; it was simply part of the rhythm, another layer in the song of Ashcliffe.

Later that evening, long after Eloise had left, and even after Albert had gone home, Stella returned to her guitar. She played the melody again, and this time she didn't try to force it. She let her fingers fall where they may, allowing the notes to guide her. As she played, she thought about what Eloise had said – about breaking things to transform them. She began to experiment, adding dissonances, unexpected chords, little splashes of noise that at first felt jarring and uncomfortable. But as she continued, she realized that those imperfections weren't weaknesses; they were strengths. They gave the melody depth, complexity, a sense of raw emotion. It wasn't just a pretty tune any more – it was something with grit and soul. It felt like it had seen things, like it had already experienced so much but was the more robust for its journey. She played for what felt like hours, lost in the music, until finally, she stopped, her fingers aching and her mind buzzing. She looked down at the sheet music, now covered in pencil markings and little notes of her own. It wasn't perfect – far from it – but it was her melody.

Out of nowhere, there was a knock on the door. It was Eloise, back again, carrying a small, chipped clay pot filled with water. "Thought you might need to wash your hands," she said, placing the pot on the table. "And I brought something for you." Eloise handed her a small, roughly shaped piece of clay. "Take this," she said. "It's been sitting in my bag all day. Just play with it." Stella took the clay, turning it over in her hands. It was cool and smooth to the touch, yielding and responsive. She began to shape it instinctively, letting her fingers guide the clay into a simple form – a small, slightly lopsided bowl. As she worked, she thought about the pot of clay, about how it had to be broken and reshaped before it could hold anything beautiful. "You know," she said, looking up at Eloise, "I think you're right. It does need to be broken."

Eloise smiled knowingly. "Of course it does. Now, go on. Break it – and then make something new."

As Stella continued to shape the clay, she realized that she wasn't just breaking a piece of pottery; she was breaking down her own expectations, her own fears. She was allowing herself to be vulnerable, to be imperfect, to be herself. A memory surfaced – a fleeting image of Alanna Brooke, standing in the shadows, meticulously arranging sheet music on a table. It wasn't a picture of triumph or success; it was a picture of someone striving for perfection, trying desperately to control everything around her. Stella felt a pang of empathy for the woman who had once owned the Siren. She hadn't realized then that sometimes, the most beautiful things were born from letting go.

Stella looked down at the clay bowl in her hands. It wasn't perfect – it was a little wobbly, a little uneven – but it felt both real and right. Just as the bowl felt complete in Stella's hands, there was another knock on the door. This time it was Albert. He held a small sketchbook and a pencil in his hand. "I had another idea," he said, handing her the sketchbook. "For the stage lighting." Stella opened the book to reveal a new drawing – a stunning rendering of the Siren's stage, bathed in a warm, golden light. But this time, it wasn't just a simple spotlight; there were layers of colour and shadow, creating a sense of depth and atmosphere. And in the corner of the sketch, barely visible, was a small, deliberately broken piece of clay – a tiny reminder that sometimes, you have to break things to make them beautiful. "It's...perfect," Stella whispered, her heart swelling with emotion.

Stella traced the outline of the broken clay in Albert's sketch with her finger. It was a small detail, almost insignificant, but it felt loaded with meaning – a shared understanding, a quiet acknowledgment of their own vulnerabilities. "You noticed," she said, a smile finally reaching her eyes.

"Of course," Albert replied, his cheeks flushing slightly. He shifted his weight, pulling the strap of his messenger bag higher on his shoulder. "It just that it reminded me of you. Like something that needed a little crack to really shine." He hesitated for a moment, then added softly, "Like your music."

Stella's smile widened. She glanced down at her hands, still dusted with clay. "I think I was trying too hard to make it perfect," she admitted. "To fit into someone else's idea of what it should be."

"And?" Albert prompted gently.

"And maybe," Stella said, turning back to him, "perfect isn't always better." She held up the clay bowl, admiring its slightly uneven form. "Sometimes, a little bit of brokenness is exactly what you need." A sudden, sharp crack of thunder echoed through the room, followed by a torrential downpour that hammered against the windows. The lights flickered once, then steadied.

"Looks like the storm's arrived," Eloise observed in her quiet and friendly way. "The Tower, remember? Change is coming." Stella nodded, feeling a strange mix of excitement and apprehension. "Do you think it's about me?" she asked, glancing between Albert and Eloise. "Maybe," he said thoughtfully, looking out at the rain-swept street. "Or maybe it's about The Siren. About Ashcliffe itself. It feels significant."

"The storm is the key!" Stella exclaimed, an idea striking her.

"Exactly," Albert said, his eyes lighting up.

"Maybe that's what I need to do," Stella said, feeling a surge of inspiration. "Not fight the storm, but work with it. Let it shape my music, let it add another layer to the melody."

She picked up her guitar and began to play again, this time incorporating the sounds of the rain – the drumming on the roof, the crashing against the windows – into her chords. It was a chaotic, beautiful sound, full of both tension and release. As she played, Albert watched her, mesmerized. He noticed how her face was lit up with passion, how her fingers danced across the strings with newfound confidence. It wasn't just music any more, it was a conversation – a chat between her, the storm, and the spirit of The Siren itself. She looked at him then, a mischievous glint in her eye. "What do you think?" she asked.

Albert stepped forward, closing the distance between them. "I think," he said softly, his voice barely audible above the rain, "that you've finally found your song."

7

CHAPTER SEVEN: BLUEPRINTS AND BONEFIRE

Predictably, the rain hadn't let up. It clung to Ashcliffe-on-Sea like a damp secret, smelling of salt and seaweed, of something ancient and slightly mournful. Stella pulled her moss-green, worn wool cardigan tighter around her, the familiar scratchiness a small comfort as she wrestled with a stubborn loose floorboard in The Saltwater Siren's main hall. Dust motes danced in the beam of her headtorch, illuminating patches of faded floral wallpaper – roses, predominantly, a little worn and bruised like they'd seen a few storms themselves. "Need a hand?" Albert's voice was low, a comfortable rumble that seemed to settle into the space surrounding him. He stood by a stack of salvaged timber, meticulously examining a piece with calloused fingers – an electrician's instinct, Stella thought, assessing him. "Just battling this recalcitrant floorboard," Stella replied, manoeuvring it slightly. "It seems determined to stay put. Like everything else in here."

Albert joined her, his movements efficient and quiet. Within seconds, he'd levered the board free with a single, well-placed tap of his hammer. "The Siren has a habit of holding onto things," he said, handing it to her. "Memories, mostly." Stella took the floorboard, turning it over in her hands – it was covered in years of accumulated grime and dust. "True that," she murmured. "It's like it wants to keep its secrets." They worked in companionable silence for a while, the rhythmic scrape of their tools punctuated by the steady drumming of rain on the slate roof. It was one of those moments – simple, unhurried – that felt unexpectedly profound. It wasn't like a scene in a grand romance; it was just being with someone, sharing a task, noticing the way he furrowed his brow in concentration, the slight twitch that danced across his lips when he smiled. "Good hands," Stella commented, glancing at Albert as he worked on stripping away some of the old plaster. "Oh, so you have noticed," he replied with a wry smile, wiping a streak of dust from his cheek. "I do spend most of my days fixing things, after all."

As they moved towards the back of the hall, where they planned to start stripping away years of accumulated grime, Albert spread out a roll of blueprints on a relatively clear patch of floor. They were yellowed and brittle with age, covered in faded ink sketches – intricate details of what appeared to be the original layout of The Siren: ornate balconies overlooking the sea, a raised stage with a small orchestra pit, even a small, almost forgotten bar tucked into one corner. "The Mariner's Rest," it was called. "Miles Thornton really had an eye for detail," Albert murmured, tracing a finger along the sketch of the bar. "He designed it himself, apparently. Said he wanted it to feel like a sailor's favourite pub – cosy and full of stories."

Stella leaned in, studying the plans. "A bit ambitious for a small-town venue, don't you think?"

"Maybe," Albert agreed. "But he clearly wanted something special. Something with character." He paused. "I'm thinking we could incorporate some of these features. Keep some of the original details, but update them for today."

"Sounds good," Stella said, feeling a flicker of excitement – and perhaps a touch of hope – as she absorbed his enthusiasm. "Less fluorescent and medical, more edgy and vibe-filled."

"Exactly," he replied, grinning. "A little bit of drama." He pointed to a section on one of the blueprints. "Original lighting scheme – gas-lit chandeliers. Fancy that."

Stella chuckled. "Miles Thornton really was a visionary."

"Definitely," Albert said, his gaze drifting towards the rain-streaked windows. "Local legend says he performed here himself, before he vanished. Always told tales about the siren – how she'd lure sailors in with her song."

Stella snorted. "Right. A bit cliché, don't you think? The siren and The Saltwater Siren – keeping the local legend alive was probably very good for his continued business!"

"Maybe," Albert said, his voice a little quieter, as if contemplating something. "But there's something to it, isn't there? Something about this place feeling connected. Like it's waiting for someone." He paused, turning back to face her fully. "I started researching the town's folklore when I arrived. The Storm of Echoes is pretty fascinating – a tempest that supposedly carries her song across the sea." Stella remembered their previous conversation about it all – how after particularly violent storms, births would spike in Ashcliffe. "The siren's longing inspires creation."

"Exactly," Albert said, his eyes meeting hers for a moment. "And I think this place has absorbed some of that energy. It's like... it wants to be remembered." He pointed to the stage sketch. "He really thought about the acoustics, too. Wanted it to feel intimate, even when it was full."

Stella found herself captivated by Albert's quiet intensity. "It's pretty special," she murmured, taking in the details of the plans. "For a bit of a wreck." He smiled then, a slow, genuine smile that crinkled the corners of his eyes. "That's what makes it interesting." He took another step closer, and for a moment, Stella thought he might kiss her.

But then he hesitated, as if considering something – or someone. "I was thinking," he said, "we could use some of those old sea shanties for the opening. Something to capture the spirit of the place."

"That sounds great," Stella replied, a little flustered with the echo of what – just a few moments ago – might have been.

Later, as they were cleaning up their tools – Albert carefully stacking the timber, Stella sweeping up the dust and debris – Stella discovered a drawer in an old dresser tucked away in a corner of the hall. Inside, amongst yellowed photographs and faded letters, was a piece of sheet music. It was handwritten on thick, cream-coloured paper, with elegant script and delicate musical notes. "Is this what I think it is?" she asked, picking it up. Albert leaned over to take a look. "Miles Thornton again," he said, his voice hushed.

"The one and only!" Stella exclaimed as she examined the music – a haunting melody, both melancholic and hopeful. "It's beautiful," she murmured, "I'll stow it with the rest!"

As the evening deepened, and the rain finally began to ease, Stella found herself sitting by the window, lost in thought. She continued to play Miles's melody, letting her fingers wander across the strings of her guitar, searching for its heart. It was then that she noticed a small sketch Albert had left on the table – a quick charcoal drawing of her, head tilted back as she played, bathed in the flickering candlelight. Beneath it, he'd written: "You found the fire." It wasn't grand or dramatic, but it felt profound. It echoed the photograph Alanna had taken years ago - the same one that accompanied the article that shattered Stella's confidence. But this time, the image held a different meaning – not of vulnerability and fragility, but of strength and resilience. Stella remembered something Alanna had said in her scathing review: "Comfortable love is hardly worth firing." A small smile played on her lips. "Well," she murmured to herself, "I guess I'm finally learning about the true meaning of comfort. But love?" she chuckled, low and breathy, "I still don't know anything about love."

The kitchen clock chimed nine, a slightly discordant sound in the otherwise quiet room. Stella glanced at Albert, who was examining a pile of old wiring, muttering to himself about grounding and insulation. He looked up then, noticing her gaze. "Almost there," he said, holding up a tangled mess of wires. "Just need to reconnect this to the main panel." Without any fanfare, Stella felt that familiar flutter in her chest again – not quite nervousness, but something akin to it. She shifted slightly, trying to appear nonchalant, but her gaze kept returning to Albert's face. He was handsome, in a quiet, unassuming way – his features softened by the candlelight, his eyes bright with concentration. "You," Stella said suddenly, a little self-consciously.

"Mmm?" he replied, still focused on the wiring.

"You look like you could fix anything."

He grinned, a flash of white teeth in the dim light. "That's my job." He finally turned to face her completely, and for a moment, Stella held her breath. "Want to help?"

"Only if you promise not to electrocute me," she said, a small smile playing on her lips before she continued, "sometimes I wonder if you can't zap things back to life with those clever hands of yours.". They knelt together, surrounded by tools and dust, working in unhurried unison.

At some point, the rain stopped completely and a sliver of moon peeked through the clouds, casting a silvery glow over Ashcliffe-on-Sea. Stella looked out through The Siren's large windows towards the sea, listening to the gentle lapping of the waves against the shore. "It's like it's waiting for something," she said softly, her voice barely audible above the sound of the tide. "Like it's waiting for its song to be finished." She turned back towards the main room of The Siren to meet Albert's warm gaze, feeling a sense of anticipation – and perhaps, just a little bit of hope – that she hadn't felt in years. The restoration would be slow going until the final moment, she was sure. With each floorboard replaced and each wall repaired, though, she felt like she would not only be bringing the building back to life, but also herself along with it. Stella found herself thinking of Eloise and how part of Ashcliffe she was, how crucial to the undercurrent of the community both Eloise herself, as well as The Chiron Cafe, was.

"For a man who is so practical, it's surprising how much you listen to Eloise's astrological pronouncements," Stella said.

"For a woman who is so open-minded and creative, it's surprising how little you think of Eloise's carefully learned skills," Albert replied, with an expression that Stella couldn't quite manage to decipher. "You know," she said, wiping a smudge of dust from her cheek, "for someone who spends his days fixing things, you're remarkably observant."

"Is that a compliment?" he asked, leaning closer.

"Maybe," Stella admitted, "It's just that you seem to notice everything." He smiled, a genuine, slightly crooked smile that made her stomach tighten into a knot. "I try. Especially when it comes to you and Eloise."

Stella chuckled, picking up another screw. "Eloise, eh? It seems as if I'm in good company there!"

"She's quite the force," Albert agreed, running a hand through his dark hair. "Like a perfectly calibrated storm. All gentle breezes and sudden flashes."

"That seems almost diabolically accurate," Stella agreed, smiling. "She just seems to get things – people, really, I suppose – doesn't she? Like, she knows you've been thinking about the wiring all morning before you even open your mouth."

"It's a surprisingly complex system," Albert replied with a hint of amusement. "And Eloise has an uncanny ability to spot a loose connection." He paused, his gaze meeting hers. "She sees things, Stella. I think it's fair to say that she sees you."

Stella felt her cheeks flush. "I hope so," she murmured, suddenly feeling self-conscious. "Because sometimes, I don't see myself very clearly any more. That means it really matters who sees me. They're the ones who have the ability to help me create myself anew."

"That's definitely where Eloise comes in," Albert said quietly, getting closer until they she could smell the faint scent of wood and rain on his clothes. "She has a way of pulling things into focus."

"Do you think it's just astrology?" Stella asked, tilting her head. "Or is there something else?"

"I don't know," he admitted, his voice low. "But when she looks at me, it always feels like there's far more there than just reading a chart. It feels like I've been known, truly. Deeply." He shifted slightly, and for a brief moment, Stella felt the warmth of his body against hers.

"She makes you feel seen," Stella said softly, and then immediately regretted stating the obvious.

"She does indeed," he replied, his eyes searching hers. "Lately, though, I've been feeling like you've been the one to make me feel seen again." He took another step closer, closing the small distance between them. "It's funny," Stella said, a little breathless, "because I thought I was just drawn to you because of the project. The restoration. You're so practical and calm – a good anchor in all this chaos."

"And what if," Albert asked, his voice barely above a whisper, "the chaos is part of the charm?"

Before Stella could respond, a cheerful voice cut through the air. "Right then! Is everyone ready for another round?" It was Eloise again, carrying her familiar tray laden with steaming mugs of tea and biscuits. "Just when I thought we were about to delve into the depths of astrological intrigue," Albert said, stepping back slightly. He turned to Eloise, offering her a genuine smile. "Always on time, as always."

"Wouldn't miss it for the world," Eloise replied, handing him a mug. "Although, I suspect tonight's conversation will involve more than just planetary alignments." She glanced at Stella and then back at Albert, a knowing glint in her eyes.

As they settled down to chat – Eloise launching into a detailed description of Saturn's current placement, interspersed with witty observations about the locals – Stella found herself stealing glances at Albert. He was completely absorbed in conversation with Eloise, his brow furrowed in concentration, a small wry smile playing on his lips. Stella noticed how Albert's hand instinctively reached out to brush a stray strand of hair from Eloise's face when she leaned forward to grab a biscuit from the tray, popping it unceremoniously into her mouth. "So, what were you two chatting about when I arrived?"

"Just about each other," Albert said simply, a slight blush rising on his cheeks.

Eloise raised an eyebrow dramatically. "Oh? Let me guess – Stella thinks you're too practical and you thinks Stella needs a bit more sparkle in her soul?"

"You've got it," Stella laughed. "Though I think 'sparkle' might be a generous description of my current emotional state."

"Well, you certainly have a way of dragging things into reality," Eloise observed, taking a sip of her tea. "A grounding force is exactly what this place needs. And who better than Albert to provide it?" She turned her gaze to Albert, a playful glint in her eyes. "He's like the Siren's anchor – steady and reliable."

"And you're the storm," Albert countered, turning his attention to Eloise. "Always shifting, always surprising, always needed to clear the air."

"Only when necessary," Eloise replied with a mischievous smile. "Besides, someone needs to stir things up a little." She paused, studying Stella for a moment. "You're awfully preoccupied lately."

"I just feel like something is changing," Stella said softly. "Like the Siren itself is shifting. Like it's finally starting to sing again."

"It always does," Eloise murmured, her gaze drifting towards the window. "It just needs the right spark." She turned back to Stella. "And you seem to be providing a rather good deal of that lately."

Silence settled over them for a moment, punctuated only by the clinking of tea cups. Then, Albert spoke, his voice quieter than before. "I notice things," he said simply. "Small things. The way you bite your lip when you're thinking, or how your hand instinctively reaches for what it wants but can't quite believe in."

Stella felt her cheeks heat up again. "You've been watching me?" she asked, a hint of amusement in her voice. "Constantly," Albert replied with a small smile. "It's what I do."

"Well," Eloise said, leaning forward conspiratorially, "it seems you two are both noticing things about each other." She glanced between them, then back to Stella. "And judging by the way you're both staring at me – there might just be a little bit of me in the mix too?" Stella and Albert exchanged a quick glance – a silent question hanging in the air.

"Let's just say," Eloise continued with a shrug, "that I have a knack for bringing people together." She took another biscuit. "It's like, I read your charts and suddenly, poof – everyone is aware of everyone else."

"You make it sound like some sort of magical ritual," Stella laughed.

"Well, isn't it?" Eloise asked, raising an eyebrow. "Don't you think that's what's happening? That we're all just pieces of a larger puzzle, and somehow, we've finally started to fit together?" She looked pointedly at Stella and Albert. "And perhaps," she added with a playful smile, "one, two, or even three of those pieces are meant for each other."

"Maybe you're right," Stella murmured. She turned to look at Albert, who was watching them both with guarded eyes. "What do you think?" he asked quietly. Suddenly, it wasn't just the music or the restoration that felt like a turning point. It was something deeper – a feeling of being seen, of being desired, of being home. And as Stella watched Albert and Eloise, she realized she hadn't just found her own fire; she'd potentially found two very different flames burn alongside. It remains to be seen, she thought, whether this particular brand of fire is destructive or necessary to survive. "I think that I didn't know how much I needed this place until this very moment," Stella said, a slow grin lighting up her face as she looked from Albert to Eloise and back again.

Later, after Eloise had departed – citing an astrological emergency reading with Krissy as the reason – leaving behind the aroma of Earl

Grey and a lingering sense of warmth, Stella was meticulously cleaning up the tea things. Albert followed her to the kitchen, carrying a sketchpad and charcoal pencils with him as he went. "I was thinking about the stage," he said, settling onto a stool near her. "And I wanted to capture something – not just its physical form, but the feeling of it." He held out the sketchpad, revealing a surprisingly detailed drawing of Stella – she was bathed in the light from the window, her hand reaching out as if to touch one of the stage beams. Stella took the sketch and looked at it, surprised. "Do I really look like this to you?" she asked.

"You really do. You look like you've just found something," he said softly, his eyes fixed on hers. "A missing piece."

"Maybe I have," Stella replied, her voice a little shy. She turned to face him fully, and this time, when he leaned in, she didn't pull away. Their lips met – a tentative touch at first, then deepening into something warmer, more sure. It wasn't a dramatic, sweeping kiss, exactly, more a quiet, intimate, kiss that was filled with the promise of something new.

When they finally broke apart, Stella found herself breathless. "Well," she said, trying to regain her composure, "that was unexpected."

"I thought you might like that," Albert murmured, his hand gently brushing a stray strand of hair from her face, an echo of his earlier motion with Eloise. Albert looked at Stella for a long moment, and for a fleeting second, Stella thought she saw something – a hint of vulnerability beneath his usually calm exterior. "It's funny," he said quietly "I've always been so good at fixing things but maybe you're the one who will finally fix me."

"And what exactly do you think is broken?" Stella teased, a smile playing on her lips.

"I think I'm in need a little bit of fire," he replied, his gaze locking onto hers. "I've long been waiting for it to be fully rekindled."

8

CHAPTER EIGHT: THE CRACKS THAT SING

Stella had been staring at the chipped paint on the back wall of The Saltwater Siren for a good ten minutes feeling like an antique herself, slightly faded and definitely needing a polish. "You look like you're contemplating the existential dread of damp plaster," a voice chirped beside her, breaking into the silence of The Siren. Stella turned to find Krissy, Ashcliffe's resident whirlwind of an illustrator, perched on a rickety stool, meticulously arranging a collection of mismatched teacups. Her hair was a riot of pink and turquoise, secured with what looked like a fishing net, and she wore a jumper covered in hand-knitted flowers. "Just thinking," Stella mumbled, feeling slightly self-conscious under Krissy's bright gaze, "about how much needs doing."

"Needs doing is an understatement! It's screaming for doing," Krissy declared, holding up a particularly battered teacup with a chipped rose. "This one just wants to be rescued. Needs a bit of glue and a whole lot of love, I reckon."

"I think the entire building needs rescuing," Stella admitted, gesturing around at the peeling wallpaper and exposed beams. "Exactly!" Krissy agreed, "I'd go so far as to say that it's got potential." Stella gratefully accepted Krissy's pronouncement, like she accepted the chaotic but genuine friendship growing between them, one that felt increasingly precious after years spent adrift.

"So," Krissy continued, tilting her head, "you were telling me about this Alanna Brooke. The potter and general cultural vulture who apparently thought you were 'pleasant clay'? She was the same Alanna Brooke who used to own The Saltwater Siren?"

Stella grimaced. "That's the one."

"Well," Krissy said, examining Stella with a thoughtful expression, "clay can be pretty strong stuff, you know? Needs the right heat to really shine. Maybe she just needed to see what you were capable of burning." The analogy, simple as it was, resonated. A small counterpoint to the persistent echo of Alanna's words in her mind. "I'm still not sure how I feel about it," Stella confessed, "it's a lot to carry around."

Making the two women jump, Albert appeared in the doorway, carrying a stack of lumber and a small toolbox. He was wearing his usual uniform – a slightly rumpled flannel shirt and worn jeans – and his dark hair fell across his forehead. "Right," he said, surveying the scene with a quiet smile. "Operation 'Stop the Siren from Collapsing' is in full swing. Krissy, are those teacups going to be contributing or just adding to the chaos?"

"They're being rescued!" Krissy declared dramatically, brandishing the chipped cup. "And speaking of rescue, Stella needs rescuing from her own melancholy." Albert chuckled and moved towards the wall, examining a particularly large crack running along its base. "This one's been bothering me," he said, tapping it with his knuckles. "Looks like water damage. Probably from the last storm."

"It's always something," Stella sighed, feeling an increasingly – and unnervingly – familiar wave of frustration wash over her.

"Well, let's fix it," Albert announced, pulling out a level and a measuring tape. "I'm thinking some patching compound, a bit of paint and maybe a touch of history." He winked. "This place has seen a lot, you know? It's got stories in its walls."

"Here we go again," Stella teased, "there's always memories in the rafters, folksongs in the plaster, with you!"Albert grinned and started measuring, his movements methodical and precise. "Just like music," he said, almost to himself. "Notes need structure to sound right."

"Glorious as it is to get a front row seat at your flirtation," Krissy chimed in, "I'm here for a reason!" Stella and Albert both gave Krissy their full attention at this. "You both must come to lunch with me, Tom, and Rita today!" Before Stella or Albert could respond, Krissy barged on, "Now, in fact – you simply must come, all the Afternooners will be there!"

And so it was that Stella and Albert found themselves dragged by Krissy to the huge kitchen of Tom and Rita, where Eloise and Eve already stood. The room vibrated with a joyous kind of mess – pots stacked precariously high, flour dusting every surface, and the air thick with the scent of baking bread and simmering sauce. Tom, a jovial fisherman with perpetually wind-chapped cheeks, was chattering with Eloise whilst Rita, Tom's wife, regaled Eve with something that had them both laughing uproariously. It was immediately evident that they were a force of nature – a loud, loving, utterly delightful mess.

"Stella, darling!" Krissy enveloped her in a hug. "Don't tell me you're still dwelling on Alanna?"

"Just reminiscing," Stella said, feeling the warmth of the kitchen and the genuine concern in Krissy's voice. "That article really was brutal. It did things to me."

"Well," Krissy declared, grabbing a slice of lemon drizzle cake, "that woman needs to learn to appreciate good music! What did she say it was? 'Pleasant clay'?" She shuddered dramatically. "That's no way to describe a talented artist! You were burning with potential, just waiting for the right spark!"

"Easier said than done," Stella murmured, taking a bite of cake – it was delicious.

Eloise joined in, shuffling a small, brightly coloured tarot deck as she spoke. "I had a feeling you needed a little perspective," she said, settling into a chair with a contented sigh. "The kitchen is lovely. Full of energy. Speaking of energy," Eloise continued after dealing out the cards, "Let's see... The Star."

Stella frowned. "What does that mean?"

"Hope," Eloise replied. "And dreams. It suggests you're on the verge of something beautiful." She flipped over the card. "But also a little vulnerability is needed."

"Vulnerability?" Stella repeated, feeling her cheeks flush slightly. It was not one of her strengths, since Alanna, allowing herself to be truly vulnerable.

Eve spoke next, as if she couldn't help herself, "I heard there was a crisis," she said dryly, surveying the scene. "What's the emergency? Another crack?"

"It's a metaphor," Eloise explained patiently.

"Right! It just felt like everyone was trying to fix something," Stella admitted. "Like I needed to be patched up."

Albert, who had been quietly observing the conversation, finally spoke. "You know what they say," he said, his voice soft, "the cracks are what let the light in."

Stella looked at him, surprised by his insight. He always seemed to see things others missed – the subtle hum of a room, the unspoken emotions beneath the surface.

"I've been thinking about that storm-birth myth again. It's fascinating – how a period of upheaval can give way to such creativity. It's like," Eloise continued, turning to Stella, "the strongest structures are often built after being shaken." She tilted her head slightly, studying Stella's face. "You seem particularly attuned to it lately."

Stella shifted uncomfortably. "I don't know about that," she said, fiddling with the strap of her bag.

"Perhaps," Eloise replied, her eyes twinkling. "Or perhaps you're about to find something beautiful hidden within. An elegant vessel amidst the rest of the kiln's reckless clay."

"Here we go again," Krissy chimed in, "with the metaphors!" Before Stella could respond, Krissy burst out laughing. "Speaking of cracks, have you seen these cookies?" She held one of the offending baked snacks up - or would have, had it not immediately crumbled to nothing in her fingers. Holding a piece of cookie dust aloft, triumphantly, she said, "I think they've been singing in the oven for too long." As Stella laughed, a small, almost forgotten melody began to form in her head – the same haunting tune from Miles Thornton's sheet music. She recognized it instantly, a feeling like a warm current rising through her. It was as if the room itself was humming with memory and possibility. She instinctively reached in her handbag for her notebook and pen, started scribbling down chords.

"What are you doing?" Albert asked, noticing her sudden focus.

"Just... thinking," Stella said, not looking up. "I think I finally heard the song as it wants to be played."

"It's beautiful watching you work," Albert said quietly, leaning over her shoulder and watching her write. "Like you're unlocking something." Stella smiled, finally feeling a flicker of that 'burning' Alanna had described. "Maybe I am," she replied.

Later that afternoon, after a lunch of effortless chaos with Tom and Rita, Stella found herself back in The Saltwater Siren, staring at the wall where Albert had mentioned the cracks. She pulled out her notebook, opened it to a fresh page, and started sketching – not architectural plans this time, but the melody, capturing the notes on paper with a charcoal pencil wasn't ideal, but it somehow felt right. As she worked, she could almost hear the music, richer and more layered than before. The door creaked open and Albert appeared. "Progress?" he asked, his eyes scanning the wall.

Stella nodded, showing him her sketch. "I think so. I've been trying to catch it – to really hear what it wants."

Albert stepped closer, studying the sketch with interest. "It's haunting," he said softly. "Like it's calling out from a long way down." He paused, then added, "I've noticed that some places 'hum.' Like this building. It has stories to tell." He ran his hand along the wall, feeling for the cracks. "And these particular cracks... they're not just weaknesses. They've been here so long that they've earned respect as part of the structure."

"You think so?" Stella asked.

"I know so," Albert replied simply. "Like I said – cracks are what let the light in." He smiled at her, and for a moment, she felt like that might be true.

The next morning, after a strong cup of tea and a particularly enthusiastic greeting from Krissy (who'd insisted on giving Stella a hand-knitted scarf adorned with tiny seashells the day before), Stella found herself back at work, patching up the wall in the back room. She was methodical and careful, using a mix of plaster and sand to fill the cracks. As she worked, she kept hearing Albert's words – "the cracks are what let the light in." Just as she finished the last patch, there was a knock at the door. It was Eloise, carrying a tarot deck. "I had a feeling you might need some guidance," she said with a smile. "The pull of the Moon is strong today."

"What does that mean?" Stella asked, wiping her hands on a rag.

Eloise shuffled the cards and dealt them out carefully. "The Ace of Wands calls out for new beginnings. It's the kind of card that comes up when you're ready to unleash your creative power." She turned over the next card – The Two of Cups. "And this," Eloise said, "suggests a deepening connection. A merging of energies. Someone is about to open the door for you," she said mysteriously, turning over the final card – The Devil. "Now, don't be terrified of The Devil's wrath or anything like that, this card is here to remind you to acknowledge your fears and shadows."

Stella frowned. "Sounds darkly ominous."

"It's not necessarily a bad omen," Eloise reassured her. "The Devil shows up when we need to confront ourselves. You've been running from something for so long—it's time to face it, head-on. It is the shadow of your past that you must conquer, not necessarily the source of the shadow itself." As Eloise spoke, Stella heard it again – the melody, louder, clearer. "I think I hear it!"

"Exactly," Eloise said brightly. "Now you're listening, you just can't help it."

That evening, after a long day of painting and patching, Stella was sitting in The Chiron Cafe, nursing a cup of tea and trying to decipher Albert's cryptic sketch – a simple line drawing of the stage with a single star drawn above it. She felt like she was slowly starting to understand – not just the building, but herself. She looked up to find Albert standing beside her table, smiling warmly. "Just finishing up some repairs," he said.

"It's beautiful," Stella said, still studying Albert's sketch. "But what does it mean?" Albert hesitated for a moment. "I just thought it needed a little light." He paused, then added, "Like you." Stella blushed, feeling a warmth spread through her chest. She wanted to tell him how she felt – to let him know that he'd helped her find something she hadn't realized was missing. But the words caught in her throat. She looked out at the gathering dusk, watching as the clouds drifted across the sky. "I just think," she said finally, "that this place, all of you – well, it's like a puzzle. And we're all trying to fit together."

"Perhaps," Albert said, his eyes twinkling. "Or perhaps we're each meant to create our own piece of the picture." He took a sip of his tea and then looked at her with an intensity that made her breath catch in her throat.

As if on cue, Eloise appeared at their table, carrying two steaming mugs of hot chocolate. "I had a feeling you needed a little sugar," she said with a smile. "to have a little astrological flirtation, if my transits are anything to go by!" Eloise's laugh was twinkly and clear. "Also," she added, flipping over the cards once again, "The Tower! Again."

Stella groaned. "Not again!"

"Don't be so quick to judge," Eloise said, handing her a mug. "It's not necessarily bad news. It signifies upheaval – something old has to fall for something new to rise." She paused, studying Stella's face. "You're about to have your foundations shaken. Prepare yourself."

Suddenly, the lights flickered and went out, plunging The Chiron Cafe into darkness. A collective gasp rippled through the room. Then, a chorus of murmurs – "Storm!" someone shouted. "It's coming!"

Before anyone could react, rain began to fall with a bleak intensity, drumming against the windows and the awning. It started as a drizzle but quickly escalated into a downpour, punctuated by flashes of lightning and booming thunder. Outside, the wind howled through the narrow streets of Ashcliffe, carrying with it the scent of salt and sea. Stella, Albert, and Eloise exchanged worried glances. "Looks like the siren's calling," Eloise said quietly.

"Let's just hope she doesn't bring a flood with her," Albert replied, heading towards the exit. "I should get back to The Saltwater Siren." As they rushed out into the rain, Stella realized that everything felt different tonight – charged with energy and anticipation. She glanced at The Saltwater Siren, its windows glowing with warm light, like a beacon in the storm.

That night, Stella slept downstairs in the Siren, the scent of wood and salt clinging to her clothes. She drifted off to sleep easily, but her dreams were restless – filled with crashing waves, swirling mist, and the echo of a haunting melody. She woke gasping for air, feeling as if she'd been pulled from the sea.

9

⟨∞⟩

CHAPTER NINE: MISSED NOTES

Stella fiddled with the strap of her bag, unable to settle – a restlessness thrumming beneath her skin. The post had been slow today, but what was new about that? A flash of turquoise caught her eye: Eve's delivery bicycle, wobbling slightly under the weight of a large brown envelope. Stella practically sprinted the last few steps to The Chiron Café, feeling a familiar flutter of excitement – and maybe a touch of foolishness – about these small, often significant, moments in Ashcliffe.

The café was its usual charming chaos. Krissy was orchestrating a miniature food fight with a stack of mismatched plates and bowls whilst Rita's booming laughter punctuating the air. Tom was meticulously arranging a collection of seashells on the counter, his brow furrowed in concentration. "She's here!" Krissy announced, brandishing a chipped ceramic spoon as if it were a trophy. "The postwoman of doom! Bring her chaos!" Eve looked around from face to face and, upon landing on Stella's, approached with the envelope. "This arrived for you... addressed to The Siren, at least" she said, her voice shrewd as always.

Stella took the letter, feeling a slight tremor in her fingers. It was thick, sealed with a dark blue wax stamp – a stylized wave cresting over a single, shimmering star. She recognized the handwriting immediately – elegant, slightly slanted, undeniably Alanna Brooke. "Well," she murmured to herself, turning to Eloise. "Here we go."

Eloise didn't look up. "Let it be a door, not a wound," she said simply, her gaze fixed on her folder of astrological charts, as if trying to call one of them to mind without actually opening the thing. Stella tore open the envelope with a little more force than necessary. The letter was a symphony in moderation, being of moderate length, moderate tone, and moderate sting.

Stella,

The Siren seems to be holding onto you now. A fitting choice, I suppose. You always were drawn to things that needed a comfortable touch.

I trust you've managed to shake off the dust and clay? It's a shame about your music. Pleasant clay without fire, wasn't it? That's what I said. A rather blunt critique, perhaps, and certainly a shocking way to cut ties... and yet I did have a point, didn't I?

Don't bother trying to fix it. Don't try to recapture anything. Just...sing, if you must.

Alanna

Stella crumpled the letter slightly in her hand, then smoothed it out again, as if hoping to erase some of Alanna's barbed comments. It wasn't an apology, not really. More like a carefully calibrated dose of passive aggression. "She's still enjoying this," Stella said, handing the letter to Eloise. Eloise took it with a practiced air, scanning the lines with a thoughtful expression. "A door," she repeated. "Exactly. She's acknowledging you, not attacking. A subtle invitation to move forward."

"Or a particularly well-crafted taunt," Stella grumbled, running a hand through her hair. "She knew exactly how to crush me."

"And you let her," Eloise pointed out gently. "You clung to the wound for years."

Stella frowned. "It felt... justified. Like she stole something from me... or even if she didn't steal it," Stella continued, a little defensively, "she certainly judged it and found it wanting."

"And you let her judge you," Eloise said softly, her fingers tracing the edges of the letter. "You allowed that one article to define your entire career." Stella looked down at her hands. It was true. It had taken so long – fifteen years – but she could still feel the sting of Alanna's words, sharp and precise. The image of herself, caught in a photo from that time – all flowing hair and with an audience hypnotised – seemed to float before her eyes: "Pleasant clay without fire."

"It was more than just an article," Stella said quietly. "She ripped apart everything I thought I was." "And you responded with?"

"Art, Eloise. Or so I thought. The song that made me 'me' – a recognisable sound, if not face – was a revenge call to arms against a scathing lover." Eloise's eyes widened as she put the clues together. "You were Stella Bright? The one with that song... But you're Sinclair now... and I would never have guessed!"

A familiar voice cut through the cafe's gentle bustle. "What's all the fuss about?" It was Albert, nursing a cup of coffee. He looked slightly flustered, as if he'd been interrupted mid-thought. "Just Alanna," Stella said, trying to sound nonchalant. "She sent a letter." Albert took the letter and read it quickly. "Ah," he said, folding it neatly. "A little bit of salt. Good." He offered a small smile, and for a moment, Stella felt that familiar warmth spread through her chest – a quiet comfort she hadn't realized she'd been craving so intensely. Chatting with Eloise always got her flustered with the sparks that flew, but Albert's solid and grounded vibe could always be relied upon, it seemed, to muddy the waters of her daydreams. "She thinks she's being clever," Stella said, feeling a surge of irritation.

"Or perhaps she just wants to see if you've finally healed," Albert replied, his eyes twinkling. "Don't let her words dictate your melody,

Stella." He turned to leave, then paused. "You know," he said, turning back slightly. "I think I'll go and check on the wiring again. There's something about that place... it feels like it's humming."

Stella watched him go, a small smile playing on her lips. Albert always had a way of cutting to the heart of things. He didn't offer platitudes or easy answers – just quiet observation and gentle encouragement. "It's like she's trying to tell me something," Stella said, tracing a finger over the blue wax seal on the letter. "But I don't know what." Eloise nodded, her gaze distant. She glanced at Stella, then back at the letter. "It's not about the words themselves, so much as what they represent. You held onto that article for so long, didn't you? Like it was a shield. You even used it as a buffer between you and your most famous song! You don't even tell the people closest to you," Eloise paused and gave Stella a long look, "that you once wrote a song that defined a generation of people's views on revenge!"

"Don't remind me," Stella groaned, "I'm fairly sure that my lyrics have become memes."

"Well, if that doesn't prove their merit," Eve joked, with a light barb to her words, "nothing will." Eve stood up and stretched before focussing her attention on Eloise. "Eloise? Can I borrow your attention to ask if there might just be anything happening up above that would make sense of all the weird stuff that's been happening to me recently. The lost packages, the flat tyres, the mislabelled post, the Wi-Fi constantly disconnecting..."

"It's just another Mercury Retrograde," Eloise said, with a smile. "Always messing with things. Especially correspondence and anything related to travel."

"So, it's not Alanna trying to torment me?" Stella bounded back into the conversation as Eve rolled her eyes. "Just the universe conspiring to make me feel inadequate?"

"Not necessarily," Eloise replied, tapping the letter thoughtfully. "It's more like she's acknowledging you. She recognized that she impacted your life profoundly. And now, she's presenting you with an opportunity to move on."

"A door," Stella murmured, echoing Eloise's earlier words. "But what if it leads back to the same wound?"

"Then you walk through it anyway," Eloise said firmly, her eyes sparkling. "It doesn't have to be a pleasant stroll. It might be full of thorns and rain. But you don't stay huddled under a bush just because it's slightly less uncomfortable than walking with yourself for a while."

"It's just... she has such a precise eye," Stella said, turning the letter over in her hands again. "That photograph Alanna took of me... it wasn't just a picture of a musician. It felt like she was dissecting me, laying me bare for everyone to see."

Eloise nodded slowly, taking a sip from her teacup. "And you let her. You allowed her to define your 'before.' For fifteen years, that photo has been the marker – the point where everything changed. But it doesn't have to be the end of the song, does it? It was just one verse."

"But what if it was a really good verse?" Stella asked, a touch of defensiveness creeping into her voice. "What if that article—that brutal assessment—wasn't entirely wrong? Maybe I hadn't had enough fire."

"Maybe," Eloise conceded, smiling gently. "Or maybe you were so busy trying to prove her wrong that you forgot to listen to your own music. To your own voice." She set down her cup and leaned forward slightly. "You opened Miles's sea-chest, didn't you? You rummaged through his belongings, discovered his unfinished song... That was the turning point – not just for hearing about him, but for feeling connected to the venue he built from the ground up, just like you're doing now. For feeling like you were part of his story."

Stella considered that, a flicker of recognition in her eyes. "I just... I felt this pull towards him," she admitted. "Like he understood something I didn't. Like he knew what it was like to be drawn to the sea and then lost to it."

"And perhaps he was," Eloise said, her voice thoughtful. "He vanished during a storm, after all. A dramatic exit." She gestured towards the window with her hand. "It's as if the sea itself wanted him to complete something – and that something was your song." A sudden gust of wind rattled the windows of The Chiron Café, scattering a few leaves from the potted plants on the windowsill. Stella shivered slightly, despite herself. "It feels... heavy sometimes," she said. "Like there's this weight on my shoulders – the weight of her words, the weight of his disappearance, the weight of the venue itself: the weight of all that has happened."

"Then let it go," Eloise urged. "Don't carry it like a burden. Let it wash away with the tide." She gestured to the letter again. "She's acknowledging you. She recognizes that she impacted your life profoundly. And now, she's presenting you with an opportunity to move on."

A small bell above the door chimed as Albert entered, carrying a toolbox and a slightly sheepish grin. "Found another frayed wire near the stage," he announced cheerfully. "Looks like I'll be spending most of my afternoon wrestling with The Siren's nervous system." He paused, noticing Stella's pensive expression. "Everything alright?"

"Just... thinking about letters," Stella said, holding up Alanna's again.

Albert took the letter for a second time and, as if to re-acquaint himself with it, scanned it briefly before folding it neatly and tucking it into his pocket. "Ah yes, that little pinch of salt," he commented. "Good. Keeps you grounded." He looked at Stella, his eyes searching. "Don't let it pull you back under, though. You're starting to find your own rhythm."

"It's just that I keep thinking about what she said – 'Pleasant clay without fire,'" Stella repeated, almost to herself. Albert walked over and gently took her hand, his touch warm and reassuring. "Then add the fire yourself," he said simply. "You have it in you, you know." He squeezed her hand briefly before turning back to his toolbox. As he turned, he caught Stella's eye again – a silent encouragement that seemed to say, 'Don't let anyone tell you who you are'.

Eloise nodded and said, "Albert's right. You do have the fire within you. If only he knew how much, eh?"

"What do you mean?" Albert asked Eloise, oblivious.

"Well, our little Stella Sinclair here was once none other than Stella Bright, of..."

"... of 'Kiln Cold' fame?" Albert looked at Stella with a renewed thoroughness.

"Yeah," Stella admitted, "that's me."

Albert paused, looking at her intently. "It wasn't pleasant, exactly, but it wasn't unpleasant either. It felt like... like you were holding something back – simmering. Like the song itself was waiting for the right heat to hit it."

"You think so?" Stella asked, a little surprised.

"Absolutely," Albert confirmed, nodding emphatically. "It's not the kind of music that grabs you by the throat and shouts at you. But it lingers, for sure. It sticks with you. Like a good piece of stoneware – strong, but with a subtle warmth underneath." He set down his wrench for a moment, turning to face her fully. "'Kiln Cold'. Well, I'll be. You know, it's funny," he said, a small smile playing on his lips. "I always thought it sounded colder than it actually was. Like someone had poured in too much ice water. That part where it goes, 'You called my chords a cradle song, / Too smooth, too safe, too sweet, too wrong / But lullabies can turn to knives / When sung beneath electric skies' – that was some shrewdly-observed stuff. Poetry."

Stella chuckled. "Well, Alanna was rather famously of the opinion that I wasn't 'heating up adequately.'"

"Well, maybe she just didn't have enough faith in your kiln," Albert replied, his eyes twinkling. "Or maybe... maybe you were deliberately keeping it cool. Saving the heat for something special."

"Knowing you," Eloise began, having followed the conversation eagerly, eyes bright, "and I feel as if I am getting to know you at least, Stella, I think that Albert is definitely onto something." Albert chuckled as the final words of Kiln Cold stuck in his brain. "*Now every note's a bitter gloss,*" he echoed, tapping his finger lightly on the counter like a makeshift metronome. "That's the line that stuck with me. Back in '07, I think I was still working nights at the lighthouse. I used to hum that part while doing maintenance checks. Couldn't get it out of my head."

"Oh no," Stella groaned, hiding her face in her hands. "Please don't tell me I haunted your lighthouse rounds with my existential breakup poetry."

Eloise grinned and leaned in, clearly delighted. "Oh, but you did. And quite stylishly too." She straightened her posture and began reciting, half-singing in a mock-dramatic whisper, "You wanted war inside a frame... Mistook restraint for lack of flame..." She pointed at Stella triumphantly. "That's a killer couplet."

Albert joined in, not to be outdone. "But there's a freeze that burns the same," he said, shaking his head with exaggerated solemnity. "You know, I think that line is actually responsible for at least two broken engagements in Ashcliffe. People took it as gospel."

"Oh dear," Stella muttered. "I was so young! I'd just discovered metaphors and vengeance in the same week."

Eloise laughed. "And you made them your entire personality. Honestly, it's iconic."

"Iconic in a slightly unhinged, melodramatic, post-conservatory kind of way," Stella muttered, though she was smiling despite herself. "Seriously, it's like hearing someone read out my diary."

Albert leaned casually against the counter, a small, amused smile tugging at his mouth. "You called my chords a cradle song, too smooth, too safe, too sweet, too wrong..." he repeated, half under his breath. "I remember thinking, 'Whoever wrote that has been burned. But not broken.'"

"That's exactly it!" Eloise exclaimed. "There's this quiet power underneath the hurt. Like a volcano that hasn't erupted yet but is very much awake."

Stella looked between them, a little stunned. "You two are impossible. I finally start to open up about my old life and now you're quoting me like I'm some kind of tragic folk legend."

"Oh, *you are*," Eloise said, grinning. "Stella: Poet Laureate of Passive-Aggressive Longing."

Albert raised an imaginary glass. "Queen of Kiln-Cold Vengeance."

Stella burst out laughing, the sound catching even her by surprise. It had been a long time since the memory of that song hadn't felt like a bruise. "Alright, alright," she said, waving them off. "You've made your point. But if either of you starts singing the chorus, I'm leaving this café and never coming back."

Eloise immediately launched in with exaggerated vibrato, "Now every note's a bitter gloss"

"A kiln-cold silence – everything lost!" Albert joined, off-key but enthusiastic.

"Oh *wow*, you're both the worst," Stella cried, laughing so hard her shoulders shook. "I was aiming for haunting and ethereal, not a local pub singalong." Eloise sobered slightly, reaching out and squeezing Stella's hand. "It was all of those things, Stella. Haunting, powerful, cold and fierce. But what I think you've forgotten... is that it was also brave. You turned pain into poetry. That's not melodrama. That's alchemy."

Albert nodded, a gentle weight in his voice. "And maybe it's time you stopped thinking of it as a response to her, and started seeing it as the first thing that was truly yours." The laughter faded into a soft, thoughtful quiet. Stella looked down at the old letter once more, fingers brushing the seal, then back at her friends – these people who were slowly helping her piece together something she didn't even realize was scattered. "Maybe it *was* the first thing," she said. "And maybe... it's not the last."

Albert raised an eyebrow. "Does that mean you'll be writing again?"

Eloise leaned forward, eyes shining. "Better question. Will you be singing again?" Stella didn't answer right away. Instead, she stood and walked to the old upright piano in the corner of the café – mostly decorative these days, though still faintly in tune. She rested her hands on the keys. "I think," she said slowly, pressing a quiet chord that resonated in the stillness, "it might be time to find out what happens... when clay finally meets fire." And with that, she played her first new note in a long time.

10

CHAPTER TEN: HEARTH SONG

Rain lashed against the windows of The Saltwater Siren, each drop a tiny percussionist joining Stella's song. It was a restless morning: the wind howled like a mournful sea creature, and the building itself seemed to vibrate with a low, resonant hum. She sat on the worn velvet stool in front of the stage, her fingers dancing over the strings of her guitar – a galaxy-bodied Lindo that she'd learned more on than she cared to admit. The melody of Miles Thornton's song, the one she'd unearthed from the sea-chest, filled the room, now richer and more defined than before.

It wasn't just chords; it was feeling. A bittersweet ache, a touch of melancholy overlaid with a surprising current of hope – all swirling together like saltwater and sand. The rain seemed to intensify as she played, each chord echoing off the damp walls, clinging to the faded wallpaper. Albert had said places "hummed," and this morning, The Siren truly sang. Stella closed her eyes, letting the sound wash over her, feeling a strange pull, a sense of recognition that went deeper than just remembering – like a half-forgotten dream trying to surface. It was both unsettling and profoundly beautiful, a reminder of the connection she felt to this place, to Miles, and perhaps, even to herself.

The melody resonated with the building's history, as if it were speaking through her fingers.

The scent of damp wool and beeswax polish hung in the air as Albert tightened the last screw on a newly installed conduit. He hadn't been rushing – his work was always methodical, careful – but now, with Stella playing, he found himself listening intently. The rain continued its steady drumming against the roof, but it faded into the background, overshadowed by the melody. He wasn't just hearing music; he felt it. A subtle shift in the building's energy, a deepening of the resonance it hummed with. He straightened, pushing a stray curl from his forehead and studying her with a thoughtful expression. It was more than just a pleasant song – there was a vulnerability to it, a quiet intensity that reminded him of the crashing waves on Ashcliffe's shore.

"That's beautiful," he said finally, his voice low. "It feels older than you think." He gestured towards the stage with a small smile, a hint of something more than simple appreciation in his eyes. "Like it's been waiting to be heard." He glanced down at his tools, then back up at her, as if unsure whether to say more. "It's like it remembers," he murmured, almost to himself. "Miles. And maybe a little bit of everything that happened here." He paused, tilting his head slightly. "You've got a good ear for it."

Stella finished the last phrase of the melody, letting the final chord fade into the rain. Albert was still looking at her, his gaze holding a depth she hadn't quite registered before. He simply nodded, then reached into his pocket and pulled out a small piece of folded paper – a haiku, scrawled in elegant, slightly messy handwriting. "I... I had it," he said quietly, handing it to her. "It just came to me."

Stella unfolded it carefully, reading the few words with their rhythmically scant syllables: "What was buried sings / fire beneath saltwater / broken notes bloom whole." The rain seemed to soften a little as she looked up at him. "That's beautiful, Albert," she said, genuinely surprised. "Did you write that?"

He nodded, a faint blush rising on his cheeks. "Just now. It felt right." He watched her closely as she turned the haiku over in her hand, searching for meaning. "It's about the song, I think," he added softly. "About unlocking something."

"'What was buried sings'..." Stella murmured, tracing the words with her finger. "Do you think it means Miles?" Albert stepped closer, the scent of wood and electricity around him. "Maybe," he said, his voice barely a whisper. "Or maybe it just means that even in the quietest places, there's always something waiting to be set free." He paused, then, emboldened by the shared moment, offered her a small, tentative smile. "And sometimes," he added, glancing at the rain-streaked window, "it takes broken notes to bloom whole. The haiku hung in the air between them, small and simple yet somehow weighty. Stella closed her eyes for a moment, letting the rain and the melody wash over her again. 'What was buried sings...' It felt...familiar, like a forgotten echo from within herself. At first, she just thought it was poetic – Albert always had a knack for finding the right words. But then, 'fire beneath saltwater...'

It connected with something deep, something she hadn't fully acknowledged. The song, Miles's song, felt less like a puzzle to be solved and more like a key – a key to something hidden within her own past, something she had long since felt was lost. She remembered the feeling of being soothed by music, how it used to feel like a shield against everything else. 'Broken notes bloom whole.' That was particularly resonant. For so long, she'd been afraid to let herself be imperfect, afraid that if she broke a little, she would shatter completely. But maybe, just maybe, the cracks weren't weaknesses – maybe they really were where the light got in. A small smile touched her lips. It wasn't a triumphant smile, not yet, but it was genuine - a flicker of hope amidst the lingering sadness. It felt right. Like she'd finally heard something that truly resonated with her, something that acknowledged both the pain and the potential for beauty. "It's beautiful, Albert," she repeated, this time with a little more conviction. "Thank you."

The rain hadn't entirely abated as they worked, instead that reliably steady drizzle clung to the windows of The Siren. Stella, having carefully laid her guitar on the stage, perched on an old stool, handing him tools with small, almost playful gestures. Albert was focused on the wiring behind the stage, tracing a frayed cable with his finger, a smudge of grease on his cheek. "You're awfully close," Stella observed, tilting her head slightly. He glanced up, a slow smile spreading across his face. "Trying to make sure it's properly grounded," he said, his voice a little deeper than usual. He reached out and gently brushed a stray strand of hair from her face – brief contact, but electric. "And, well," he added, returning to the wiring with slightly more urgency, "it feels like a good idea."

Stella didn't move away. "It always does when you're around," she admitted, her own smile widening. They worked in comfortable silence for a moment, the only sounds the rhythmic click of tools and the drumming rain. Then, Albert reached for a particularly stubborn connection, his hand brushing against hers as he tightened it. "You know," he said, his voice low, "this building... it feels like it's holding onto secrets."

"Like it remembers," Stella echoed his familiar cadence, leaning slightly closer to him.

Albert straightened up then, turning to face her fully. "Maybe it's remembering the feeling of music being created under its beams." He stepped a little closer, the scent of wood and rain mingling in the air. "It felt like it wanted to show me something."

"And what did it show you?" Stella asked, meeting his gaze.

He hesitated for a moment, then said, "That you have a beautiful melody waiting to be unleashed." He reached out again tucking more unruly strands of her flowing hair away, neatly behind her ear, "And I think," he murmured, his eyes sparkling with amusement, "I'd like to help you unleash it."

"Speaking of unleashing – have you ever wondered what exactly Miles's creative process was like?" Stella murmured, her gaze drifting towards the rain-streaked windows. She was fiddling with one of Albert's tools – a small screwdriver – lost in her own undercurrent of swirling thoughts. "His workshop, for example," she began.

Albert paused his work, turning to watch her. "You've been there?" Stella nodded, a faint smile playing on her lips. "Not really. But... I imagined it. It was down by the docks, you know, according to Krissy. Small and cluttered – rolls of canvas, half-finished sculptures, tools scattered everywhere." She closed her eyes for a moment, as if reliving the memory. "And always this scent – linseed oil and salt air."

"What did you feel?" Albert asked softly.

"Passion," she said immediately. "A real, raw passion for his work. He was completely absorbed in it. Like he was talking to something bigger than himself." She pictured him – a tall figure with dark hair, large and capable hands stained with paint, lost in concentration. "But also... loneliness. It wasn't just passion; there was this quiet sadness about him. Like he was carrying a secret."

"He seemed to find solace in his art, by all accounts," Albert observed.

Stella nodded emphatically. "It felt like... he was trying to capture something elusive – the feeling of the sea, maybe? Or of himself, at least. And he wasn't always sure he succeeded." She shifted slightly, as if still feeling the pull of the memory. "There was this one time I thought I saw him – just for a second – and he looked up, like he sensed someone watching. It was intense." She opened her eyes, meeting Albert's gaze. "It's funny," she said quietly. "Like I knew him, even though I'd never met him. Like there was a connection – a shared understanding of that passion and that loneliness." She took a deep breath. "And now... I feel like he's waiting for me to finish his song."

The rain had softened to a gentle drizzle by now, casting a warm glow over The Siren as Stella sat by the window, lost in thought. Albert was back at his wiring, but he seemed to be listening more intently this time, as if absorbing every word she'd said about Miles's workshop. He paused in his work, turning towards her with a small smile. "I was thinking about that haiku," he said quietly, holding up the folded paper. "Let me read it to you again." His voice held a little more warmth this time, and as he recited the words – "What was buried sings / fire beneath saltwater / broken notes bloom whole" – Stella felt a subtle shift in his gaze. It wasn't an intense look, not like before, but there was something like recognition. Like he'd heard it somewhere before, perhaps within himself.

"It feels different now," she murmured, watching him carefully. He nodded slowly, returning to the wiring for a moment before meeting her eyes again. "Maybe," he said, his smile widening just a little. "Or maybe it's just that you finally understand it." He reached out and gently brushed a stray strand of hair that seemingly couldn't help but take up residence in front of her face – this time the motion was far longer, more deliberate. "It felt like it wanted to show you something," he repeated, his voice low and intimate. "Like it was waiting for you to hear it." Stella's breath caught in her throat for a moment. It wasn't just the words; it was the way he said them, the way he looked at her – as if he knew her, truly knew her, better than she knew herself. "Do you think it's just about music?" Stella asked softly.

They stood close now, the scent of the rain and the sea hanging heavy in the air. The silence between them wasn't awkward, but charged – thick with unspoken possibilities. Albert's hand had lingered on her cheek for a few moments longer than necessary. Then, it slowly moved to cup her face, tilting it slightly towards him. Stella held her breath, anticipation fluttering in her stomach. He leaned in, his eyes searching hers. It felt... inevitable. Like they had been moving towards this moment. But as his lips brushed against hers – a brief, gentle touch – she hesitated. A second kiss... what would it mean? Would it be a simple confirmation of the attraction that had been simmering between them, or something more?

A flicker of vulnerability crossed Albert's face – a hint of hope mixed with perhaps a little apprehension. Stella realised that Albert hadn't rushed; he'd waited for her to lead. They'd both enjoyed their first kiss, out in the rain at the cove, hadn't they? But would a second signal an expectation? A desire for something deeper? She could feel the warmth of his lips, the soft press of his forehead against hers, and a wave of conflicting emotions washed over her. Part of her wanted to surrender completely – to let go and allow herself to be swept away by the feeling. But another part – the guarded, cautious Stella – was hesitant, afraid of revealing too much, of opening herself up to the possibility of more pain. She pulled back slightly, just enough to break the contact, her cheeks flushed. "You have a beautiful voice, you know, it's got echoey depths" she said softly, turning away for a moment to gaze out at the rain. Albert didn't immediately move towards her. He simply watched her, his expression thoughtful. "And you," he replied quietly, "have a very beautiful melody."

A small smile played on her lips. It was a tentative smile, not quite as confident as before. She realised now that the hesitation wasn't just about fear; it was about wanting to be sure – sure of her feelings, sure of him. A second kiss would solidify things, yes, but it would also change the dynamic. Taking a small step back, she met his gaze again. "It's... nice," she said softly, a hint of uncertainty in her voice. "Very nice." The rain continued to fall, now a gentle whisper against the roof of The Siren. For a moment, they simply stood there, suspended in the aftermath of their almost-kiss. Albert's eyes held hers, a quiet intensity that felt both familiar and new. A faint blush dusted his cheeks, and he shifted slightly, bringing his hand up to adjust the collar of his shirt – a small, unconscious gesture.

Stella's own face was flushed, and she found herself instinctively fiddling with the strap of her guitar bag. She avoided direct eye contact for a moment, glancing down at the worn velvet stool before returning her gaze to his. There was a subtle shift in the atmosphere – a palpable tension, but not an unpleasant one. It felt charged, like the air after a thunderstorm. She noticed he hadn't moved away, but also that he hadn't rushed to recapture the moment. He simply held her gaze, allowing her to decide. A small smile played on his lips, hinting at amusement and perhaps a touch of nervousness.

Albert tilted his head slightly, as if inviting Stella to step closer – but she didn't move. Instead, she offered a small, almost shy smile in return. It was a smile that said, "I enjoyed that," and "I'm not quite sure what it means yet.". Or, at least that's what she hoped it conveyed. A silence settled between them, punctuated only by the steadily gentle drumming of the rain. Albert's hand moved to rest lightly on the back of her stool – a simple touch, but one that spoke volumes. It was a silent question - "So?" – and Stella felt herself drawn into the quiet space between them, aware of the lingering warmth of his touch and the promise of something more to come.

Stella picked up her trusty Lindo guitar again, its familiar weight grounding her. Taking a deep breath, she began to play Miles Thornton's song. But this time, it was different. There was more confidence in her touch, more feeling in her strumming. The notes flowed out of her with a newfound assurance, as if unlocked by the almost-kiss and Albert's lingering gaze. She closed her eyes for a moment, letting the melody wash over her, remembering the warmth of his hand on her cheek, the way he'd read her the haiku. It wasn't just playing any more; it was sharing – sharing the song, sharing herself. The melody rose and fell, imbued with a depth she hadn't quite captured before. It spoke of longing and hope, of loss and rediscovery. As she played, she could almost hear Miles himself, his passion and loneliness echoing through the strings. She felt connected to him, to this place, to Albert – as if they were all part of a single, beautiful song.

When she reached the final chord, she opened her eyes, a genuine smile gracing her lips. The room seemed brighter now, filled with a warmth that hadn't been there before. Albert was watching her intently, his expression thoughtful and appreciative. As if on cue, he raised his hand slightly, a silent invitation to continue – or perhaps, to share in the moment more actively. And Stella knew, with a certainty that surprised even herself, that she wanted to. The rain had softened even further now, painting streaks of light across the windows of The Siren as Stella finished playing. Albert stepped forward, reaching into his pocket – and handing her back the small piece of paper: the haiku.

But this time, it felt different. It wasn't just a casual offering; he seemed to be presenting it to her like a small treasure. He looked at her while he handed it over, his eyes filled with genuine curiosity - as if waiting for her reaction. There was something deliberate about the gesture, a quiet intention that made her heart skip a beat. "I thought you might want to see it again," he said softly, his voice carrying a hint of warmth. "It just felt right to give it back to you properly." He held her gaze for a moment longer than necessary, letting her take in the haiku – and perhaps, him. Stella took the paper slowly, turning it over in her fingers. It was as if she were examining a precious stone, searching for hidden meaning. "It really is beautiful," she murmured, looking up at him. "Thank you."

A small smile touched his lips. "You're welcome," he said simply. "I just... I wanted to see if it meant anything to you now." He tilted his head slightly, a playful glint in his eyes. "Did it?" Stella met his gaze again, and for a moment, she felt like she understood – not everything, perhaps – but something. Like he was trying to read her thoughts, to connect with her on a deeper level. It wasn't just about the haiku; it was about the shared space between them, the unspoken questions, and the growing feeling that they were both starting to unravel the secrets of The Siren together.

The rain had almost completely stopped now, leaving a glistening sheen on the cobblestones outside The Siren and a feeling of hopeful dampness in the air. Stella sat by the window again, turning the haiku over and over in her mind. "What was buried sings / fire beneath saltwater / broken notes bloom whole." It felt layered now, richer than it had before. It wasn't just about Miles any more – although he was certainly central to everything that was going on. It was about her. About the music she'd tried so hard to keep hidden, the "pleasant clay" Alanna Brooke had called her work. The 'fire beneath saltwater' that

Albert now remade her into – was that his recognition of her longing for something more? For connection? Or was it the sea itself, pulling at her memories and emotions?

Then it clicked. "Broken notes bloom whole." It reminded her of Eloise – with all her sharp observations and astrological readings. Eloise had immediately seen through her carefully constructed walls, hadn't she? She'd recognized the dissonance within Stella's music, the fear of letting go. And yet, Eloise was so wonderfully, beautifully layered herself – a blend of intuition and practicality, of dreamy insight and grounded knowledge. Stella picked up the small chapbook of poetry that Albert had given her – a gift from his own collection. She'd been meaning to read it properly, but hadn't made time. Now, she flipped through the pages, captivated by his simple, elegant verses. They were filled with observations about nature and quiet moments – themes related to his fascination with the town's folklore.

It was like there were layers to Albert, too – a past love that burned him, a love for poetry and wiring, a quiet intensity beneath a carefully measured exterior. And she found herself wanting to unpack them all, one by one. A new question bubbled up, and it felt both exciting and slightly daunting. How did her continued fascination with Eloise fit into this? Was she simply enjoying the witty banter and shared observations, or was there something more – a subtle competition for Albert's attention? Or perhaps, did Eloise's insightful readings about Albert offer a clue to her own feelings? Stella glanced over at Albert now, who was meticulously cleaning one of his tools by the workbench. He looked so focused, so comfortable in his own skin. There was something inherently appealing about that – a sense of quiet confidence and a gentle warmth.

It wasn't just attraction, she realized. It was curiosity. She wanted to know everything about him, just like she wanted to discover all she could about Miles, about this town steeped in secrets and song. And perhaps, a little bit about herself. The rain had stopped completely now, watery sunlight took the rare opportunity to stream in through the window, kissing both Stella and Albert's skin. Stella smiled. The "almost-kiss" hadn't solved anything, not really, but it had opened up another layer – another question to explore. And for the first time since arriving in Ashcliffe-on-Sea, she felt like she was finally starting to feel truly seen.

11

CHAPTER ELEVEN: LIVING MELODIES

Inside The Chiron Cafe on the windswept evening of its semi-regular Open Mic Night, there was a chaotic blend of warm light from mismatched lamps and the comforting aroma of strong coffee and slightly burnt sugar. A small crowd had gathered, mostly locals nursing mugs and listening attentively, their faces illuminated by the flickering candlelight on the tables. The air buzzed with a quiet anticipation, punctuated by the occasional clink of cutlery and the murmur of conversation. Albert sat at a corner table, sketching in his notebook – a focused furrow in his brow as he captured the scene before him with quick, confident strokes. Stella felt a familiar flutter of nerves as she adjusted her microphone again, the worn wood cool beneath her fingertips a small comfort against the rising tide of anxiety. It was like seeing the room for the first time – not just the cosy chaos of The Chiron Cafe, but this – a room full of people actually listening to her. She kept glancing around, taking in the faces, noticing details she'd missed before: Krissy's bright scarf, Eloise's knowing smile, even the way Albert was sketching, completely absorbed.

Stella's fingers tightened around the neck of her guitar, a nervous habit. A small tremor ran through her hand as she checked the tuning for what felt like the tenth time. It all came back then – the initial swell of praise for Kiln Cold, followed by the sharp edges of the criticism, the feeling of being both lauded and dissected. She remembered the suffocating pressure to be 'perfect,' to fit a mould. A quick flash of memory struck her: London, a packed but indifferent club, the echoing silence after she finished playing. Then, the quiet routine – record stores, records, the shield of anonymity. This felt different. Vulnerable. She smoothed down her dress, a small, almost unconscious gesture. It was more than just a performance; it was a return – a hesitant step back into the spotlight after years spent hiding in its glare.

Her microphone finally meeting her approval, Stella walked to the bar to pick up her water. "You seem haunted by something familiar tonight," Eloise observed quietly, her eyes fixed on Stella with an unnerving accuracy. "Like you're listening to a song that's both known and just out of reach." She gestured vaguely towards the stage, Stella's guitar was leaning in wait. "It's as if Kiln Cold is trying to tell you something new." Eloise radiated a calming presence, a gentle warmth that seemed to settle over the room. With a quick glance at Stella's chart – a swirl of rings and symbols she usually kept hidden – she murmured, "Ah, yes. A strong Capricorn Ascendant – giving you that natural sense of self-assuredness, the ambition. And your Sun in Sagittarius is radiating tonight; you believe you can do this." She tapped a finger on Stella's chart. "Jupiter in Pisces adds a touch of expansive possibility, suggesting you believe in achieving great things... even if you occasionally doubt it yourself."

"But," Eloise continued, her voice dropping slightly, "there's a beautiful tension there. Your Leo Moon – that's where the vulnerability lies. You crave recognition, don't you? And your Scorpio Venus... you feel everything intensely." She paused. "And look at this – Saturn in Sagittarius retrograde! That's key. Making you feel like you're not doing enough, that you haven't quite earned the right to shine."

Stella shifted slightly, feeling Eloise's words sink in. "It's like... a balancing act," she finally said, her voice barely above a whisper. "Confidence when I want to be seen, but then... vulnerability creeps in. Like I'm afraid of being judged."

"Exactly!" Eloise exclaimed softly, a small smile playing on her lips. "It's the dance between showing up as the capable artist you are and allowing yourself to be truly vulnerable – to let people see the notes that aren't always so bright." She leaned forward slightly. "Tonight, don't fight it. Embrace both. Let the vulnerability fuel the confidence. It will make your music all the richer."

"It's about recognizing," Eloise concluded, "that being brave doesn't mean you're not afraid. It means you do it anyway." She gave Stella a reassuring nod, her eyes twinkling with insight. "Now go on! Let that song tell its story." Albert was there, as always, radiating a quiet sort of encouragement that felt surprisingly potent. He was meticulously fiddling with the sound system, adjusting the levels just so, his brow furrowed in concentration. Stella noticed he hadn't spoken much tonight, but he seemed to be absorbing everything. With a wink, Albert left the stage as Stella returned to claim it. Then, as she began to play – those familiar opening chords of Kiln Cold – Albert's expression shifted. A small smile touched his lips, and he subtly adjusted the lighting, dimming it just slightly to create a warmer glow on stage – remembering Stella's request from earlier for something a little less harsh.

It was a small thing, but it spoke volumes. It was that song. The one that had launched her into the spotlight, and then knocked her down. Kiln Cold, the revenge hit she'd penned about Alanna, a song that still carried a faint sting after all these years. As Stella's voice rose, strong and clear, Albert's encouragement grew subtly. He gave a small, almost imperceptible nod of approval, his eyes fixed on her with genuine admiration. It wasn't boisterous or effusive; it was simply knowing. Like he recognized the battle she was fighting – the balance between confidence and vulnerability, ambition and insecurity - and believed in her ability to win. He seemed to be saying, "You've got this."

As Stella stepped up to the microphone, a hush fell over the room. She took a deep breath and offered a brief explanation, her voice a little tentative at first. "I hadn't really listened to Kiln Cold in, well let's just say over a decade," she said, glancing down at her guitar. "It felt a bit daunting, almost. But tonight I just feel compelled to play it, so I hope you'll bear with me in case my fingers have forgotten it!" A ripple of curiosity went through the audience. It was that song – the one that had defined how a generation understood the concept of revenge – was Stella Sinclair really Stella Bright? "It's... a complicated memory," Stella continued, a small smile playing on her lips, "but it felt like the right choice to make tonight." She looked out at the faces in the crowd, a flicker of vulnerability in her eyes – and then, with determination, Stella began to sing.

As the opening chords flowed, Stella's performance began tentatively, almost hesitant. But as she moved into the first verse, a shift occurred. "You touched the edges, never deep / Mapped my skin but not my heat," she sang, her voice gaining strength with each word. It resonated deeply – recalling the feeling of being observed, judged, yet never truly seen. "Spoke in fires, lit with pride / But never saw what burned inside." The lyrics mirrored her own past, a constant striving to impress, to project an image of confidence, while concealing the vulnerability beneath.

She continued, "You called my chords a cradle song / Too smooth, too safe, too sweet, too wrong," her voice resonated with a newfound conviction. It was about the pressure to conform, to play it 'safe' – a feeling she recognized acutely. "But lullabies can turn to knives / When sung beneath electric skies." The line hung in the air, capturing the sharp sting of criticism and the realization that even something seemingly gentle could be weaponized. The chorus hit with a powerful surge. "You chased the flame, but feared the slow / The steady pulse, the undertow / Now every note's a bitter gloss / A kiln-cold silence—everything lost." Stella's voice soared as she sang of being dismissed, of feeling like her passion was constantly underestimated.

"You wanted war inside a frame / Mistook restraint for lack of flame / But there's a freeze that burns the same / A hush so loud it haunts your name," she delivered with a touch of steel, referencing Alanna's judgment – and the lingering effect it had on her. "You wrote the script, then shut the play / Declared me dull, then walked away / But silence has its own decay / And now it's yours to hold—okay?" Stella paused, letting the last word hang in the air. It was a challenge, an acceptance – and a release. As she moved into the final chorus, her voice filled with a quiet strength. "You lit the fuse, but missed the melt / Dismissed the world I slowly felt / Now every note's a bitter gloss / A kiln-cold silence—everything lost."

By the end of the song, Stella was radiating confidence – not the forced, polished version she'd presented to the world for years, but something deeper and more genuine. It was as if Kiln Cold itself had chipped away at her defences, revealing the fire within. The room was silent for a moment, then erupted in applause – a warm, appreciative sound that wrapped around her like a comforting blanket.

The applause that followed Kiln Cold was different – warmer, more sustained than anything that had come before. It wasn't just polite appreciation; it felt like genuine recognition. The audience remained quiet for a moment longer, captivated by the lingering notes of the song and Stella's performance. They looked, each in their own way, deeply moved by the raw emotion she'd laid bare. Krissy was visibly struck, perched on the edge of her seat with Rita sitting beside her, openly sobbing. Even Tom, usually a whirlwind of boisterous laughter, looked shaken, his hand resting thoughtfully on Rita's arm. Even Eve, typically observant and detached, wore a look of quiet contemplation – a subtle softening around her eyes that suggested she, too, had been touched by the song. A few people in the audience were wiping away tears.

The shift was palpable. It wasn't just that Stella had played well; she'd connected with them by revealing a vulnerability they hadn't known she possessed. The Kiln Cold performance felt like a turning point, not just for Stella, but for the entire room – a shared acknowledgement of a story told, and finally, allowed to breathe. It was as if the song had cracked open something within them all. After the last echo of applause faded, Albert approached Stella. He held out a small sketchpad, open to a drawing. It was a simple one – a quick charcoal rendering of Stella mid-song, her head thrown back, lost in the music, a single spotlight illuminating her face. Beneath it, he'd scrawled "You found the fire."

"I wanted to capture that," Albert said quietly, his eyes holding hers for a moment. "The way you just let go." He gently placed the sketchpad in her hands, and Stella turned it over, examining it closely. A wave of surprise washed over her – not an overwhelming one, but a gentle recognition. It was like looking at a photograph of herself from another lifetime, yet instantly familiar. A touch of nostalgia bloomed as she remembered the first time she'd seen that famous photo of her that Alanna had taken – the initial shock and then... something else. But beneath the memories, there was a spark – a flicker of hope. It wasn't just a reminder of the past; it felt like a validation of the present. A small smile touched Stella's lips. "It feels like that photograph," she said softly, turning the sketch over in her hands again. "But... warmer." She glanced up at Albert, a question in her eyes. "Do you think I actually did find it?" As Stella continued to gaze at Albert's sketch, Eloise drifted over, a knowing smile playing on her lips. "That song...," she murmured, as if speaking of a well-worn favourite, "it held so much of you back then." She recognized it immediately – the subtle shift in Stella's expression, the way she was holding the sketch.

"You're finally letting it go," Eloise continued, her voice gentle and perceptive. "Not running from it, exactly, but... acknowledging it. Accepting that part of yourself." She paused, tilting her head slightly as if consulting some unseen celestial map. "You know, when you played Kiln Cold, it wasn't just about Alanna. It was about letting go of the need to prove yourself, to be seen in a particular way. It's like," Eloise elaborated, gesturing with a graceful hand, "that sketch... it's not just a portrait of you playing music. It's a reminder of how far you've come – and how much more is still waiting for you." She offered Stella a large encouraging smile. "You opened up Miles Thornton's sea-chest," Eloise reminded her softly, "and that was the turning point. You started to let in the echoes."

Suddenly, Stella felt a brief, sharp inner pull – a flicker of something familiar and intensely vivid. It was like stepping into a photograph from another lifetime. She was younger, standing in front of a flashing camera crew. The air buzzed with the excited chatter of reporters, the clatter of microphones. It was the day Kiln Cold made it to the top of the charts. The screen behind her flashed images: Stella, radiant and poised, then close-ups of the album cover, then snippets of interviews. Critics were already lining up to dissect her music – praise for its boldness mixed with criticisms about its bitterness. She remembered the conflicting emotions swirling within her – relief at finally releasing something so personal, coupled with a nagging sense of vulnerability.

Stella saw herself clutching a glass of champagne, forcing a smile as she spoke to a reporter, trying to project an image of confidence despite feeling utterly exposed. There was a flash of Alanna's face – sharp and critical, the article that had both launched and haunted her career. Then, just as quickly as it began, the flashback faded. Stella blinked, momentarily disoriented, until the scent of rain and charcoal filled her senses again, grounding her in the present. Kiln Cold hadn't just been a song; it had been an event – a crucible that had both forged and tested her. Stella caught Albert's eye. For just a fraction of a second, he seemed to be watching – not with judgment or criticism, but with a quiet understanding. A small, almost imperceptible acknowledgment flickered across his face. He didn't smile, nor did he offer any words of encouragement. It was subtle—a slight tilt of his head, a brief tightening around his eyes – but Stella recognized it immediately. He'd caught on to her unspoken reference, to Alanna, to her. It wasn't an accusation or a challenge; it felt like a shared secret, a recognition of the past that had shaped her present. A small smile played on Stella's lips – a silent acknowledgement of their intertwined stories.

It wasn't just that she'd played the song; she'd lived it. And looking down at Albert's sketch, nestled in her hand, everything clicked into place. The charcoal lines, the way he'd captured the intensity in her eyes – it mirrored the photograph Alanna had taken of her back then, the one that had launched and haunted her career. It was more than a coincidence. It was an echo – a tangible link to her past, to the day Kiln Cold had first been unleashed upon the world. Suddenly, the song wasn't just about Alanna's criticism; it really was about her. It was about her fear of vulnerability, her relentless need to prove herself worthy – a desire rooted in that initial feeling of being observed, judged, and perhaps not quite good enough. "It's... it's like you captured the whole thing," Stella said softly, turning the sketch over in her hands again. "The praise, the criticism... everything."

Without meaning to, Stella came to the realisation that Alanna hadn't just been a critic; she'd been a mirror – reflecting back Stella's own insecurities and ambitions. And Kiln Cold wasn't simply a reaction to that critique; it was an expression of those same feelings – the desire to be seen, to be heard, to leave her mark. But as she looked at the sketch, she also saw something else: it was as if Albert had understood not just what she'd been feeling then, but why. "It's funny," she mused aloud, "I always thought it was about her. About how she'd dismissed me." She paused, taking a deep breath. "But... it's really about me, isn't it? About letting go of that need to be validated." A slow smile spread across her face. "Ashcliffe-on-Sea... I thought it was just a place to hide. But maybe... maybe it's been waiting for me all along – waiting for me to finally sing my own song." She glanced at Albert, who met her gaze with a knowing smile. "It's not about escaping the past," she continued, "it's about accepting it – and using it to fuel something new."

She looked at Albert and Eloise, seeking confirmation of what she'd been feeling for so long. "I built this whole anonymous life in London," she explained, her voice a little huskier now. "Record stores, records... carefully crafted normalcy. It was my shield – against the memory of that song, of Alanna's words. And, I think now, against letting anyone really see me." Eloise nodded thoughtfully, stirring her tea. "It's a common trap," she said, her voice gentle. "To use art as armour. To hide the most vulnerable parts of yourself."

"Exactly!" Stella exclaimed, a little more animatedly. "'Kiln Cold'... it felt like a cage to me. I was so determined to impress, to prove I deserved to be heard, that I built this incredibly safe, almost sterile melody. But it wasn't me. It was polished and pleasant, but underneath... there was nothing." She continued, her fingers nervously tracing the lines of Albert's sketch. "I was afraid to let anyone see the 'fire' inside – the messy, uncertain, sometimes a little bit prickly parts. I thought if I showed them, they'd just walk away."

"It's a brave thing to admit," Albert said quietly, his eyes holding hers for a moment. "And it's a beautiful song, despite – or perhaps because – of that cage." He paused, a small smile playing on his lips. "You were trying so hard to control the sound, you forgot to feel the rhythm." Stella laughed softly, feeling lighter with each word. "Thank you," she said, turning to Eloise. "That's exactly how it felt!" With a wink, Albert rose, a little awkwardly at first, and stepped up onto the small stage at The Chiron Cafe. He adjusted the mic and, without a word, began to read – his voice rich and resonant, filled with the quiet observations of a man who truly saw the world around him. It wasn't flashy or dramatic, but it was honest, stark, and true. Stella was spellbound.

12

CHAPTER TWELVE: CURRENTS UNCHARTED

The dusk along Ashcliffe-on-Sea's shoreline felt particularly weighted that evening, a grey blanket draped over everything after a day of intermittent rain. Stella walked with Albert across the sand, the dampness clinging to her boots and drawing the colour from her cheeks. The tide was low, revealing patches of slick, seaweed-covered rock, each stone whispering secrets to the retreating waves. It wasn't a dramatic sunset; just a slow bleed of colour – bruised purples and muted oranges – across the horizon, mirroring the feeling in Stella's chest. "It always feels heavier at dusk here," Albert said quietly, his voice barely audible above the rhythmic sigh of the sea. "Like everything that's been held onto all day finally settles." Stella nodded, pulling her cardigan tighter around her. The memory of the last time they'd been alone together for any length of time – the almost-kiss, the haiku, the lingering warmth of his hand on hers – felt both exhilarating and slightly daunting. It was a new current, pulling her in a direction she hadn't anticipated. "It's... comforting, I think," she admitted, watching a lone gull wheel overhead. "Like it's okay to feel a bit... exposed."

Albert stopped walking for a moment, turning to face her. The last rays of light caught the flecks of grey in his hair. "You are," he said simply, and then, almost shyly, brushed a strand of damp hair from her cheek. "More than you realize." Stella's breath hitched. It wasn't a passionate embrace, not yet – just a brief, gentle touch that sent a pleasant shiver down her spine. But it was enough to make the weight in her chest feel a little lighter. "Some things take root slower," he continued, resuming their walk. "Like a stubborn sea-root." She'd been writing late into the night, a messy scrawl of words filling a notebook she'd found in The Siren – another one of Miles Thornton's. It wasn't a masterpiece, not by a long shot, but it felt brave. A small victory against the years spent building walls. "I dreamt of the sea singing last night," Stella said suddenly, breaking the silence. "Just...singing." Albert stopped again, turning to look at her with an expression she couldn't quite decipher. "It always sings here," he replied, a hint of a smile playing on his lips. "Doesn't it?" The applause at The Chiron Cafe still echoed faintly in Stella's ears as she walked on, a pleasant warmth spreading through her despite the lingering damp-ness. It hadn't been a roaring ovation – more of a quiet appreciation, a collective understanding. But it felt genuine. More than any polite clapping after a polished performance in London.

There was a definite contentment settling over Stells, a lightness she hadn't experienced in years. The song had felt true, stripped down to its core. Not just a reaction to Alanna, but a release of something within herself – the fear, the insecurity, the armour she'd spent so long constructing. But beneath that contentment lay a touch of melan-choly, too. It wasn't painful, not exactly, more like a gentle recognition of how much she'd been hiding. The vulnerability had felt both terri-fying and liberating. As if, for the first time in a long time, she'd truly allowed herself to be seen – flaws and all. She stopped by the water's edge, picking up a smooth piece of sea-worn glass from the tideline. It was cool and smooth beneath her fingers, polished by countless tides. She turned it over, examining its subtle swirl of blues and greens, a miniature reflection of the sky and sea. It felt familiar somehow – like a small piece of Ashcliffe itself had found its way into her hand.

"It's funny," she murmured to herself, "all that noise and attention, and really, it was just... letting go." She thought about the younger Stella, back in London, terrified of exposing herself through her music. The memory felt distant, almost hazy. It wasn't devastation now; more like a wistful fondness for a past self she barely recognized. She held the glass tighter, feeling a small connection to the sea, to the town, and – perhaps – to a future that was still unfolding, one hesitant note at a time. "I think I actually felt a bit exposed."

Albert chuckled, a low rumble in his chest. "You were brilliant. Raw, but brilliant. And you didn't even seem to notice everyone staring." He gestured towards the sea. "It was a good storm for it too – always adds drama to a performance."

"The rain really did feel like it was listening," Stella agreed, glancing up at the sky which had cleared slightly, revealing patches of blue. "Like it understood." She picked up another piece of sea-worn glass, this one speckled with white. "Do you ever just... watch the waves and think about all the things they've seen?"

"Constantly," Albert replied, his gaze fixed on the water. "They've witnessed centuries of storms and sunshine, lovers and losses. They hold onto everything, don't they? Like Ashcliffe does." He paused, considering. "Did you notice how the tide went out so far tonight? Almost like it was trying to reveal something." "It felt...hungry," Stella said softly. "Like it wanted to eat away all the grey and leave just the blue." They walked side-by-side in silences for a few minutes, the only sound the gentle lapping of the waves. Then, Albert stopped abruptly, pointing towards a small cove nestled into the coastline. "We're nearly there," he said quietly, gesturing with his hand. "That's where we shared that...brief moment."

Stella's smile tightened slightly. She still didn't know how to feel about the repeated moments she'd had with Albert, let alone that rainswept first one! "Right," she replied, a little too quickly. "It was rather surprising, wasn't it?" Albert continued, his voice low and thoughtful. He didn't seem to notice her hesitation. "A sudden burst of rain, and then...that." Stella shifted her weight, picking at the hem of her cardigan. "It was... nice," she conceded, avoiding his gaze. "But I don't really do 'returning,' you know? Not any more."

"You don't have to," Albert said simply, turning to face her again. His eyes were gentle, not probing. "Just thinking out loud. It just struck me how the light catches that cove differently now." He paused, letting the silence hang in the air for a moment. "It's funny how places can hold onto things."

Stella looked down at the glass in her hand, turning it over and over. "I like to think of it as... collecting new stories," she said finally, her voice soft. She didn't elaborate, offering no invitation for him to pry. He simply nodded, letting her feel comfortable in her own thoughts, a small smile playing on his lips – waiting patiently for her to decide if she wanted to share more. "It wasn't just about the memory," Stella said quietly, her voice barely audible above the sound of the waves. She finally met his gaze, and it felt easier than she expected. "That was a big part of it, certainly. But I wanted more than just anonymity. I think I needed to be known."

Albert nodded slowly, understanding dawning in his eyes. "So, not just escaping, but seeking?"

"Exactly," Stella confirmed, taking a small step closer to him. "London was... . Predictable. But also... grey. Everyone had their routines, their little shields. I wanted something with colour, with feeling. Something that would actually matter." She paused, her fingers tightening around the glass. "I spent so long constructing this quiet life – the record stores, the records, the carefully chosen normalcy – as armour. It worked, in a way. No one knew anything about me."

"And what did you want them to know?" Albert asked gently.

Stella shrugged, a small, self-conscious movement. "I don't know exactly," she admitted. "Maybe that I used to play music. Maybe that I was scared. Maybe...that I still have a little bit of fire left inside." She looked out at the sea, a wistful expression on her face. "But here? It feels like everyone in Ashcliffe has a story, a connection to something bigger than themselves. I just want to feel that again – not to just be part of it, but truly seen for who I am."

"I do agree that it's more than just the legends, you know?" Albert said, turning to face her fully. "Ashcliffe... it just feels right. There's a quietness here, a stillness that I find comforting. It's not exciting, not always brimming with possibilities like London, but it has a certain...possibility." He paused, his gaze drifting out towards the sea. "I was born and raised here. My family's been in Ashcliffe for generations. It wasn't a grand plan – just a slow settling. A feeling that maybe, if you listen closely enough, you can find something worthwhile hidden beneath the surface." A hint of melancholy touched his features. "There's a bit of loneliness to it too, I suppose. But it's a good kind of lonely – one that allows you space to breathe, and to hear yourself think." He offered her a small smile. "It's a place where the past isn't quite as insistent as it is elsewhere."

"Oh, it feels pretty insistent," Stella replied, thinking of the mystery of Miles Thornton and of his connection, too, to both the siren and The Saltwater Siren, "but it also feels like home."

"Somewhere where legends get stuck in the tide," Albert began, before Stella cut in with a sigh. "It's... it's just the way you say 'legends,'" Stella murmured, gazing out at the sea. "It just brings it all back."

Albert tilted his head, noticing her sudden shift. "What does?"

It wasn't the memory of the devastating review that had shattered her, not this time – it was smaller, quieter. A local open mic night, her first ever performance in London. She'd been nervous, acutely self-conscious, feeling every glance from the small audience. And then, she'd caught the eye of a man in the front row – a critic, really – who gave her this almost imperceptible nod after her song. It felt like judgment, not encouragement. "I just wanted to disappear," she whispered, clutching the glass tighter. "Like I hadn't ever existed. Like I never even mattered at all."

Albert reached out and gently touched her hand. "You always did," he said softly. "And you always will."

The air in The Crooked Note had been thick with summer sweat, dried and covered in over-used perfume, and anticipation, Stella remembered. Stella felt it clinging to her skin again – in place of the fresh salt air that was brandishing her skin now – prickly and uncomfortable. It was her first open mic night – a terrifying plunge into a sea of faces she didn't know, all judging, all waiting. She was still a teenager, clutching her guitar like a lifeline, the wood smooth and warm beneath her fingers. The stage lights were harsh, exposing every imperfection: the slight tremor in her hands, the nervous fidgeting with her shoelaces. She could hear her own heartbeat drumming against her ribs, loud and insistent. A few polite coughs rippled through the small crowd – a mix of students, retirees, and couples nursing lukewarm pints.

She'd taken a deep breath and began to play – a song she'd poured her heart into, a simple melody about longing and searching. Her voice was shaky at first, then gained strength as she lost herself in the music. She closed her eyes for a moment, letting the chords wash over her, trying to block out the faces in the audience, the low murmur of conversation. Then, she opened them again. And there he was – a man in a tweed jacket, sitting in the front row, his expression unreadable. He gave her a small nod – almost imperceptible – as if acknowledging something. It wasn't a smile, not exactly, but it felt like judgment. Like she hadn't quite measured up. The feeling of being exposed intensified. Every note, every lyric, felt laid bare for all to see. She finished the song, the applause polite and unremarkable. As she walked off stage, her cheeks flushed, she caught his eye again – he was still watching, a faint smile playing on his lips. And in that moment, surrounded by strangers, she knew – truly knew beyond a shadow of a doubt – that she'd revealed everything, and it wasn't enough.

The last note of the flashback seemed to hang in the air between them. Stella stood there for a moment, still clutching the glass, her gaze fixed on the sea. Her expression was... complicated – a mixture of vulnerability and something else, something she hadn't quite managed to hide. Albert noticed it immediately. He didn't say anything at first, simply watching her with quiet attentiveness. "What were you thinking about?" he asked softly, his voice gentle as the sea breeze. Stella hesitated for a moment, then turned to face him. "Just... how easily it felt like everyone was judging," she admitted quietly. "Like I wasn't good enough. Like they could see right through me."

"It's funny," Albert said thoughtfully, "how those small moments can stick with you. They build up over time." He paused, his eyes searching hers. "You felt like you were showing them everything, didn't you? All your hopes and fears and it wasn't enough."

The air between them thickened with unspoken things – the memory of her past, the tentative connection they'd been building, and something more that was starting to feel undeniably present. Stella shifted slightly, drawn to Albert's gaze, which seemed to hold a warmth she hadn't realized she craved. He mirrored her movement, taking a small step closer until the distance between them felt almost negligible. Their hands brushed briefly as they walked – a fleeting contact that sent a surprising little jolt through Stella's arm. It wasn't forceful, just a gentle graze, but it lingered in the air between them. Albert slowly extended his hand, offering her his wrist – an invitation to touch him, to bridge the space that had seemed so vast just moments before.

Stella didn't hesitate this time. Her fingers curled around his wrist, a light pressure, and she met his eyes again. This time, there was something more in his gaze – a hint of desire, of anticipation. A small smile touched his lips – a genuine, unguarded smile that reached all the way to his eyes. He didn't pull away. Stella's breath caught in her throat, and she found herself leaning into his touch, wanting – needing – to feel him closer. The silence stretched for another moment, electric and heavy. Stella felt Albert's thumb gently trace circles on the back of her hand – a small, grounding touch that pulled her back from the edge of something. He was holding his breath, she could feel it. And then, without warning or fanfare, he leaned in and brushed his lips against her forehead.

It wasn't a passionate kiss. Just a fleeting touch - brief and light – like a feather brushing against skin. It was warm, surprisingly so, and utterly unexpected. Stella froze for a fraction of a second, caught completely off guard. A small gasp escaped her lips, a mixture of surprise and something deeper – a warmth that spread from behind her ears down to her chest. It wasn't the long, lingering kiss she might have dreamed of, but it was perfect in its simplicity. It felt... intimate – like he'd finally allowed himself to acknowledge the connection they'd both been subtly nurturing. She tilted her head slightly, allowing him to deepen the contact for just a moment longer, feeling the warmth of his lips against her skin. He gently pulled away, his eyes searching hers. There wasn't any pressure, no demand – just an acknowledgment of the moment, a shared understanding. "Some things take root slower," he whispered, his voice low and husky.

Stella nodded slowly, her heart beating a little faster now. She lifted her hand to touch the spot on her forehead where his lips had just been, feeling the ghost of his warmth lingering there. It was a small thing – a simple and almost chaste kiss – but it felt like a shift, like something had finally clicked. A genuine smile touched her lips, a hesitant, hopeful smile. "It does," she agreed softly, and for the first time since arriving in Ashcliffe-on-Sea, Stella felt truly settled – grounded by the sea, by the rain, and by the quiet certainty that maybe, just maybe, she was finally home.

"Some things take root slower," he whispered, his eyes searching hers. He offered her a small, reassuring smile – a hint of warmth and understanding. "It doesn't mean they're not there. Just... that they need time to grow." She lingered on the feeling of his forehead against hers, trying to capture it, to hold onto it like a precious jewel. It hadn't been a dramatic, sweeping kiss – no passionate tangle of limbs or breathless sighs. Just that small, perfect touch – and yet, it felt as significant as the times their lips had touched, perhaps even more so. Like a tiny seed planted in fertile ground, waiting for the right conditions to sprout. It wasn't the instant fireworks she might have expected, not after years of hiding, of building walls around her heart. It was quieter, more subtle – like a slow burn that promised warmth and depth. It felt reassuringly unhurried, as if he understood that she wasn't rushing into anything.

She considered what it meant—that simple gesture. Was it a sign? A promise? Or simply a small acknowledgement of the quiet pull they'd been feeling for each other? Maybe it was all those things, combined. It felt like permission – permission to be vulnerable, to let go just a little bit, to allow herself to feel. To feel that maybe, just maybe, she was finally ready to let something beautiful grow, even if it took its own, deliberate pace. It simply was.

Back at The Saltwater Siren that night, Stella felt inspiration grip her hard and fast. Albert's words and actions that day – from that forehead kiss, to "Some things take root slower," felt... weighty. Like a tiny seed planted in soil that had been stubbornly dry for years. Stella was at the small writing desk by the window, the candlelight painting flickering patterns on the pages of her notebook. The air smelled faintly of beeswax and salt from the sea – a comforting combination now.

She chewed on the end of her pencil, staring at the half-formed lines in front of her. "You, the hands I didn't seek..." She'd written that down a few times already, tweaking it, searching for the right note. It felt true – Albert's touch wasn't flamboyant or demanding; it was simply... present. Steady. Like he knew exactly where to place his hand without her having to ask. "I came with hands too tired to hold / The fire I once called mine..." It felt good, that line. Familiar. A little bit sad, but honest. She pictured herself in London, gripping her guitar as hard as she dared, desperately trying to coax a spark from her fingers, building up walls of silence and anonymity around herself.

She paused, tilting her head. It was coming together. The song wasn't about escaping, it was about acknowledging the echoes, letting them shape you. About recognizing that even the storms could be beautiful, and that they always, eventually, led somewhere. She chewed on her pencil again, considering. "Wreckage turned to light..." It felt right. Like taking something broken and transforming it into something new. Something brighter. She looked back down at the page, adding another line: "Not every fire burns to ash / Not every wound must scar..." The words felt more like half a song than a full one, but they would do. For now. A little bit raw, perhaps, but undeniably hers. She closed her notebook and went to bed.

PART THREE: STARDUST IN THE TIDES

13

CHAPTER THIRTEEN: ROMANCE ON THE CARDS

"Right, just need to angle this a bit," Albert murmured, fiddling with the dimmer on one of the exposed bulbs in the corner of The Saltwater Siren. "Less 'haunted venue,' more 'cosy listening room'?" Stella leaned against a newly painted – but thankfully dried – shelf, arms crossed, watching him. "You're doing a fantastic job, actually. It's... brighter. And less like we've been wrestling with cobwebs all afternoon." She offered a small smile, a genuine one that reached her eyes. "Just trying to banish the gloom," he replied, turning to face her. His brow was slightly furrowed in concentration, and his hands were dusted with a fine layer of plaster. "And you, it seems, are slowly being lit up." He gestured towards her with a paint-stained hand. "Slowly is good," Stella agreed, a little playfully. "Better than a sudden, blinding flash. Like my music career." She paused, then added softly, "Though, sometimes, a little brightness isn't such a bad thing."

The invitation arrived mid-afternoon, a brightly coloured card with a slightly wonky illustration of tarot cards. "Game Night at The Chiron Cafe!" it proclaimed in Krissy's exuberant handwriting.

Stella almost crumpled it in her hand. Game night. Of all the things… She glanced over at Albert, who was meticulously cleaning a vintage microphone stand. "You going?" she asked, trying to sound casual. "Wouldn't miss it," he replied, without looking up. "Though, I must say, this is a bit fancy for me. Usually, it's just Krissy and a chaotic assortment of board games." Albert chuckled, taking the invitation and examining it with mock seriousness. "An official invite? I've never received an official invite before! Does this mean she thinks I'm unworthy of her celestial scrutiny?" He grinned at Stella, a hint of playful teasing in his eyes.

Stella read the invitation, letting the words wash over and through her.

Dearest Stella,

I hope this finds you well – and not too overwhelmed by your newfound glow! I wanted to personally invite you to our regular Friday game night at The Chiron Cafe. It's always a wonderfully chaotic mix, and I think you'd enjoy the company (and perhaps a little friendly competition, eh?).

From my astrological reading, I sensed it would be particularly auspicious for you this week – with your Leo Moon craving a need to step outside of your comfort zone and connect with some playful energy. With Mercury Retrograde still swirling, it's wise to gather with friends and let the good vibes flow!

Plus, honestly, it's been too long since we last properly chatted - and I could use another dose of your sharp wit. Think tarot readings, questionable board games, and plenty of gossip.

It would be lovely to see you there. Let me know if you can make it!

Warmly,

Eloise

P.S. – Don't worry about being official; I just have a feeling you need a little bit of lightheartedness in your life right now!

"'A little bit of lightheartedness in your life right now?'" she murmured to herself, a small smile playing on her lips. It was typical Eloise – both insightful and slightly tongue in cheek. "I wouldn't worry about how she worded it," Albert said, matter of factly. "She probably just wants you to come."

"It's a bit... much. Like she's trying to force me into something." Stella hesitated, then added quietly, "It's also good that she thinks I need lightheartedness."

"Well," Albert said, holding up the card for inspection, "I suppose it's better than being ignored entirely. And frankly," he added with a wink, "I could use some astrological justification for spending an evening surrounded by board games."

"But it's just a game night," Stella said, trying for nonchalance but blushing slightly. "It'd be nice to just be part of things."

"It's a good step," Albert agreed, his eyes holding hers for a moment. "Ashcliffe seems like it's been waiting for you. And I'm glad you're letting yourself feel that little bit more connected." He gestured towards the invitation in her hand. "Looks like Eloise is particularly keen to get you out of your shell."

"She has a point," Stella admitted, smiling shyly. "It's just... not always easy, stepping outside."

"I'll be here to catch you if you fall," he said simply, his gaze warm and reassuring. "No pressure either way."

Krissy burst into The Chiron Cafe with a slightly freaked out Stella on her arm. Stella had been slowly walking to the games night alone when Krissy, a chaotic whirlwind of enthusiasm and half-empty mugs, swept her up and propelled her through the door. "Right, game night can officially begin!" Krissy announced, immediately making her way to greet Eloise, holding her familiar deck of tarot cards and waiting for Albert to finish setting up the tables. "And look who it is," Krissy chirped, giving Stella a quick hug that smelled faintly of lavender and sea air. "You look like you've seen a ghost! Or maybe just a particularly judgmental dust bunny." Stella laughed, feeling the tension begin to ease. "Just... a lot going on. And I almost didn't make it."

"Almost? Nonsense!" Krissy declared, pulling her gently towards the table where Albert was arranging cards and dice. "That's why we're here – to ensure you *do* make it." She plonked herself down with a happy sigh, immediately surveying the scene. "Right, let'a see who can predict the most chaos tonight!" The game began with a few rounds of Major Arcana – mostly friendly competition between Stella and Eloise. Eloise was clearly enjoying herself, laying down dramatic gestures as she played, declaring each card with theatrical flair. "Ah, The Emperor! A force to be reckoned with!" she exclaimed, pointing dramatically at a card featuring a regal figure in armour.

Stella, meanwhile, was focusing, trying to remember the meanings of the cards that she'd seen Eloise draw before. "The Moon," she announced after drawing a card, "Definitely about illusions. Or maybe... echoes."

"Ooh, cryptic!" Eloise said, tilting her head thoughtfully. "I love it! It's saying you're wrestling with something deep, Stella – something tied to your past, perhaps?" Albert, who had been quietly observing, chimed in. "Or maybe," he suggested with a smile, "it's just saying the lighting is a bit dim."

Krissy erupted into laughter. "Always the pragmatist, Albert!"

Stella drew a card – The Lovers. She glanced at it briefly, a flicker of something akin to recognition passing over her face, before focusing on her next word. "Hmm," she murmured, considering. "Connection. Choice." Eloise dramatically shuffled the deck with a flourish, scattering a few cards onto the floor. "Oh, this is perfect!" she declared, pointing to The Lovers with a triumphant grin. "The Lovers!" For a moment, the usual chaotic energy of The Chiron Cafe seemed to quieten. Everyone looked at the card – Stella, Albert, Krissy, even the usually stoic Eve. It was a beautiful card, depicting two figures intertwined beneath a golden archway. "It's telling us that something significant is coming," Eloise announced, her eyes sparkling with insight.

"A decision, perhaps? Or maybe... a deepening of an existing bond." A comfortable silence settled over the table as they all absorbed the meaning. "I knew it!" Eloise exclaimed, beaming. "My intuition never fails!" Albert chuckled, reaching for a stray card from the floor. "Well, you certainly have a knack for dramatic flourishes, Eloise."

"That's not all I have 'a knack for', Albert – and I won't have Stella believe that it is!" Eloise retorted, playfully. Krissy, ever perceptive in the face of potential drama, leaned forward. "It's about Stella," she observed quietly. "Don't you think?" She glanced at Stella, her gaze encouraging. "It feels... important."

"Obviously," Eloise said, beaming, "a significant choice! A connection! A merging of energies!" She glanced pointedly between Stella and Albert. "It could be romantic, of course, but it's also about aligning with your true self – or finding someone who helps you do that." Her eyes twinkled with amusement as she watched for Stella's reaction. Stella shifted slightly, a touch defensive in her posture. "Right," she said, fiddling with the rim of her mug. "Well, I've got a perfectly good life as it is." She took a small sip of tea, trying to appear nonchalant, but a faint blush crept up her neck. "I don't necessarily need another decision." The word 'decision' felt loaded, carrying with it the weight of past choices and anxieties.

Albert spoke up. "It's just a card," he said calmly, his voice measured and reassuring. "But it is suggesting something is brewing." He looked directly at Stella, his gaze warm and perceptive. "And sometimes, the most significant things in life arrive when you least expect them." He paused for a moment, letting his words sink in. "It's not about adding to your life, Stella; it's about recognizing what's already there, waiting to be nurtured." Krissy leaned forward, her eyes bright with curiosity. "Maybe it's Albert," she suggested, grinning at Albert playfully. "He's been awfully attentive lately." She shot a teasing glance at Stella. "Don't you think?" Stella felt a warmth spread through her chest – not just from the tea, but from Albert's quiet observation. She glanced between Eloise and Albert, suddenly aware of their shared glances. "Well," she said, trying to sound casual again, "I'm perfectly happy with my life as it is. It's... quiet." She hoped 'quiet' sounded less like 'isolated' than it actually felt. "And I don't tend to make rash decisions." Eloise raised an eyebrow, a knowing smile playing on her lips. "Everyone makes 'rash decisions', Stella. It's what makes life interesting!" Eloise continued with a gentle encouraging gaze. "Don't you think? Don't you want to see where these decisions of yours might lead?"

"Oh, come on!" Stella playfully protested, stirring her tea with a little more force than necessary. "I'm perfectly happy being single!" She shot a quick glance at both Eloise and Albert, trying to project an air of resolute contentment. "Are you?" Eloise countered, raising an eyebrow with a mischievous glint in her eyes. "Or are you just avoiding commitment? It's a classic Lovers dilemma – choosing between two paths." She leaned forward slightly, studying Stella intently. "It's like a beautiful melody," she mused,"Do you stick with what you know, or do you let it take you somewhere new?" Albert chuckled, leaning back in his chair and taking a sip of his tea. "Perhaps Stella is contemplating whether to choose between a perfectly good record player and a handsome electrician?" He offered a charming smile, his eyes twinkling with amusement. "Both have their merits, you know."

"You're trying to distract me with wiring," Stella said, rolling her eyes playfully. But there was a definite hint of warmth in her expression – and she found herself smiling again.

"Well, someone has to make sure your tunes sound good!" Albert retorted, his gaze lingering on hers for a moment. "Besides," he added, a playful note in his voice, "I'm pretty sure you'd find my wiring rather... captivating." He winked.

"You're terrible," Stella said, shaking her head and letting out a small laugh. "Absolutely terrible."

Albert's gaze lingered for a moment, then he looked away, his expression unreadable. Stella felt the warmth in her cheeks settle into a quieter kind of hum, like the echo of a song you hadn't realised you'd memorised. The laughter around the table resumed – Krissy brandishing another card and declaring it "an omen of total game-night domination" – but Stella felt herself drifting slightly. The Lovers card sat on the table like a weight. Not heavy, exactly, but certainly present.

She reached for her tea and took a sip, saddened to discover that it had long since gone cold. Eloise leaned over and tapped the card gently. "You know," she said in a softer tone, "it doesn't have to mean anything scary."

Stella raised a brow. "I'm not scared."

"Sure you're not," Eloise replied lightly, her eyes scanning Stella's face with that unnerving kind of knowing. "But sometimes, the idea of possibility is more terrifying than any closed door."

Before Stella could answer, Albert stood, stretching his arms above his head. "Think I need a bit of air," he said. "The Chiron's roof is probably dry now, if anyone fancies a change of atmosphere."

Eloise was already gathering her mug. "Perfect." Stella hesitated. The idea of escaping – even just for a moment – was deeply appealing. She followed them, the inside warmth of the café giving way to the cool hush of the evening as they climbed the narrow back stairs to the rooftop.

The rooftop of The Chiron Cafe was slick with recent rain, puddles catching the reflections of scattered stars. The air was soft, smelling faintly of salt and jasmine from the nearby potted plants that Krissy had taken upon herself to garden, insisting on keeping them alive. Stella stepped out last, hugging her arms to herself. "Still feels like a place out of time," she murmured.

Albert smiled. "That's why I like it."

They moved quietly at first – just three silhouettes framed by the low rooftop lights. Albert settled near the railing, sipping the rest of his tea, while Eloise wandered, her fingers trailing across the tops of damp wooden crates. Stella leaned against a post, exhaling slowly. The sky above was a wash of dark indigo, clouds moving sluggishly.

"I'm not very good at... this," Stella admitted.

Eloise turned. "Which part?"

Stella gestured vaguely. "Opening up. Letting people in. I did all that in London, and then everything felt like it collapsed on top of me. I kept pretending it didn't hurt, because people needed me to be... composed. Polished. And now I just –" She broke off, laughing quietly. "I don't want to go back to that. To performing myself."

Eloise walked toward her, her expression softer now. "You know, in astrology, when someone has a Leo Moon, it usually means they crave recognition – but not just applause. It's about being seen for who they really are."

Stella blinked. "And you think I'm not letting that happen?"

"I think," Eloise said gently, "you're trying. Which is enough. For now."

There was a quiet pause, punctuated by the far-off cry of a gull. Albert glanced over from the edge. "It's brave, you know. Choosing not to run."

Stella looked at him, her voice low. "It doesn't feel brave."

"It never does," he said simply. Eloise stepped closer, close enough for Stella to see the way her curls caught the light, the faint smudge of lavender beneath her collarbone. "Can I ask you something?" Stella nodded. "Have you ever wondered what something could feel like... if you weren't overthinking it?" The question wasn't pointed, but it landed with precision. Stella hesitated, then said, "Maybe."

Eloise smiled—not smug, but soft. "Just once," she murmured. "I'd like to stop wondering."

Eloise leaned in gently, her hand brushing Stella's wrist. The touch wasn't demanding, only asking. Stella inhaled – and didn't pull away. The kiss was quiet. A question more than an answer. Tentative, a soft press of lips that held no promises, only curiosity and presence. The rooftop disappeared for a moment – the puddles, the sounds below, the distant creak of the café door – all blurred behind the hush of breath and the taste of Eloise's chamomile tea. When they parted, Eloise smiled faintly. "There. Not the end of the world."

"No," Stella said, dazed but honest. "It wasn't." Albert had turned away, his gaze on the skyline. If he'd seen, he gave no indication.

Later, after they'd descended back into the warm clatter of The Chiron Cafe, Stella lingered in a quiet corner, arms loosely folded. Her lips still tingled, her heart felt oddly buoyant – and unsettled. Not in a bad way. Just... incredibly aware. She picked up a napkin left folded on the table. Scrawled in tight, precise handwriting was a haiku: 'Rain kissed the rooftop / but it wasn't the water / that made the air hum'. Albert's name wasn't on it. It didn't have to be. Stella looked across the room and Albert caught her gaze. He didn't smile, not fully. But he gave her a small, knowing nod. Something inside her stirred. Not certainty. Not yet. But maybe, just maybe, possibility.

Stella didn't sleep that night. She tried. She closed her eyes. Turned over. Even listened to the soft clinking of wind chimes from the neighbouring balcony as if they might lull her into unconsciousness. But her mind refused stillness. The image of Eloise's kiss replayed again and again – not in some grand, cinematic montage, but as a memory on loop. The sensation of breath before it happened, the impossible hush of everything around her, the press of lips like the start of a note held too long in the throat. And then, the look Albert gave her – that almost-smile. That nod. As dawn crept in, she sat by the small kitchen table in her flat above The Saltwater Siren, nursing a second cup of tea. She felt suspended between heartbeats. Not caught between two people, exactly, but between two versions of herself — the one she had always been, and the one still becoming. Outside, the tide was coming in. The sea, ever a mirror to her shifting interior landscape, lapped gently at the shore.

Later that morning, Krissy showed up at the shop carrying a ridiculous number of pastries and humming what could only be described as a disco remix of a sea shanty. "You didn't sleep," Krissy observed, squinting at Stella as she arranged the pastries in a crescent on the counter. "Either that or you fought a sea witch in your dreams."

Stella blinked. "You are... very specific."

Krissy wiggled her fingers mysteriously. "I'm connected to the ether." She paused, watching Stella with more sincerity than usual. "You okay?"

"I'm... recalibrating," Stella admitted. "Emotionally. Possibly romantically. Existentially, too."

Krissy leaned across the counter. "Wow. That's a whole pie of '-allys.' Is this about Eloise? Or about Albert? Or both?"

Stella opened her mouth. Closed it. "Yes."

Krissy let out a low whistle. "Hot damn, Ashcliffe really is working its magic on you."

That afternoon, The Saltwater Siren was filled with the soft murmur of music and the smell of lemon oil and old wood. Stella adjusted the microphone on the refurbished stand — Albert's handiwork — and tested a few chords on her guitar. Her voice, tentative at first, warmed into the small room. As she played, the door creaked open. Albert stepped in, a wrapped bundle of new string lights under one arm. "I come bearing gifts of illumination," he said, holding the box aloft. "Figured the back shelf could use some sparkle."

Stella gestured to the stage. "There's room for more light." Albert set the box down, then paused, hands in his pockets.

"You played beautifully last night," he said. "Even if most of it was tarot-based warfare."

Stella laughed. "Eloise is a dramatic opponent."

Albert smiled. "She is." There was a pause. Not uncomfortable – just full.

"Did you know?" she asked quietly. "About her and me? I mean... last night?"

"I suspected." His voice was steady. "I saw something shift. And then you came back with stars in your eyes."

She turned to face him fully. "Is that... okay?"

Albert tilted his head. "You don't need my permission, Stella. You're allowed to feel something. For whoever makes you feel alive."

"And if that's... complicated?"

He gave a soft chuckle. "Complicated is the default in Ashcliffe."

"I don't want to hurt anyone," she said.

Albert looked at her for a long moment. "Then don't. But don't hurt yourself trying to avoid what you want, either." He moved to leave, then paused at the door. "You're not someone who chooses lightly, Stella. So whatever you choose... I trust it will be real."

That evening, Stella found herself walking through Ashcliffe with no clear destination. The sky was bruised with the colours of dusk — lavender, gold, rust. Her feet carried her past the local archives and the sleepy post office. Everything felt quieter, as if holding its breath. Eventually, she reached the cliffs. The wind whipped her coat open, and she pulled it tight. Below, the waves churned, a rhythmic heartbeat. She stood there, silent. Behind her, footsteps. "I thought you might be here," said Eloise.

Stella didn't turn immediately. "You always know where I'll be."

Eloise stepped closer. "Not always. Just sometimes. The important times."

Stella looked at her then. The wind had mussed Eloise's hair, and her cheeks were pink with cold. She was holding a thermos. "Chamomile," Eloise said. "Didn't want to assume you'd want it, but... I hoped."

Stella took it. "Thanks."

They sat in silence on a bench overlooking the sea. Eventually, Stella spoke. "What do you want from me?"

Eloise didn't flinch. "Honesty. Connection. Maybe a little mess. Not perfection. Never perfection."

"I don't know how to do this without thinking it to death." Stella admitted.

"Then think it to death," Eloise said gently. "Just... don't let the thinking be louder than your heart."

Another pause. "And Albert?"

Eloise smiled, a bit wistfully. "Albert is steady. Kind. He sees you. I think... he loves you, in a way. Maybe not confessed, but there."

Stella closed her eyes. "That doesn't help."

"No," Eloise agreed. "But it's true." She stood, brushing salt-sprayed dust from her trousers. "You don't have to choose right now. The Lovers card isn't always about picking between people. Sometimes it's about choosing yourself. Choosing what you need to feel whole." She leaned down, kissed Stella's forehead, and whispered, "You already know. Deep down." Then she left.

The next few days were filled with a hush that Stella couldn't quite shake. She found herself drawn to music – old records, songs she hadn't written yet, Miles Thornton's melodies that hovered just beyond her reach. She journaled obsessively. Walked at odd hours. Sometimes she saw Albert, quietly fixing something, never pushing. Other times, she caught glimpses of Eloise at the café, reading under the stained-glass skylight. Ashcliffe, as ever, held its breath. One evening, Krissy cornered her. "This isn't a triangle," she said bluntly. "This is a compass. You're just trying to figure out where north is."

Stella blinked. "That's... surprisingly poetic for you."

"I've been reading," Krissy said. "Don't make it weird."

14

CHAPTER FOURTEEN: FAULT LINES

The rain hadn't let up all morning, clinging to The Saltwater Siren like a particularly heavy memory. Stella was nursing a mug of lukewarm tea as she watched Albert. He was hunched over his well-used workbench, meticulously polishing a brass fitting for one of the antique lamps – a task he usually tackled with booming enthusiasm and plenty of chatter. Today, his movements were measured. His usual solid grace seemed tinged with something else – a quietness that felt unfamiliar. It wasn't anger, or sadness, not exactly. More like a slight detachment, as if he was observing himself from just a little way off.

He hadn't said much at all to her recently, Stella was beginning to notice, and when he had spoken, his voice held a subtle pause between the words. Stella shifted on the stool she was perched on. It felt like a small shift in the tide – something, or someone, was pulling away, just slightly. She wondered if she'd missed a sign, or if this quietude was simply Albert's own way of contemplating the secrets of Ashcliffe-on-Sea. What stung, Stella realised, was that for once, Albert wasn't sharing those secrets with her.

Stella tried a gentle attempt at normalcy. "You seem particularly focussed recently, if you don't mind my saying."

Albert didn't look up. "Just getting ahead of things."

Stella offered a half-smile, warming her hands around the mug. "Everything okay?"

"Busy day," he replied too quickly. His eyes flicked up, met hers, and just as quickly dropped again.

Something inside her shifted. This wasn't the Albert who shared blueprints at midnight or offered her driftwood metaphors about healing. He wasn't sketching. He wasn't tinkering. Just... polishing a brass fitting. Over and over, like it held answers. Her gaze drifted down. In his other hand, mostly hidden beneath the table, he was turning over a small, smoothed piece of sea-glass. It had been worn well by the combined kisses of both sea and time. She'd seen it before – she was sure it was one of the pieces she had picked up during their last walk along the beach... when he'd kissed her forehead and made her feel... well, he certainly made her feel.

That afternoon, the rain came harder, a silver sheet against the stained glass and warped panes of the old venue. Stella found Albert in the main room, staring out at the storm, hands shoved in his jacket pockets. She stepped softly, but firmly. "Okay," she said, arms crossed but voice gentle. "'Nothing's wrong' is getting old." Albert didn't turn around right away. When he did, his expression was guarded. But there was something behind his eyes – not avoidance, exactly. More like hesitation. "I care about you," he said finally. "Probably more than I should. That doesn't usually make me shut down, but I'm out of practice."

Stella exhaled. "You think I'm not? I'm still learning how to feel anything again. I get flashes, moments of joy or panic or... interest. And then I clamp down." He tilted his head, listening. She stepped closer. "It's not that I don't want to feel it," she whispered. "I'm not numb. Just... unpracticed."

Albert smiled, just barely. "You said once that you didn't know if the Siren was a curse or a gift. Maybe that applies to feelings too." A beat passed. He reached out, fingers brushing hers. Just once. Then gone. "Maybe you just need to let yourself go a little," he said. As if the touch of their hands had forced the weather to remember something crucial, a storm broke with startling intensity. Water drummed on the roof like a thousand tiny fists. A leak burst through in the corner of the rehearsal space. "Oh hell," came Krissy's bellow, as she stomped in through the front door, soaked to the knees. "It's pissing down harder than a nervous ghost on a date!" Immediate chaos surrounded them. Towels were hastily thrown, buckets reliably fetched. Eloise arrived with a scarf over her head and laughter bubbling out of her like soda. "Well, Mercury Retrograde strikes again!"

Albert skidded into the room with an armful of sandbags, almost colliding with Stella. "Sorry! Sorry. Door wouldn't shut."

"You're charmingly damp," Eloise quipped.

"You're unreasonably cheerful," he muttered, but his smile was real. Stella found herself laughing, genuinely, as she knelt to mop up water pooling on the centre of the stage. Her hair stuck to her face, and her jeans were drenched to the thigh, but she felt alive. No masks. Just movement, mess, and company. Buckets clanged. Krissy cursed colourfully. After her postal round was completed, even Eve showed up with fresh towels and a flask of something undoubtedly stronger than tea. In the madness, Stella caught Albert's eye across the room. He looked tired, damp, and oddly at peace.

By early evening, the worst had passed. The Saltwater Siren glowed with warm, flickering candlelight. The smell of damp wool mingled with the salt air. Eloise, ever graceful, wiped a streak of mud from Stella's cheek with her sleeve. "You survived your first real Ashcliffe flood. Congratulations."

Albert appeared beside them with a dry pair of socks. "They're clean. Probably. And warmer than what you're wearing."

Stella blinked. "You carry spare socks?"

He shrugged, smiling sheepishly. "Local wisdom."

A shared laugh broke the last of the earlier tension. Stella accepted the socks, heart thudding with something like comfort. Balance, perhaps. A kind of beginning again. Stella was sitting near the window, watching the sea reflect candlelight through the warped glass. Eloise was spinning some nonsense about Saturn returns in the background. Krissy was dramatically squeezing water from her bra into a teacup, to Eve's horror. And in all of it, the warmth inside Stella didn't feel borrowed. It felt earned.

The morning after the flood, Ashcliffe-on-Sea woke beneath a low-hanging mist. The sea was calmer, apologetic almost, as if embarrassed by its previous outburst. Stella padded barefoot through the main hall of The Saltwater Siren. The wood beneath her feet creaked with tired familiarity, and the water-lines of puddles still lingered like ghosts refusing to leave. Someone – likely Eloise – had lit incense in the corner, and its tendrils curled through the air like lazy dancers. The Siren felt less like a performance venue and more like an eccentric grandmother's living room after a particularly rambunctious storm. But Stella didn't mind. There was something sacred about the aftermath. The quiet hum of resilience.

Albert wasn't in the workroom. His tools were lined up precisely, the brass fitting finally finished and gleaming like a trophy. Stella ran her finger along the edge of the bench, half-expecting the sea-glass to still be there. It wasn't. She found him on the roof. The access ladder was slick with dew, but she climbed anyway, her old, oversized flannel shirt snagging briefly on a nail. At the top, Albert was sitting cross-legged with a thermos beside him, staring out over the town. His hair was still damp, curling slightly at the edges. He didn't turn when she emerged. "Morning," Stella said, settling beside him. Albert held out the thermos. "Still warm." She accepted it, grateful for the heat. "Do you always climb up here after storms?"

He nodded. "Helps me remember things aren't always falling apart. Just... shifting." They sat in silence for a while, watching as the mist began to rise. Ashcliffe's rooftops poked through like timid swimmers. Gulls wheeled overhead, their cries mournful but familiar. "I thought about leaving once," Albert said suddenly.

Stella turned. "The Siren?"

"The town." He scratched his jaw, thoughtful. "Not long after I finished my electrician's apprenticeship there was that incident... those damned Christmas lights... her burnt skin... her father's face when he told me that I'd put her in danger... That I'd always keep putting her in danger. So even after the whole family left, it felt like the walls here were made of her memory. I couldn't walk five steps without bumping into her ghost." He sighed deeply, shaking his head. "I know she didn't die, but part of me did that day."

"What made you stay?" Stella asked, quietly but pointedly.

Albert exhaled slowly. "A dream. Sounds mad, I know."

"Try me."

"I dreamt I was underwater. Deep. Cold. Everything above me had gone quiet. But when I looked up, there was this light filtering through. And something – a voice maybe – was calling me back."

Stella tilted her head. "Back to Ashcliffe?"

He nodded. "Back to here. To the Siren. I woke up that morning and started repairs on the roof. First time I'd picked up a hammer in months. It didn't help that nobody had asked me to – I must've looked like a ghost, hammering away on the roof to drum out the heartache."

Stella studied him. "Was the voice hers?"

"I thought so at first. But I think it was mine. The part of me I'd buried."

The vulnerability in his words was so open, so unguarded, Stella found herself reaching out before she could think twice. Her hand found his. This time, he didn't let go.

Below, the town began to stir. Shop shutters opened with metallic clatters. The scent of bread from Mrs. Hargrave's bakery wafted through the air. The normalcy of it all grounded them both. "I'm scared of how much this place is starting to feel like home," Stella admitted.

Albert smiled. "That's not a bad thing."

"It is when you're not sure how long you'll stay."

His fingers tightened around hers. "Then stay a little longer."

Two days later, the Siren hosted its first post-storm gathering. Not a performance exactly—more like a community patch-up. Locals arrived with donations: old rugs, vintage lamps, spare tools, and the kind of pastries that only exist in small-town lore. Krissy led the charge with a bucket of paint and her sleeves rolled to the elbow. "If this place is going to flood every Mercury Retrograde, we might as well make the walls waterproof and fabulous." Eloise floated through the crowd in a velvet cape, offering people 'cleansing rituals' involving lavender sprigs and clove oil. Eve manned a tea station with military precision, although she kept getting swatted at by Krissy when she attempted to spike the Earl Grey with rum. Stella watched it all from the corner of the stage, heart swelling. The Saltwater Siren wasn't just a venue. It was alive. Beating. Breathing. And in some small way, healing her.

Albert found her near the stage ropes, holding a can of paint she hadn't opened. "We never did finish the lighting grid," he said, nodding to the ceiling.

Stella smiled. "Think we can still rig it?"

He looked up. "With help? Probably. With coffee and pie? Definitely."

She nudged him. "I'll bring the pie if you bring the existential metaphors."

"Deal." As they moved through the day – laughing, sweating, painting – Stella felt herself ease into the rhythm of belonging. People didn't ask for her résumé. No one cared who she had been before Ashcliffe. Here, she was just Stella. Quiet. Kind. Capable. A part of something.

With alarm, Stella realised just how long she had been able to feel the clay-covered fingerprints Alanna had left on her life, smudging everything she touched. "I need to get some air," she said, her voice tight. Eloise and Albert both rose slightly in response, but Stella waved them off with a fragile smile. "I'm alright. Really. I just... need a moment." Out in the drizzle, the air hit her like a gulp of cold water. She leaned against the brick wall beside the cafe, heart pounding. How could Alanna have owned the very building she'd poured her soul – and savings – into? Had Alanna known? Was it some twisted joke? Or a peace offering that Stella herself had never asked for? A strange, sharp laugh escaped her lips. The rain didn't care. It traced her cheekbones with reverence, like a lover who knew all her soft spots. She was so tired of being haunted – by a face, a voice, a critique that had burrowed its way under her skin and refused to be washed away.

Behind her, the door creaked open again. "Stella?" It was Eloise. Stella didn't turn around. "I wasn't going to follow," Eloise continued, stepping lightly beside her, "but your chart's screaming out that something needs to break. Not in a destructive way — in a 'something old has to shatter so something honest can rise' kind of way. A Tower kinda way, if you will let me borrow a tarot image."

Stella chuckled mirthlessly. "Fault lines, right?"

"Exactly. And you've been walking around trying to convince everyone you're made of polished stone when actually, you're lava – glowing, dangerous, alive."

Stella finally turned to face her. "What if I don't want to erupt? What if all I want is peace? A venue with working wiring and dry walls. A quiet life."

Eloise smiled, but her eyes were impossibly soft. "You wouldn't have come to Ashcliffe-on-Sea if you wanted quiet. You came to a town haunted by music and storms. To a building called The Saltwater Siren. You knew – even if you didn't know you knew – that you needed to be cracked open." They stood in silence for a while, the rain drizzling a rhythm over the slate rooftops. "I kissed you," Stella said, suddenly.

"I think you'll find that I kissed you," Eloise corrected gently.

"Well, whoever it was that did the actual kissing, I'm the one who doesn't know what it means." "You don't have to." Eloise's voice was steady. "You're allowed to be in-between." A warmth kindled in

Stella's chest – not desire, but relief. Eloise always seemed to have the exact words that let her exhale. "Come back in," Eloise urged. "Albert's got a tape deck and a stack of cassettes with sea shanties and weird storm ballads that sound like they were recorded underwater. It's utterly compelling. You'll love it." Stella hesitated, then nodded.

Inside, the tapes hissed and crackled with ghosts. Music from another time filled The Saltwater Siren – low, mournful harmonies wrapped in static. Eloise sat on the windowsill, arms around her knees. Albert gestured toward the table where a hot mug waited. As Stella made herself comfortable, Albert slid over a page torn from his notebook. It was a haiku. 'The sea takes its time / but always returns again. / Memory sings salt.' She read it twice. Something inside her, long-locked, stirred. "I think," she said slowly, "that I want to write again." She paused. "Properly, I mean, not just dancing around Miles Thornton's old melodies." Albert and Eloise exchanged a glance, but said nothing. Stella exhaled. "I want to write something that doesn't sound like fire smothered in clay. Something real. For me." Her eyes welled, but she didn't look away.

"Then let's start small," Eloise whispered. "Let's begin with listening."

"You're a wonderful listener, Stella." Albert agreed, "perhaps you just need to trust yourself a bit more."

"Exactly," Eloise said. "The tide has pulled you here, to us. You've been swimming against the current and then treading water, don't you think it's time you let yourself come to shore? Shake off the storm clouds once and for all?" Stella looked between Eloise and Albert, their faces both focussed on hers. If only you both knew, she thought, that the storm clouds I'm caught under are the pair of you. One rumbles with low, steady thunder, the other flashes with inspiration like lightning.

"It's funny," Stella said, tracing the ink on the page with her finger. "I always thought 'writing' was about expressing something – big or small. Not...recording it."

"It's about capturing a feeling, a moment," Albert replied, his voice softer than usual. "Like this rain. It feels like it's saying something, doesn't it? About letting go."

"Or clinging on," Eloise added, tilting her head. "A bit of both, probably. Like the sea itself – sometimes turbulent, sometimes utterly still."

Stella laughed, a genuine sound this time. "You and your metaphors, Eloise. You're exhausting."

"That's my job," Eloise said with a grin. "Besides, you need someone to translate the cosmic chaos into something you can actually sit down and write about."

"So," Stella said, turning to Albert, "what do you think I should write? About... this?" She gestured around the room – the candles, the rain, the tapes. Albert shifted slightly, considering. "About the feeling of being grounded, maybe. Even when everything feels like it's shifting beneath your feet. Like here. In Ashcliffe."

"Or about how you're always remembering something," Stella prompted gently. He nodded, a flicker of vulnerability in his eyes. "It's not always bad. Sometimes it helps me feel less alone." He paused. "Do you ever think about the people who came before? All the acts that played here? The lovers who whispered secrets in these walls?"

"All the time," Stella admitted. "I keep finding little scraps – a faded ticket stub, a broken button – like pieces of their stories are still clinging to the place."

"It's like the building remembers," Eloise said thoughtfully. "And it shares those memories with whoever's here."

"Maybe that's why I was drawn to it," Stella mused. "Like it knew I needed a little bit of history, a little bit of echo."

The silence that echoed around the three of them was punctuated by the hiss of the tapes and the steady drumming of rain on the roof. "You know," Albert said finally, "I was going to try and fix that leaky pipe in the back room this afternoon."

Stella raised an eyebrow. "And?"

"And I thought about it. Then I remembered you were here." He offered a small smile. "Didn't want to bother you with my usual chaos."

"Your 'chaos' is part of what makes it interesting," Stella countered, smiling back. "Besides, I might need your help wrestling with the thing."

"Deal," Albert said readily. "I'll bring my toolbox and a healthy dose of optimism." He glanced at Eloise. "You think she'll let us borrow her tarot deck for a bit of divination?"

"Absolutely," Eloise declared, re-entering the conversational fray with vigour. "We need to know if the pipe is leaking with sadness or with simply, well, water."

Stella chuckled. "Okay, okay. So, you're saying I should write about a leaky pipe and a little bit of memory? Grounded by the rain?"

"Or a haunted building, a touchy electrician, and a whole lot of sea-glass," Eloise added helpfully.

Albert reached out and gently squeezed her hand. "Or a jaw-dropping astrologer whose talents with the stars are barely comparable to her talents with a teapot." He looked between the two women carefully before continuing. "Just write what feels true." Stella looked down at his hand on hers and gently reached for Eloise with her free hand. She looked up at their faces, then – Albert's quiet strength, Eloise's sparkling intuition. "It's funny," Stella said softly, "I used to think I needed a big, dramatic event to feel something. Now... it feels like it's in the small things."

"Like a good cup of tea," Eloise offered.

"Or a leaky pipe and a shared toolbox," Albert added, grinning.

"Or a hand that doesn't let go," Stella whispered, a warmth spreading through her. "Maybe I'll start with that." She took a deep breath, and for the first time since the rain began, it felt like she was breathing in Ashcliffe itself.

15

CHAPTER FIFTEEN: THE ARCHIVE

Stella felt a little restless, like a note slightly out of tune. It wasn't quite dissatisfaction, more…a gentle pull, a subtle resonance echoing from somewhere deep within The Saltwater Siren. It was the kind of feeling that made her want to just know, to dig a little deeper into Ashcliffe's secrets. That feeling led her back toward the familiar glow of The Chiron Cafe, and to Krissy, already nestled amongst Rita and Tom at their usual table. "You look like you could use a strong cup," Krissy diagnosed, already halfway through a slice of lemon drizzle cake, Tom's friendly laugh punctuating her words. Rita offered Stella a generous spoonful of the lemon drizzle cake. "Just arrived from another corner of your mind, I reckon?"

"Something like that," Stella replied, accepting the cake with a smile. Krissy, ever observant, continued, "You're always drifting toward that archive by the butcher's. What is it about that dusty old place that intrigues you so much?"

"I don't know," Stella admitted, swirling the foam on her latte. "Just a feeling. Like there's something connected to Miles Thornton in there."

"I should say so," Krissy agreed enthusiastically, "Emily Thornton runs it now – Miles Thornton's cousin. She's got all sorts of local oddities – old photographs, letters, newspaper clippings..."

Tom nodded thoughtfully. "He was a strange one, by all account. Miles, I mean. Obsessed with capturing the siren's song, my granddad said. More than that, he said that Miles would sit out on the beach for hours, just listening."

Rita added, "They say he vanished with the storm – like he'd been swallowed by it."

"I need to know more about him," Stella said firmly. "About what he was trying to capture."

The idea of digging through old records felt almost comforting – a tangible link to the past and a potential key to unlocking The Saltwater Siren's secrets. She thanked them for the chat, promising to tell them all about her discoveries. As she stepped back out into the rain, she couldn't shake the feeling that the archive held more than just dusty documents – that it might just hold echoes of Miles Thornton himself.

The archive itself was exactly as Krissy had described – cramped and delightfully chaotic. Dust motes danced in the shafts of light that pierced through the grimy windows, illuminating shelves crammed with boxes, folders, and rolls of faded maps. The air hung thick with the scent of paper, glue, and a hint of something vaguely floral – probably Emily Thornton's perfume. A small, elderly woman with spectacles perched on her nose looked up from a pile of documents as Stella entered. "You must be Stella Sinclair," she said, her voice a little creaky. "Krissy told me you were interested in exploring."

"I am," Stella confirmed, smiling warmly at Emily. "I'm hoping to find out a bit more about Miles." "Of course, of course," Emily said, "follow me!" Stella found herself following the surprisingly nimble woman deeper into the archive. The storeroom smelled of dry paper and something faintly like lavender – Emily Thornton's scent, Stella recognised with a smile. It was a glorious mess, a curated chaos of forgotten Ashcliffe. Boxes overflowed with brittle newspapers tied with faded ribbon, shelves groaned under the weight of rolled maps depicting long-gone coastlines, and oddities – a chipped porcelain doll, a rusted fishing net, a collection of smooth sea stones – were stacked haphazardly on every surface.

Stella moved through it all, running her fingers along the spines of ancient folders. "It's been a while since anyone really dug here," she commented, pulling out a box filled with photographs. "Indeed," Emily agreed, peering over Stella's shoulder. "Most people just come in for the obvious – birth certificates, property deeds. But Miles always had a penchant for collecting the unusual." Stella's fingers rested upon a stack of old reel-to-reel tapes labelled simply "Siren Melody – 1938." They were tucked away in the back of a particularly dusty crate, almost hidden beneath a pile of brittle maps depicting Ashcliffe's coastline from the early twentieth century. A slightly faded photograph accompanying the tapes showed Miles Thornton himself, his young face alight with concentration as he held a microphone to his lips on Ashcliffe's windswept beach.

"These weren't on anyone's list," Emily said, peering over Stella's shoulder. "He must have been hoarding them." Stella carefully examined the notes attached to the tapes – handwritten in a neat, slightly slanted script. They were filled with Miles Thornton's observations about the wind speed, the tide, and the 'emotional resonance' of the sea on that particular day. "'The grief hangs thick in the air today,'" she read aloud, a shiver tracing its way down her spine. "It's fascinating."

"He was meticulous," Emily confirmed, nodding approvingly. "Obsessively so. He believed the siren wasn't just a mythical creature – she was an embodiment of Ashcliffe's collective memory, its hopes and sorrows." A small thrill ran through Stella as she traced her fingers across Miles Thornton's handwriting – familiar, almost comforting. It felt like a connection across time. "Do you think it would be alright if I took these back to The Siren and listened to them there?" she asked, clutching the stack of tapes to her chest.

"Absolutely," Emily beamed, her spectacles glinting in the weak light. "It will probably feel most at home there. He spent so much time on that beach – it'aut like they're waiting for him." She paused, a thoughtful expression on her face. "But still be careful with them! They've been gathering dust for almost a century."

"Of course," Stella replied, carefully placing the tapes in a small, padded bag. "Thank you so much." As she turned to leave, Emily added, "And don't be surprised if it speaks to you. Miles felt a very deep connection to that song. It was his obsession." As she left the archives, clutching the tape, Stella felt a thrill of excitement. It wasn't just about Miles Thornton anymore; it was about uncovering layers of Ashcliffe's story, one forgotten artifact at a time. And she had a feeling that tape held a key – a beautiful, haunting key – to unlocking everything.

Back at her flat above The Saltwater Siren, a rush of anticipation propelled Stella through the narrow staircase. It wasn't glamorous, far from it – just a small room crammed with the detritus of her creative life: half-finished sketches leaned against the walls, sheet music spilled from overflowing shelves, and her beloved acoustic guitar rested on a stand by the window. The scent of salt and beeswax mingled with the faint aroma of lavender – a lingering reminder of Emily in the archive. She hauled an ancient speaker system up from the basement, a relic from a bygone era that promised to deliver authentic sound, and set it up on a wobbly table, connecting it precariously to a tangle of wires. "Albert would not approve of this setup," she murmured with a wry smile.

As she popped the tape into the deck, a hiss of static filled the room before settling into the familiar melody – "The Siren's Lament." It was hauntingly beautiful, imbued with a palpable sense of longing and melancholy. Stella closed her eyes, letting the music wash over her, feeling an immediate connection to Miles Thornton. He hadn't just recorded it; he'd felt it. As the song progressed, she noticed subtle shifts in the sound – a slight crackle here, a brief drop in volume there.

It wasn't just the ageing tape; it felt like the room itself was responding to the music, as if it was absorbing its emotions. A creak from the floorboards below, a gentle sigh of wind through the open window – it all seemed to weave into the tapestry of the song. A warm smile played on her lips. It wasn't just sound; it was memory, longing and perhaps, even a little bit of the siren herself. She felt a pull, a resonance that deepened with every note – as if she'd finally found a piece of herself in the echoes of The Saltwater Siren.

Stella leaned forward as she played the song for a second time, immediately following this first. She held her breath as the opening notes of "The Siren's Lament" re-filled the room. The initial static cleared, revealing a sound that was both achingly beautiful and subtly unsettling – like a memory glimpsed through a rain-streaked window. It wasn't pristine; far from it. The melody was slightly muffled, as if heard through layers of damp wool or perhaps even saltwater. There was a certain distance to it, a feeling that Miles Thornton hadn't just recorded the song, but captured a fleeting moment in time – a specific storm, a particular tide. The notes themselves were exquisite - haunting and mournful, with a delicate vibrato that hinted at both passion and vulnerability. It spoke of vastness – of the sea, certainly, but also of something deeper, something almost lonely. Stella recognized it immediately, yet it felt alien too, as if she'd heard it before in a dream or a half-forgotten song.

As she listened further, she noticed subtle textures within the recording – the gentle hiss of the tape, the faint sound of waves crashing against the shore, almost like an echo layered beneath the music. It wasn't just a performance; it was an atmosphere. She closed her eyes again, letting the sounds wash over her, and felt a strange tug – a pull towards the past, towards Ashcliffe itself. "It's beautiful," she murmured to herself, almost afraid to break the spell. "But so sad." A shiver traced its way down her spine. It was familiar, undeniably so – like a piece of her own heart had been echoed within the melody. But it was also distant, as if belonging to someone else entirely – someone lost to time and the sea. A feeling settled over her, a sense that she wasn't just listening to a song; she was eavesdropping on a secret, a whispered story from centuries ago. "It's like he's still out there," she breathed, captivated by the haunting beauty of Miles Thornton's lost lament.

A sense of restless energy propelled Stella to grab her own guitar. The first two listens had been about absorbing the melody, letting it sink in. Now, she wanted to respond to it. Taking a deep breath, she hit record on an old portable recorder she'd brought with her – a relic from her London days. As the original tape continued, she tentatively added a simple harmony, layering her voice over Miles's melancholic notes. At first, it felt awkward, almost intrusive. She adjusted the volume carefully, striving for a balance that wouldn't overwhelm his song but would complement it. But as she listened back, she noticed something remarkable – her voice wasn't competing; it was joining in. It was like two currents merging, creating a richer, fuller sound. Encouraged, Stella began to experiment further. She added subtle embellishments, little flourishes and runs that echoed Miles's phrasing. As she played, she felt a strange connection to him – as if he were listening along, approving of her interpretation. It was more than just technical skill; it was an emotional resonance, a feeling of shared longing.

Stella let herself feel the music fully, allowing her own vulnerability to bleed into the recording. The melody shifted slightly under her touch, gaining a new layer of depth and emotion. A small smile played on her lips as she realised she wasn't just replicating his song; she was adding to it, building upon it with her own voice. With growing confidence, Stella began to harmonise more boldly, locking in with Miles's original part. It felt natural, effortless – as if she'd been playing the song alongside him all along. A genuine smile spread across her face as she realised she was not just hearing the siren's lament – she was becoming a part of it. "Okay," she murmured to herself, feeling a surge of excitement, "let's see what you've really got."

As Stella layered her voice over "The Siren's Lament," a profound sense of emotional resonance washed over her. It wasn't just hearing the song; it was feeling it – a deep, aching sadness that resonated with something buried within her own heart. The melancholy was palpable, laced with longing for a lost love, a forgotten dream, perhaps even a piece of herself. But as she continued to play, something shifted. Mixed with the sorrow was a current of hope – tentative at first, then growing stronger with each note. It felt like Miles Thornton wasn't just lamenting his loss; he was also looking towards the future, towards the possibility of reunion or renewal. As if in response to her playing, the room seemed to deepen around her. The shadows lengthened, pooling in the corners and dancing across the walls. A subtle chill filled the air, as if the temperature had dropped a few degrees. It felt thicker now, heavier – as if laden with forgotten memories and hidden emotions.

Stella noticed the dust motes swirling more noticeably in the shafts of light, illuminated like tiny spirits caught in the music. The old furniture seemed to sigh softly, as if remembering its own past. She glanced out the window and saw that the rain had intensified, drumming a steady rhythm against the glass – a perfect accompaniment to the song. "It's...it's like the building is listening," she whispered, feeling a prickle of goosebumps on her arms. "Like it remembers." The melody swelled, and for a moment, Stella felt as if she were standing on the shore of Ashcliffe Bay, swept away by the tide – carried back in time to join Miles Thornton in his search for the siren's song. It was a powerful, almost overwhelming sensation – a feeling that she wasn't just playing music; she was unlocking something ancient and profound.

The final chord faded into the rain-streaked silence, leaving a lingering echo of melancholy and hope. Stella leaned against her guitar, feeling slightly breathless from the intensity of it all. Just as she was about to switch off the recorder, a gentle knock echoed through the room. "Just popping in to see if you were battling with the blues," Eloise announced, stepping into the room without invitation. She'd clearly been drawn by the sound – her eyes were wide and focused, and a faint smile played on her lips. "I just had to hear it!" Eloise settled onto Stella's wobbly stool, closing her eyes as soon as Stella restarted the recorder, letting the song wash over her. The room seemed to hold its breath as Eloise listened intently, lost in the music. When Stella finally stopped recording, a comfortable silence hung in the air for a moment before Eloise spoke, her voice quiet and thoughtful. "It's like grief healing itself," she said softly, opening her eyes and fixing Stella with a knowing gaze. "Bittersweet, isn't it? Like remembering something beautiful that you almost forgot."

Stella felt a warmth spread through her – a welcome feeling of validation and understanding. "I know," she replied, surprised by the emotion in her own voice. "It just felt familiar. Like I'd heard it before somewhere deep down in my soul."

Eloise nodded sagely. "This place is full of echoes, you know. And melodies. It's waiting for them to be rediscovered." She glanced around the room, taking in the scattered sheet music and sketches with a thoughtful expression. "It feels like you're starting to hear it too." A playful glint sparkled in her eyes.

Stella tilted her head, intrigued by Eloise's observation. "Me? What do you mean?"

"It's not just the melody, Stella," Eloise replied, gesturing vaguely with a hand. "It's you. You're channelling something – a resonance, a memory... a piece of Miles himself." She paused, letting her words sink in. "You've been carrying his song around for so long, without even realizing it. It's not just about the music; it's about unlocking your own song."

"But I didn't know him," Stella said, a touch of defensiveness creeping into her voice. "Not even you or Albert knew him, he disappeared nearly a century ago!"

"Maybe you didn't know him consciously," Eloise countered gently. "Or even in this life, but you feel it, don't you? That pull towards the sea, that longing... it's in your blood, perhaps." She smiled knowingly. "And I think, with this music, you're finally letting it out." A final glance at Stella and a small smile, as if sharing a secret. "You're part of the song now, Stella. A vital note."

With a flourish, Eloise produced a Thermos of some sweet-smelling chamomile concoction from the depths of her large handbag – 'for the soul,' she declared – and settled onto the floor. Stella, having wandered to the kitchen to grab a pair of mismatched mugs, returned to sit with Eloise. The rain continued its steady rhythm against the windowpane, insistent in its intimacy. "So," Eloise began, taking a sip of her tea, "you handled that open mic night in The Chiron Cafe amazingly well – it can't have been your first time? What was that like?" Stella hesitated for a moment, then began to recount the story – the fear, the self-doubt, the desperate desire to disappear. As she spoke, she felt a surprising sense of release, as if sharing the memory with Eloise was finally letting it go.

"It's funny," Eloise observed, "you built this whole wall around yourself—using music as armour. But you can't fight your fears forever." They fell into a comfortable rhythm, talking about everything and nothing – their hopes, their anxieties, their pasts. Stella confessed her initial fear of returning to music, admitting that she'd been terrified of failing again. "But now," she said with a small smile, "it feels...different."

"It always does when you let go a little," Eloise replied. "When you allow yourself to feel the joy alongside the fear." They talked about their connection to Ashcliffe, to The Saltwater Siren – and to each other. Stella found herself opening up in a way she hadn't felt comfortable with in years, drawn to Eloise's perceptive gaze and genuine warmth. "It's like," Stella murmured, swirling the tea in her mug, "everything feels... lighter." A shared glance passed between them – a silent acknowledgement of the growing connection that was blossoming amidst the rain and the music. The night, and their journey with it, felt poised to begin.

As the two women talked, their bodies seemed keen to join in the conversation. Through lingering glances and brushes of hands, ones that started accidental and ended up as needy caresses, Stella found herself feeling both intrigued and slightly nervous. It had been a long time, longer than she cared to even attempt to remember, since she had taken this particular step with someone. Sure, she had shared some kisses – some chaste, some less so – with Albert recently... but this? This, Stella realised, was a different beast entirely. A quiet moment lingered between them, stretched thin with tension and possibility. Stella's fingers brushed against Eloise's once more, slower this time, more deliberate. Eloise's gaze didn't waver, and when their eyes locked, something unspoken passed between them – a question, an answer, a breath held too long.

Then the kiss came. Not tentative, not uncertain – it was urgent, raw, and filled with all the emotion they hadn't dared to name. Stella leaned in first, drawn by the magnetic pull of need and familiarity, and Eloise met her halfway with a soft gasp. Their lips collided, tasting of chamomile and electricity, and the room seemed to lean into them, shadows folding in as though offering privacy. The first kiss that night was all fire – a release. The second was deeper, hungrier, Stella's hands tangling in Eloise's hair as they stumbled back against the wall, knocking loose a sheaf of music pages that fluttered to the floor like forgotten feathers. Breathless laughter slipped between kisses, mingling with the steady rhythm of rain outside and the muffled hum of "The Siren's Lament" still looping faintly in the background.

Clothes were tugged loose in between gasps and giggles. Buttons gave way to trembling fingers. Scarves and sweaters were pulled over heads, dropped carelessly beside cushions and cables. There was nothing practised or perfect about it – only realness. Heat and vulnerability mingled in equal measure, every brush of skin like striking flint. Stella's breath hitched as Eloise traced a path along her collarbone, a gentle press of lips and palm grounding her even as her senses threatened to spin away. Eloise's hand trembled slightly, not from hesitation, but from the weight of emotion behind every touch. It wasn't just desire; it was memory, grief, joy, longing – a symphony of feeling conducted in silence. They collapsed onto the tangled blanket strewn across the floor, their bodies fitting together in a way that felt both fated and familiar. The music faded, but the rhythm between them continued – skin on skin, breath on breath, heart to heart. They moved together with a reverence that bordered on sacred, as if this was something ancient being rediscovered, not for the first time but for the first time in this life.

Stella pressed her forehead to Eloise's, stilling them both. Her voice came soft, warm against Eloise's cheek. "Thank you," Stella whispered, "for not asking me to decide. For not putting a limit on this... thing." Eloise swallowed hard, threading her fingers gently through Stella's hair, her heart pounding. "There's no limit," Eloise murmured back. "Not here. Not with you." Later, they lay tangled in the fading warmth of the moment, a hush settling over the room like a lullaby. Rain still tapped at the windows, gentle and insistent. As they pulled apart just enough to breathe, Stella caught the way Eloise looked at her – that same quiet confidence, that knowing light in her eyes. "The sea herself is limitless," Eloise said, voice low and certain, "as is the sky." And in that moment, Stella believed her.

16

CHAPTER SIXTEEN:
STARDUST IN THE TIDES

The air inside The Saltwater Siren was thick and expectant, a salty-sweet blend of beeswax polish and sea spray. It clung to the tongue, a tangible anticipation for the night ahead. Outside, a persistent drizzle painted the windows with shifting grey, and the fog machine hummed, already weaving its way through the room, promising a theatrical backdrop. Stella ran a hand over the worn velvet of her seat, feeling the familiar texture beneath her fingertips – a small comfort in the rising tide of nerves. The stage lights, warm and amber, cast dancing shadows on the walls, highlighting the peeling paint and exposed brick – evidence of the building's long and somewhat turbulent history.

Albert was a flurry of focused energy, his brow furrowed as he meticulously adjusted a tuning peg on Stella's guitar. "Just right," he murmured, testing the sound with a practised ear. "Little bit more resonance there." The note that emerged was clean and bright, a small victory in the face of the growing chaos. The room itself felt alive, humming with low-level energy. Small details stood out to Stella – the way the candlelight flickered on the brass fittings, reflecting tiny golden sparks, the faint scent of lavender from the diffuser Eloise had insisted on "To soothe the nerves and attract good vibes," she'd declared. Funny, Stella thought, to think that Emily Thornton's signature scent was going to be used with such power that night. Would Emily approve? Stella hoped so, just like she hoped to see the elderly archivist's kind face in the crowd during her performance.

Then, Stella noticed it: nestled amongst her guitar picks in a worn leather case, was it – The Photograph. The one that had haunted her for fifteen years. Alanna's photograph, really, more than it was hers. It showed her, younger, more confident, bathed in the golden light of stage lights before she'd ever even conceived of "Kiln Cold". Her body radiated both vulnerability and a fierce determination. Stella hadn't consciously thought about it until now, but as she pulled it out, a familiar tremor ran through her. The photo itself was faded, the edges slightly frayed – a testament to its journeying. It captured that moment perfectly – poised on the edge of something big, before the shadow of Alanna's critique had fallen. It felt heavier in her hand now than she remembered.

Stella glanced over at Albert, who was still meticulously adjusting her guitar's strings, oblivious to her internal turmoil. He seemed so calm, so grounded – a steadying force amidst the swirling anticipation. Stella took a deep breath, trying to push back on the memories – the feeling of being exposed, judged, smaller somehow. Less real. The sound of muffled chatter and excited voices drifted in from the small crowd gathering near the bar. Tonight wasn't just about reopening a music venue, it was about reclaiming something: herself. And maybe, just maybe, finally letting go of the past. The rain continued to fall outside, as if urging her on. The scent of salt and beeswax faded slightly as a sharper memory pierced through – a shard of ice in Stella's chest. Suddenly, she was back. Back in the sterile, bright light of The Quill's office, fifteen years ago. The air had been thick with tension then, the kind that clung to your skin like damp wool.

Stella remembered the feeling most vividly: the tightening in her chest, a dull ache that spread outwards, making it hard to breathe. It hadn't been a dramatic reaction – no screaming or tears. Just a subtle constriction, as if someone were slowly and deliberately squeezing the air from her lungs. A snake's favourite finishing move. Alanna Brooke stood before her, impeccably dressed and radiating an effortless cool – a stark contrast to Stella's slightly rumpled appearance. The photograph lay on the desk between them - The Photograph – capturing that iconic shot of Stella mid-performance, guitar slung low. "Pleasant," Alanna had said, her voice laced with a carefully measured disdain. "But safe, Stella. Pleasant. You've built an empire on pleasant. Where's the fire? Where's the grit?"

Stella remembered gripping her guitar tighter then, instinctively shielding herself. It was a small gesture, almost unconscious – but it had felt monumental at the time. She recalled the way the words had landed – sharp and precise, dissecting her art, her identity. "Kiln Cold" - Alanna had called her. And it was true, to an extent. She'd retreated after that, seeking anonymity in London – a deliberate shedding of skin, a conscious effort to disappear.

The flashback sharpened, pulling her further back into the moment. She remembered the flicker of defensiveness that had flashed across her face – a brief, almost imperceptible tightening of her jaw. It wasn't anger, not exactly. More like a feeling of being exposed, of having her most vulnerable self laid bare for all to see. "It's easier to be liked than loved," she'd mumbled, avoiding Alanna's gaze. A half-truth, perhaps, but it captured the essence of her strategy. Alanna had simply raised an eyebrow – a gesture that felt like a judgement in itself – and continued, "You've built a comfortable cage for yourself, Stella. Don't let it trap you." Stella remembered the feeling of being trapped then – not just by Alanna's words, but by her own fear. The fear of failing, of being judged, of exposing that vulnerable core that she had so carefully guarded.

It was a deliberate choice, she realized now – building that wall. Layering it with anonymity and pleasantry. It had worked, to an extent. She'd found peace in obscurity. But tonight, standing in the warm glow of The Saltwater Siren, surrounded by the echoes of its history, she wondered if that peace had come at too high a price. The sound of Alanna's voice - "pleasant but safe" – echoed faintly in her mind, a reminder of the potter-turned-critic who'd shaped so much of her life. She tightened her grip on the photograph, a small smile playing on her lips. It wasn't just a reminder of a past critique, it was a symbol of everything she had left behind – and everything she hoped to reclaim.

The stage lights warmed as Stella stepped forward, adjusting her strap one last time. The crowd, a mix of familiar faces and curious newcomers, buzzed with anticipation – a low hum that vibrated through the floorboards. It wasn't quite the roaring applause she remembered from before, but tonight felt different – more intimate, warmer. As she began to play, a slight tremor ran through her fingers. Nothing dramatic, just a subtle flutter, like nervous butterflies taking flight. It was a familiar sensation – a reminder of her first performance, all those years ago, when the pressure had felt almost unbearable. The opening chords resonated – clean and bright, but with a hint of melancholy. As she started the first verse, "You touched the edges, never deep...", her hand movements were tentative at first, almost hesitant. But as she sang, they grew more assured, her fingers dancing over the fretboard with a growing sense of confidence. The room seemed to dim slightly, bathed in shades of grey – reflecting the imagery of the song. A subtle misting effect from the fog machine added to the atmosphere, creating an illusion of depth and distance. Outside, the rain continued its steady drumbeat against the windows, as if accompanying her on stage.

"Mapped my skin but not my heat..." Stella's voice was smooth, a little huskier than she remembered – seasoned by time and experience. She caught the eye of Albert in the crowd, and for a fleeting moment, their gazes locked in silent acknowledgment. Of who she was now, of who she was then - of how far her journey to find herself had taken her from the path that she'd expected. As she moved into the chorus, "You chased the flame, but feared the slow..." her voice gained strength, filling the room with its resonance. This time, she didn't hold back – letting the emotion flow through her. She held that final note for just a beat longer than before, allowing it to linger and hang in the air. The audience seemed to respond instinctively, leaning forward slightly, captivated by her performance. A ripple of recognition passed through the crowd – smiles, nods, a few knowing glances.

"Now every note's a bitter gloss / A kiln-cold silence—everything lost," she sang, injecting a hint of vulnerability into her voice. Her hand moved to brush away a stray strand of hair – a small, almost unconscious gesture that spoke volumes about the years of carefully constructed restraint. During the second verse, "You wanted war inside a frame..." she closed her eyes for a moment, drawing on memories of that critical moment. She could almost feel Alanna's cool gaze upon her. The lighting subtly shifted – a brief flicker of shadow across her face – mirroring the feeling of being judged. As she reached the final chorus, "You lit the fuse, but missed the melt / Dismissed the world I slowly felt..." Stella opened her eyes, and met the gaze of several faces in the crowd – Krissy, Tom, Rita, Eve, Albert, and Eloise, the family that Ashcliffe had tied to her. Her voice soared, filled with a quiet strength – "A kiln-cold silence – everything lost." She held it for a beat longer still, letting the weight of the words sink in. As the final chord faded, a collective sigh swept through the room – followed by enthusiastic applause, warm and genuine this time. Stella offered a small, grateful smile, acknowledging the audience's appreciation. She caught Albert's eye again – a quick nod of encouragement. It wasn't just a performance now; it was a reclamation—a step towards letting go of the "kiln-cold silence" that had haunted her for so long.

Buoyed by the success of Kiln Cold, Stella continued to play the song she had been working on recently. She knew that if she waited too long, she'd talk herself out of performing it at all. As Stella began to play, the room seemed to soften, bathed in a shifting palette of greys and blues. The fog machine intensified its work, swirling tendrils of mist curling around her feet like sea spirits – clinging to her clothes, dancing across the stage. It wasn't just atmospheric, it felt connected, as if the building itself was breathing with the music. "I came with hands too tired to hold / The fire I once called mine..." Stella's voice started softly, a little tentative at first – like she was rediscovering her own sound. Her fingers moved gracefully over the guitar strings, each note imbued with a quiet longing.

"Found echoes in a salt-worn hall / And chords beneath the brine..." As she sang these lines, she tilted her head slightly, as if listening intently for something – or someone – within the room. The visuals intensified – streaks of light catching on the damp walls, creating an illusion of shimmering water. "The walls remember lullabies / That never found an end..." Stella's voice gained a little more strength here, a hint of nostalgia creeping in. Eloise, seated near the side of the stage, subtly nodded her head – picking up on the connection to "Kiln Cold." A small smile played on her lips. "But storms that sing don't break a thing – / They shape the way we mend" – Stella's hand rose slightly as she sang this line, reaching towards something just beyond her grasp. It was a gesture of both vulnerability and hope. As the chorus began, "And we were / Stardust in the tides...", Stella opened herself to the music fully. Her voice soared, filled with a sense of wonder and recognition. "Wreckage turned to light" – she held that note for just a moment longer, letting it resonate through the room.

Throughout the song, Albert's gaze followed her every move. His eyes – usually calm and observant – held a hint of something else tonight: a shared understanding, a gentle warmth. When she sang "You, the spark that caught the sound" he offered a subtle nod – acknowledging the unspoken connection between them. "You held the wire, you read the stars / You both saw who I'd been...", Stella's voice gained confidence with each repetition. She wasn't just singing about her past; she was inhabiting her future and the roles that both Albert and Eloise might have to play in that future. "I wasn't built for staying still / But you let me belong / A home not made of roots or walls

– / But harmony and song," – As she sang these words, Stella turned slightly towards Eloise, a fleeting moment of eye contact that seemed to hang in the air. Both Stella and Eloise shifted their eyes to Albert in the same moment. He, feeling the heat of their combined gazes, blushed.

As the music built to the final chorus, "'Cause we are / Stardust in the tides...", Stella's voice grew richer and more powerful – filled with emotion and conviction. She closed her eyes for a moment, lost in the music, as if she were floating on the ocean itself. "Falling, then we rise / You, the hands I didn't seek / But found me when I couldn't speak / A love that never hides – / Stardust in the tides." – Her voice cracked with emotion at the end of this line – a moment of raw vulnerability shared with a room of her closest friends and most casual acquaintances. As the final note faded, the fog seemed to swirl around her even more intensely, as if celebrating the revelation. The audience was silent for a beat – then erupted in applause – a wave of warmth that washed over Stella, feeling both familiar and new.

As the final notes of Stardust in the Tides lingered in the air, Stella stepped forward slightly, a small smile gracing her lips. A soft spotlight illuminated her face – highlighting the subtle emotion that still clung to her. "I... I wrote this," Albert murmured, stepping up to the microphone with a little hesitation. He held up a small, folded piece of paper – simply inscribed with his haiku. He paused for a moment, taking a deep breath – as if gathering his thoughts. Then, in a quiet, measured tone, Albert began to read: "Storms that don't destroy / only root us deeper still / stardust in the tides." The words hung in the air, simple yet profound. For a beat, it felt like time itself slowed down – as if everyone in the room was holding their breath, waiting for something – or someone. The sound of the rain against the windows seemed to intensify, adding to the sense of anticipation.

As he finished, there was a collective intake of breath from the audience – a shared moment of reflection. Then, slowly at first, it began: a ripple of applause – starting with a few scattered hands, then growing in intensity until it became a warm, enveloping wave. It wasn't a boisterous, celebratory roar like after "Kiln Cold," but something quieter, more considered – as if they were acknowledging the depth and resonance of the moment. Stella watched him, her eyes meeting his for a brief second – a small smile playing on her lips. She seemed to understand immediately what he was trying to say – that even after the storms, they were stilling rooted—stronger than before. As the applause began to subside, Albert offered a shy grin. "Just... a thought," he said quietly. Then, looking at Stella directly, he added, "It felt right." The audience erupted in another round of applause – this time led with whoops and yells from Krissy – as if celebrating not just the song, but the connection between them all. It was clear that Stardust in the Tides wasn't just a song: it was a feeling, a shared experience that had resonated deeply with everyone who heard it.

The applause began to fade, leaving behind a warm glow and a sense of shared emotion. Stella leaned into Albert, offering him a small smile as they stepped offstage – the scent of wood polish and sea air clinging to her clothes. "It felt complete," she said softly, gesturing towards the audience. "Like it was always meant to be." Eloise appeared beside them, swirling in a cloud of chamomile and woodsmoke. "Well, obviously," she declared with a playful grin. "You were bathed in moonlight, darling Stella – all moonbeams and whispers. You needed your celestial spark." Stella chuckled, turning to meet Eloise's knowing gaze. "And you've been keeping me grounded," she teased. "Naturally!" Eloise replied, tilting her head. "Without my constellations, you'd be drifting aimlessly. You needed the moon, Stella – a steady presence." She shot a playful glance at Albert. Albert stepped forward slightly, a subtle smile playing on his lips. "I provided the electricity," he said quietly, his gaze lingering on Stella for a moment. "The spark that caught your sound."

"Oh, really?" Stella asked, raising an eyebrow. "And did you also provide the grounding?"

"Perhaps," Albert replied, a hint of amusement in his voice. "Sometimes, all it takes is a steady hand to bring out the fire." He offered her a brief, almost shy smile.

"So," Eloise chimed in with a mischievous sparkle in her eye, "we each played our part – celestial, electric, and...well, you'd be the one to decide what you were."

Stella paused for a moment, considering their words. She felt a warmth spread through her – a comfortable blend of affection and curiosity. "I think," she said finally, turning to look first at Eloise and then at Albert, "I was just... found."

"And perhaps," Albert murmured, stepping closer, "you were always meant to be found." He let his hand brush against hers for a fleeting moment – sending a pleasant shiver through Stella.

"It's funny," Eloise observed, watching them. "Like the song itself – a blend of moonbeams and sparks."

"Exactly," Stella agreed, turning back to face them both. "And it feels like... like we all fit together."

"We do indeed," Albert said quietly, his gaze holding hers for a moment longer.

"Though, I think you're the one who really captured it," Eloise added with a wink. "You were the tide itself."

Stella laughed softly, feeling a warmth spread through her. "Maybe," she said, "but we all helped it flow."

Stella stepped away from the stage lights, seeking refuge in a small alcove overlooking the hall. The sounds of chatter and laughter still drifted to her, but they seemed softer now, less insistent – like a gentle current rather than a rushing tide. She leaned against the cool brick wall, closing her eyes for a moment – letting the memories wash over her. It wasn't just about the music, she realized. It was about herself. For so long, she'd been hiding – building walls of silence and anonymity to protect herself from judgment, from vulnerability. Kiln Cold had been a shield – a way to keep people at arm's length, but it had also trapped her. She opened her eyes and looked out at the audience. They weren't looking at her – not with the critical gaze she remembered. Instead, they were looking through her – as if seeing something deeper, something more authentic. She saw smiles, nods of recognition, a few misty-eyed faces – all sorts of evidence of connection.

It was a subtle shift - but it felt profound. It wasn't just about pleasing them; it was about sharing a part of herself, letting go of the fear that she wouldn't be accepted for who she truly was. "'I wasn't built for staying still... But you let me belong'," she murmured to herself, repeating the lyrics from Stardust in the Tides. It hadn't just been a line from a song; it had been a truth – a revelation. She hadn't found belonging – she'd allowed it to be found in her. She thought of Albert's quiet strength, his steady gaze, and the way he seemed to see through all her defences. And Eloise, with her sparkling observations and celestial wisdom – always reminding her to embrace the magic within. "It's not just about leaving behind the past," she realized, a small smile playing on her lips. "It's about accepting it – and letting it shape you." The fear hadn't vanished completely, there was still a flicker of vulnerability beneath the surface, but it felt smaller now. Somehow less daunting. Stella recalled the feeling of standing on stage, bathed in the spotlight, as Stardust in the Tides filled The Saltwater Siren. It wasn't just about performance, it was about release – letting go of the tension, the fear, the need to be perfect. "It's okay not to be perfect," she whispered to herself. "It's okay to be a little messy, a little flawed – a little stardust." She thought back to her initial reaction to Alanna's critique – that feeling of being exposed, of having her creative spirit judged. But now, it didn't feel like the end of the world. It was just a memory – a stepping stone on her journey. "It wasn't always about avoiding fire," she mused. "Sometimes, you need to embrace it – to let it burn away the old and make way for something new." She looked out at the crowd one last time - feeling a sense of gratitude, of connection. "Finally, I belong," she whispered, a genuine smile spreading across her face. "Not just here, in this room...

but somewhere within myself." It wasn't a grand declaration or a triumphant pronouncement – it was simple, honest, and deeply felt. It was the realization that she hadn't just found a new home at The Saltwater Siren; she had finally found herself. And maybe she was finally ready to let the stardust shine in its own right, and not just settle for a reflection of light in the tide.

By the end of the night – a resounding success in Stella's book – the rain had eased to a gentle drizzle, leaving behind a glistening sheen on the cobblestones. Stella stepped outside, set her feet towards the seafront. A few lingering candles flickered in the windows of the nearby buildings, casting a warm, golden glow over everything – painting the scene in hues of amber and rose. She tilted her head back, allowing herself to be enveloped by the vastness of the ocean. The waves crashed against the breakwater with a steady rhythm – a comforting heartbeat beneath the small town. It was a moment of quietude – a chance to simply be. The moonlight, filtering through the clouds, danced on the water's surface, creating shimmering patterns of light and shadow. It felt familiar, as if she had known this place – this feeling – all along. Stella closed her eyes for a moment, inhaling deeply – the salty air filling her lungs with each breath. It was more than just the scent of the sea; it was the scent of memory, of possibility, of homecoming all rolled up into one. With that, she was excited to see what tomorrow would bring. Opening her eyes again, she focused on a single point in the distance – a star glowing extra brightly, or perhaps it was a planet. Eloise would know, Stella thought. Maybe Albert would too, now she came to think of it. For a brief moment, she felt a sense of connection – as if the shining celestial light, and everything around her, were part of a larger, interconnected whole. She smiled – a genuine, unguarded smile that reached all the way to her eyes. It wasn't a forced or practised smile; it was as if something within her had finally loosened – allowing a little bit of joy to shine through. "Finally," she whispered to herself, her voice barely audible above the sound of the waves, "I'm not just singing to the sea, but with it." It wasn't just about capturing its beauty or echoing its rhythm; it was about becoming part of its melody – a small, shimmering note in its vast and ancient song. It was a feeling of belonging – a sense that she had finally found her place, not just in Ashcliffe, but within herself. Stella found herself wondering if Miles Thornton had found this kind of sweet clarity before he disappeared... she hoped he had. Stella took one last lingering look at the ocean, then turned back towards The Saltwater Siren – a beacon of light and music in the gathering dusk. A single thought resonated in her mind: "Home."

17

❧

CHAPTER SEVENTEEN: AFTERGLOW

Upstairs in The Saltwater Siren, night had softened everything. The walls, the breath in their lungs, even the wood beneath their feet seemed to hold less tension now. Outside, the rain had ebbed into a damp whisper, puddles collecting quietly under the eaves. Wind murmured against the windowpanes like someone humming just under their breath. Inside, the only real sound was the soft scrape of a broom across the floor. The lights were low – not off, but low, like the room itself knew the hour. Mismatched lamps cast warm puddles across the scuffed floorboards and worn rugs, shadows bending long around the corners of furniture. A record spun somewhere in the background — not playing, just turning, letting the last groove hum in lazy circles like it wasn't quite ready to sleep either.

Stella moved slowly, folding linens that still held the scent of smoke and salt. Her hands were sure but unhurried, smoothing each crease with a kind of reverence. She didn't look up when Albert passed behind her with an armful of tea cups, or when Eloise clicked the tarot box shut and placed it gently on the windowsill, like it too needed to rest. No one said much. They didn't have to. The silence wasn't awkward — it wrapped around them like a blanket, shared and sacred. It was a silence earned, the kind that followed something good and left no room for guilt or analysis. Just being. Just now. Albert crossed the room to blow out one of the candles near the old piano, and Stella reached at the same time, fingers brushing his. "Sorry," she murmured.

He smiled. "It's okay." They didn't move apart right away. Eloise chuckled from the couch, lazy and warm, her feet tucked beneath her. "You two trying to extinguish each other?" Eloise teased. "No," Albert said, glancing over his shoulder with the softest smile. "Just synced up." It was true. They'd moved all night like this – a kind of unspoken choreography. Stella passed the empty mugs to Albert without needing to look. Eloise picked up the blanket Stella had dropped and folded it before she'd even noticed it had fallen. When they crossed paths in the narrow hallway between the upstairs bath and the main loft, no one bumped into anyone. It was as though their bodies remembered each other's presence before their minds did. Shoulder to shoulder, they moved through the space.

Eloise padded barefoot to the corner bookshelf and began stacking stray books into neat little towers. Her skirt rustled like leaves. Stella reached to help but paused as Eloise's fingers brushed her forehead. "Hold still," Eloise whispered, brushing a curl away. "You always get this one little halo strand when you're tired." Stella didn't move, didn't breathe. The touch was light – barely there – but grounding, like a hand against her spine saying, stay. You're okay here. Albert emerged from the kitchen with a half-finished bottle of something sparkling and raised an eyebrow. "Anyone still thirsty?" Eloise shook her head, nestling into the couch now that her tarot had been put to bed. Stella took the bottle from him, their fingers grazing again. She sipped without speaking, then handed it back. "Thanks." He nodded and didn't step away. Instead, he reached a steady hand toward her elbow, guiding her around the uneven floorboard that always creaked louder than it should. "Careful," he said softly. "That one's a trap."

"I remember," Stella said. She hadn't remembered. But the warmth of his hand on her arm made her forget the lie.

The air felt heavier than it had all day, but in a good way – like gravity had thickened, making everything slower, quieter, more honest. Outside, waves moved in their ancient rhythm, echoing the rise and fall of lungs. Wind pulled at the glass but found no cracks to slip through. Inside, breath moved the same way. Stella inhaled, and Eloise's chest rose beside her. Albert exhaled, and Stella followed half a second later. Syncopated, but close. Three notes of the same chord. No one said it out loud, but they all felt it: the room had stopped performing. This was the part after the curtain call – not the aftermath, not the crash, just the after. When the show is over and the world doesn't end. When applause is replaced by the quiet thud of boots on stairs and the rustle of fabric being put away. The realness that settles once the glitter's gone.

Stella folded one last linen and placed it in the wicker basket at the foot of the stairs. She turned slowly, letting her eyes sweep over the room. Eloise was half-reclined on the couch now, tracing a finger along the hem of her sleeve. Albert leaned against the door-frame, thumbs hooked into his belt loops, eyes unreadable but soft. Stella realized she was smiling. Not the practised smile she once wore on stage. Not the wary smile she used in green rooms or bars or press junkets. This one was different. It didn't pull at her. It didn't hurt. I've never felt this kind of peace, she thought. Not after a show. Not even alone. It wasn't adrenaline any more. It was something older, quieter. A part of her that had been waiting – not for a performance, but for a place to be still. A place where silence didn't demand to be filled, and closeness didn't have to prove itself with declarations or metaphors or need. It felt like being inside a song she hadn't written yet. One made of breath and creaking floorboards and the memory of rain on the roof.

Stella moved toward the couch, and Albert joined her. Eloise lifted the edge of the blanket like an invitation. No words. Just the warmth of woven cotton and the echo of their shared breath. As she sat between them, their bodies barely touching, Stella let her head fall back against the couch and closed her eyes for a moment. She thought about all the stages she'd stood on. All the songs she'd bled into microphones. All the times she'd tried to make people see her. And now – here – when the eyes of the world weren't watching, and she'd never felt more seen. She didn't need to say it yet. The words were forming, slow and sure, like tide over rock. But she already knew the truth of them. She wasn't whole despite the broken pieces. She was whole because of them.

The clean-up had finished hours ago, but none of them had moved far from where they'd landed – a soft collapse into the old cracked leather couch that groaned under the added weight, as if resigned to holding them all one more night. The wind outside had gone quiet, muffled under a thick curtain of fog pressing against the windows, moonlight filtering through in slow, sleepy slants. They were tucked under the same worn knit blanket – one of those impossibly heavy ones stitched with memory and time. It smelled faintly of lavender and old books. The kind of scent that made you exhale a little slower. Albert handed a mug of tea across the small nest they'd made. His fingers brushed Eloise's, who passed it to Stella without looking. No ceremony. Just nearness. No one had said much since they sat down. There hadn't been a need. The hush between them wasn't silence any more; it was its own kind of language. "Tonight smelled like dust and rain," Eloise murmured, her voice scratchy with sleep and tea. "You ever notice that? Right when the crowd clears out and the windows fog up – it always smells the same." Stella sipped, her fingers curved around the mug like it held more than heat. "It smelled like something was ending. But not in a bad way." Albert leaned back, one ankle crossed over his knee. "It smelled like something was settling. Like the room finally exhaled."

They were all still dressed, but softer now – sweaters slipped loose off shoulders, shoelaces undone, boots kicked off. The fire downstairs had been banked hours ago, but the upstairs held warmth like a held breath. "You think it went well?" Stella asked, quieter now.

Eloise chuckled softly. "You mean the show, or all of this?"

"All of it," Stella said. Albert shifted beside her. His knee bumped hers and didn't move. "There was a moment during the second set," he said. "You looked out past the lights like you saw something no one else did. And then you sang like you believed it."

"I didn't see anything," Stella said. "I just stopped needing to pretend."

Albert nodded, slowly. "That's everything." The tea cooled in Stella's hands. She didn't drink more.

Albert's voice had the weight of someone who'd been holding something too long. "I used to think if something broke, it was ruined. People. Plans. Places. That you had to hide the cracks or throw things out because of them. But lately..." he looked down at his hands. "Lately I think maybe everything I've ever loved had a flaw in it. A chip, a bend, a scar. Nothing pristine. But still loved." Eloise turned toward him, her face unreadable in the low light. "You ever see one of those old Roman mosaics up close?" he asked. "They're a mess. Just pieces. Jagged glass, broken tile. It doesn't make sense when you're staring at the damage. But if you step back far enough –"

"– it's a pattern," Stella finished, voice barely a whisper.

"A masterpiece," Albert said. "Because of the pieces. Not in spite of them." They didn't speak for a long moment.

Outside, fog clung to the glass in thick layers. Inside, breath moved through the trio in slow synchronization, matching the rhythm of the couch's gentle creaks as weight shifted, legs stretched, heads leaned. Stella looked down at her wrist. There was a line there. Not grotesque. Faint, even. You might miss it if you weren't looking, but she always noticed it. A healed-over seam that once meant "stop," and now meant something else entirely. "This isn't where I broke," she said, tracing the line with her thumb. "It's where I was rewritten." Eloise didn't gasp. Albert didn't reach to fix anything. Instead, Eloise gently placed her hand over Stella's. Not pressing down. Just there. Stella's eyes stayed on the blanket. "I used to be afraid that if I stopped hurting, the music would stop. Like I'd lose the edge, the urgency. But tonight..." She looked up. "Tonight felt different. Like maybe it's not the pain that makes the song matter. Maybe it's what you build after."

"You can build cathedrals from rubble," Albert said, softly.

Eloise added, "And call it home."

Stella blinked once, slow. "What about you, Eloise? What keeps you building?"

Eloise smiled – not a bright thing, but deep. Private. "I think astrology saved my life," she said simply. "Not in a cosmic way. Just... it gave me names for things I didn't know how to feel. Helped me understand the parts of myself I used to think were broken. My fear, my chaos, even my hunger. They weren't flaws. Just placements."

Stella tilted her head. "And us?" Eloise looked at the two of them – her fingers still resting over Stella's hand, Albert's knee nudging hers. "We're a transit," she said. "An alignment. Not perfect. But meaningful. Held together by gravity and choice." Albert looked like he wanted to speak, but didn't. He just reached out, let his hand rest lightly on Eloise's knee. Her other hand found his wrist. And Stella, in the middle, felt every point of contact like a steadying pulse. No one shifted away.

The couch groaned as they adjusted, settling deeper. Stella leaned into Albert's shoulder. His body was solid, warm – the way anchor stones feel in the palm before being skipped across water. Eloise curled inward just enough that her knee brushed Stella's thigh, her arm drawn loosely over her own ribs like she was keeping her own secrets close. Eloise began to trace slow, meaningless shapes on Stella's knee with her fingertip. Not flirtation. Not performance. Just presence. Albert bent his head and kissed the crown of Eloise's hair. Not with urgency. With reverence. The heat between them wasn't sharp. It didn't buzz like early lust. It settled like embers, warm and glowing. Like the aftermath of a storm you thought might kill you, and now you're sitting in the calm, letting your skin dry in moonlight. Stella felt the shift inside herself before she could put words to it it. This – this right here – this is what real love feels like. Not a rush. Not a performance.

Not the high and crash of adrenaline and applause. Just a quiet yes across three hearts. She didn't speak it aloud. She didn't need to. Her head was still on Albert's shoulder. Eloise's fingers still drew circles she didn't understand and didn't need to. Outside, the fog thickened. Inside, not one of them pulled away.

The night had thinned to its softest hour – that quiet blue space where time felt fluid and the rest of the world with its bubbling insistencies had slipped away. Stella's flat above The Saltwater Siren held onto the final notes of warmth like a secret, its bones creaking softly with the shifting wind. A basket of thick, mismatched quilts — left thoughtfully by Krissy near the stairs — waited as if it had known they'd end up here. Eloise spotted it first, a gleam in her eye as she nudged Albert with her foot and pointed. "Sanctuary," she said. Albert chuckled and helped lift the bundle. Stella followed, her laughter low, amazed at how the simplest things – a shared look, a blanket, a small domestic task – now felt holy in a very real and robust way. They arranged the nest slowly, deliberately, like a spell being cast. Cushions pulled from old chairs, pillows scavenged from upstairs bunks, a tapestry flung down as a makeshift mattress. Eloise shook out a quilt, letting it fall like velvet rain. Albert dragged a small space heater closer. A dim fire burned low in the hearth, shadows painting soft gold across the floor. The sea breathed steadily against the cliffs outside – not roaring, not restless. Just present. They collapsed into the pile like leaves in the wind. Stella landed between them, her body folding naturally into theirs. Legs brushed. A hand grazed the small of her back. Albert's chest rose and fell beneath her cheek. Eloise's foot hooked behind her calf. No choreography – just gravity.

Touch came instinctively, never asked for, never demanded. The warmth of knees pressed close. A palm resting at the curve of a waist. The rise of goosebumps not from cold, but from closeness. No one needed to ask permission. They were long past that. Stella's breath hitched only once – a brief flinch of disbelief, of awe – before she exhaled into the softness and hardness both. "I still don't know how this is real," Stella whispered.

"You don't have to," Eloise murmured back. "You just have to be here."

Albert's fingers brushed Stella's arm. "We choose this," he said. "Not because it's easy. Because it's true." Stella closed her eyes. Her mind tried, briefly, to reach for what came next – the need to narrate, to define, to control – but it faltered in the face of this: the quiet grace of being held. They kissed like it wasn't new, but not old either. Just right. Eloise pressed her lips to Stella's cheek, then paused, letting Stella turn and meet her mouth in return – tentative at first, then deeper. Not hunger, not performance. Just presence.

Albert watched them for a moment – not possessive, not removed. Just witnessing, then joining, his hand at the base of Eloise's skull, guiding her gently toward him. Their kiss was slower still, built from years of trust and the gentleness of something just beginning. No rush. No firestorm. Just the heat of a match struck in the dark, enough to warm, not consume. The weight of arms around waists. The press of skin against skin. Eloise's hand tangled in Stella's waterfall of hair. Albert's mouth against her collarbone. A moan, low and startled – not from pain, but from the unbearable relief of being wanted exactly as she was.

Stella reached for both of them at once – fingertips trailing down Eloise's spine, then brushing Albert's chest, settling there as if anchoring herself to two constellations at once. They moved together in a slow, unhurried weave – not a spectacle but a communion. Breath was its own rhythm. Hands explored without conquest. Every kiss asked a question. Every sigh answered it. Between Albert and Eloise, the chemistry was deep, long-worn grooves that fit together like tide to shore. Between Stella and each of them, it was newer – not unsure, but reverent. Tender. Like writing the first lines of a song you already know the melody to. Eloise pressed her forehead to Stella's, her voice a hush of warmth. "You're not intruding. You're belonging." That unlatched something in Stella's chest. She made a sound, small and open, and Albert caught it with a kiss, slow and grounding. His hand ran the length of her spine. Eloise kissed her shoulder, then her jaw, her breath trembling with care. They touched with the kind of gentleness that only comes from people who have known firing – and survived.

Bodies pressed closer — not for display, but for nearness. The brush of lips down a neck. A palm flattening against ribs. The kind of softness that unravelled everything harsh. Hands. Hips. Breaths. The thrum of three heartbeats, braided like chords. And then? Stillness. Not the absence of motion. The fullness of it. Albert lay on his back, arms cradling them both. Eloise's head tucked against his chest, her leg slung over Stella's. Stella, curled between them like something precious, her fingertips tracing patterns into skin without needing to finish them. The fire had dimmed to coals. Their skin glowed from it. Outside, the sea kept breathing. The old wood of The Saltwater Siren creaked, not from weather, but from satisfaction. As if the place itself exhaled. A quilt shifted as someone reached for another edge of warmth.

A hum – Eloise, barely awake – stirred the air. Stella let her eyes close. Everything in her life had felt like proving something – surviving, performing, striving. This moment asked nothing of her. It only welcomed her in. She let herself believe it was safe. She let herself believe she was enough. And for the first time in a very long time, she felt whole. Not in spite of what she'd lost. But because of what she'd become. Her body melted deeper into theirs. A kiss against her shoulder. Fingers entwined with hers. Stella barely spoke, only mouthed the words. But they heard her. "I've never felt more like myself," Stella whispered, eyes fluttering closed. Sleep took the three of them – not as an ending, but as a promise.

18

CHAPTER EIGHTEEN: LETTERS IN THE RAIN

The Saltwater Siren was never quieter than it was the morning after a show. Not dead, exactly — it was never that — but settled, like the sea after a long night of weather. The stage still smelled faintly of smoke and sea salt, lights dimmed but not off. A stray sequin glinted on the floor like a half-buried star. Somewhere near the back, a speaker hummed a low, contented buzz, like it hadn't realized the night was over. Stella sat on the velvet couch with a blanket around her shoulders, Albert's socked feet nudging her thigh, Eloise curled beside her, head on her shoulder. Between them, a candle guttered inside an old jam jar. Someone had made coffee – strong, gritty, slightly burnt – and no one had bothered to find mugs that matched. They drank in silence, steeped in that rare kind of quiet that only came after something real had broken open.

Rain tapped the windows in a steady rhythm. Soft, unhurried. Eloise stretched, slow and catlike. Her cardigan slipped off one shoulder. "What time is it?"

"No idea," Albert muttered, not moving. "Somewhere between too early and just late enough." Stella smiled faintly but didn't answer. Her eyes were still a little glassy from the night before – not from tears

174

now, but from the kind of emotional saturation that left everything feeling soft-edged and sacred. Then the bell above the front door jingled. All three of them turned their heads slowly, like waking animals unsure if the sound meant danger or breakfast. Eve stood in the entryway, framed by the grey outside. Her hair was wet, curling from the rain, her coat dark with water. She held a small stack of mail in one hand, wrapped in a plastic bag, and a suspicious expression on her face. She blinked at them. Took in the blanket. The candle. The half-dressed, half-awake tangle of limbs and closeness. "Am I..." she said slowly, "interrupting something?" A beat. Then laughter – not guilty, not defensive. Just soft and shared, something cracked open wide enough to let the light in.

Eloise waved her in. "Come out of the storm, Eve. You look like a soggy ghost."

"I feel like a soggy ghost," Eve muttered, stepping inside and shedding her coat with a dramatic sigh. "It's post'o'clock. Mostly boring. Flyers, bills, a pizza menu someone hand-delivered like it was a love letter." Eve shook the bag, pulled out the bundle, and began flipping through. "But... this one stood out." She held it up between two fingers – a wax-sealed envelope, the colour of dried rose petals. No return address. Just the bare minimum, written in slanting, deliberate script: **Stella, The** Saltwater Siren, Ashcliffe-on-Sea. Stella didn't reach for it right away. She just stared. Albert sat up slowly. Eloise took the coffee cup from her hands and set it down on the floor. Eve looked between them. "You okay?" Stella nodded once, then reached out and took the envelope. It was Alanna's handwriting. No mistaking it. The room seemed to still, the rain outside growing louder in contrast. Stella ran a thumb over the edges before sliding a finger beneath the wax. It split cleanly — a soft crack that echoed more than it should have. She opened the envelope and pulled out a single folded sheet. Cream-coloured. Heavy stock. Alanna's script marched across the page with its usual precision – like she'd trained her pen to behave. Stella read silently at first. Her eyes flickered line by line, pausing in strange places. She didn't cry. But her jaw flexed once, ever so tightly. Then, after a few moments, her face was back to normal. Albert didn't speak. Neither did Eloise.-After a long moment, Stella inhaled – steady, quiet – and began to read aloud.

Dear Stella,

I don't expect you to read this. I only hope that if you do, it finds you somewhere with light. I was never very good at building things. Better at breaking, or judging the broken. I think you already knew that. The Saltwater Siren was never mine to save. I see that now. I only ever saw what it had been – not what it could be. The rust, the ghosts, the echo of voices. I couldn't imagine it reborn because I couldn't imagine myself changed. That was my failing. Not the building's. Not yours.

And you – I was cruel to you, even in kindness. I offered critique dressed up as care. But I was never listening. Not really. I heard you through the filter of my own fear. And so I labelled you "safe," when in fact, I was terrified of what you might become. Of what it would mean for me if you became it. So I didn't save the Siren. I didn't even try. But I knew, eventually, that someone would. Someone who saw the heat still glowing beneath the ash. It seems that someone was you.

If you're reading this, it means you've done it. You've brought the Siren back, or brought yourself back to it – which might be the same thing. I don't know. I won't ask for forgiveness. That's a kind of vanity I'm trying to grow out of. But I want you to know this: I was wrong. I was so completely wrong. You were never safe. You were molten. And only fire sings through salt.

Yours (if you'll have it),

Alanna

When Stella reached the final line, her voice trembled – not from pain, exactly, but from release. The words sat in the air like heat, rising off coals that had burned for a long time without flame. She folded the letter slowly. Held it to her chest. Eloise reached over, took one of her hands. Albert mirrored her, taking the other. Outside, the rain kept falling. But inside, something had lifted.

The Saltwater Siren was hushed, lit only by the dull silver of rain-light and the amber glow of a few surviving candles. The clink of water in the eaves, the faint creak of wood cooling after the night's heat – all of it wrapped the space in a kind of hush, not unlike reverence. Stella sat on the edge of the stage. Her guitar lay across her lap like a sleeping animal, untouched. One hand rested gently on its neck. The other hovered, listless, as if unsure whether to play or simply let it be. Beside Stella on the floor, Alanna's letter sat folded. Neat. Undisturbed. As if waiting to be buried. She stared out across the empty room. Rows of chairs half-shoved out of line. The echoes of applause still lived somewhere in the walls – but they were quiet now. Letting her be.

The first tear slipped down without warning. She blinked and let it fall. No sobbing. No great wrench of sound. Just the slow, inevitable tide of something breaking loose – gently. As if grief had been held too long, and was now leaking out from under the seams. Her shoulders rose with breath, fell with memory. A second tear. A third. Then the rest. Eloise came without sound. No heels today, no statement coat. Just soft socks, old jeans, the same cardigan from the night before. She didn't speak. She simply stepped onto the stage, knelt beside Stella, and placed a hand over hers. Stella didn't startle. Didn't speak. Her fingers shifted just enough to lace between Eloise's. Albert followed a minute later. He climbed the steps slowly, like approaching a sacred space, and placed a candle near their feet. It cast a soft halo around the three of them. He didn't stay, but pressed a kiss to Stella's crown and stepped back into the wings, where Eve stood quietly with her arms crossed. The four of them were still, held in a kind of orbit. One centre, three satellites. Bound not by explanation but presence. After a long silence – not awkward, just full – Stella spoke. Her voice was low and even, like wind moving through reeds. "It's not that I forgive her," Stella said. "It's more that I don't need to be angry any more."

Eloise gave her hand a gentle squeeze. "That's something better than forgiveness." They sat there a while longer. Not saying anything. Just listening to the rain.

Evening at the Siren carried a different kind of hush. Not silence, exactly — the building had never known that. But a hush, like a breath held at the edge of something sacred. Candlelight flickered in sconces and little tea tins. Rain had faded to a fine mist, the kind that blurred the world but didn't dampen it.

Stella stood at a corner table, a slip of paper before her and a pen in hand. She had rewritten the note three times. Crossed out whole thoughts. Started again. And now, she simply wrote what she'd known from the moment she read Alanna's final words: "I was always ready for firing,
but now I know I can weather real storms, too." She folded the note slowly, placed it atop the letter. Alanna's envelope was still wax-sealed, still heavy in the hand. The kind of permanence that paper rarely carries. It looked like it wouldn't be out of place in Emily Thornton's archive. Albert emerged from the backstage hallway holding a small crowbar and a flash-light. "I found the panel," he said. "There's a hollow behind the risers – used to be where the old fire curtain was bolted in. Apparently, people have tucked things in there for decades." He smiled at her, soft and sure. "It's as close to a time capsule as we've got." They crossed the stage together. Eloise followed with a small square of muslin cloth, the kind they used to polish brass mic stands and old guitar strings. Carefully, Stella wrapped both the letter and her note in it, like she was swaddling something too fragile to touch bare wood.

Albert crouched and wedged the tool under the panel, revealing the small, dark hollow. Inside, old playbills curled with age, a rusted lighter, a photograph of someone's band from 1973. The kind of detritus that becomes relics if you love a place long enough. Stella placed the bundle inside. She didn't hesitate. Her hands were steady now. She paused, just a moment, and whispered – not for the others, not for herself, but for the quiet, listening wood: "Stay safe." Albert resealed the panel with slow, deliberate pressure. It creaked home like it never meant to open. Not again, maybe not ever. And that was the point. It wasn't buried. It was planted.

Later, Stella stood alone on the stage. The others had drifted off – Eloise back to the kitchen to boil water, Albert checking the fuse box like he always did before locking up. The space had emptied out but hadn't gone cold. She ran her fingers along the smooth lacquered edge of her guitar where it leaned against a stool. Breathed in the scent of candle-wax, old wood, and rain-damp velvet. This was the room that had held her for months without asking her to be more or less than she was. She looked out at the rows of empty chairs, each one like a held breath. She said it aloud again. Not softly – but not loud, either. Just enough for the Siren to hear. "Only fire sings through salt." The words hung in the air. Not a question any more. Not a riddle. A truth, finally understood.

The breeze shifted, just enough to lift the edge of the sandwich board outside. It clacked softly against the wall, a heartbeat. The Siren was still cracked open to the morning, air moving through like breath through lungs. Eloise leaned, coffee in hand, sleeves pushed up, her hair catching sunlight in loose waves. Stella joined her, arms folded, their shoulders brushing with a kind of practised ease – no performance, no hesitation. They didn't speak for a while. Just watched the town unfurl around them. A gull screeched somewhere out over the water. Someone walked by with a dog in a tartan raincoat. A window opened and music drifted out – scratchy vinyl, probably Krissy's doing. "You know," Eloise said eventually, "it's kind of wild. That she just posted it here. Like she knew this was the last address that mattered."

Stella smiled, soft but sure. "It was the only one that ever did." They stood like that – soaking in the light, the quiet, the knowing – until the door behind them creaked. Albert emerged, stretching like a cat in yesterday's hoodie. "We're doing a roast," he declared. "Sunday. Proper sit-down. Gravy, the works."

Eloise raised an eyebrow. "For the three of us?"

"No," he said, eyes twinkling. "For the six."

"Six?" Stella echoed.

Albert gestured broadly at the air. "Us. And the other trio."

Eloise snorted. "You mean Krissy, Tom, and Rita?"

"They've gone full constellation," Albert said, sliding in beside them. "Playing together. Living together. Calling each other 'my guy' in public without any context."

"And no one's confused by it," Stella said. "Like everyone just accepts that's what it is."

"Exactly," Albert said. "Ashcliffe's got a new tempo. The siren's still the heart of it, but the pulse is wider now. It's not just about this place any more. It's about the dynamics. The orbit people fall into."

Eloise looked out at the street, at the people moving through it like notes in a score. "It's a town with new rules. Or maybe just better instincts."

Stella said, almost offhand, "So what if we stop pretending we're just a jam session?"

Albert blinked. "Meaning?"

"I mean us," she said, more certain now. "This – what we've been doing. The playing, the building, the nights I don't even realize I'm writing songs until someone hums them the next day."

Eloise turned to face her more fully. "You want to go official."

"I do," Stella said. "Not just emotionally. Publicly. I want people to know we're a thing. Creatively. Personally. Something with shape. With name."

Albert whistled low. "Damn. That's a real announcement."

"It's not sudden," Eloise said, nudging him. "It's been happening. We've just been letting it happen without naming it."

"Well," Albert said, standing straighter. "If we're naming it — I want something fierce."

"Something elemental," Stella agreed. "Something that says we burned, but we held." Eloise squinted at them. "Alright, my wild wordsmiths. So what do we call it?" There was a pause. Then Stella said, without hesitation: "Salted Fire."

Albert grinned, wide and unstoppable. "Yes. That's it. That's us."

Eloise nodded slowly. "Hard and soft. Heat and presence. Flame and shore."

"And it fits what people are already feeling," Stella said. "That this town isn't just rebuilding – it's transforming. That we're not survivors any more. We're signal flares."

Albert reached out, took each of their hands. "So. Salted Fire. Let's light it up." They stood there as the sun broke over Ashcliffe – three people who had lost things, and found each other. No rush. No stage yet. Just the certainty of something real beneath their feet. The wind moved through them like a promise.

19

⚬⚬⚬

CHAPTER NINETEEN: THE LOW TIDE TRUTH

The hush that followed dawn settled like salt on skin – barely there, but felt all the same. In the main hall of The Saltwater Siren, a gentle warmth radiated. Mismatched cushions, some threadbare, some gaudy in velvet and fringe, were strewn across the floor in a loose sprawl of intimacy. Stella lay half-draped in a crocheted blanket, one leg peeking out, toes twitching. Albert's head rested on her thigh, soft snores tugging at his lips. Eloise leaned against the back of the couch, mug in hand, steam curling past her cheek like a ghost's whisper. A half-eaten pack of bourbon biscuits lay open beside them. Someone had crushed a custard cream underfoot during the night, the imprint still ghosting the wooden plank. It looked like a scene from a storybook told sideways—a tender chaos, familiar and unfiltered.

Eloise reached for the last biscuit without moving much. "So," she said, voice still thick with sleep, "are we all pretending that last night was just a very well-lit dream?"

Albert cracked one eye open. "If it was, I've never had one that included nearly knocking over a vintage lava lamp mid-orgasm." Stella giggled – a real, belly-deep one that caught the other two by surprise. She slapped Albert's arm lightly. "You're such a menace."

"And yet," Eloise said, dryly, "you both keep inviting him back." There was no shame, no awkwardness. Just a stillness between them that pulsed with understanding, like the space between waves. It wasn't about what they'd done. It was about what it had opened. Outside, gulls cried. The wind stirred gently at the loose latch of the front door. Stella's gaze drifted toward the ceiling beams, then back to the faces that had, over months, become her anchors. "I don't know what this is, but I don't want to go back to pretending."

Albert reached up to brush a crumb from her jaw. "No one's asking you to."

Before anything else could be said, the front door banged open with the sound of a cymbal crash. Krissy swept in, her scarf fluttering like a flag behind her. She stopped dead at the sight of them, a knowing grin spreading across her face. "Aha!" she declared. "How very Ashcliffe this is! Do you have the proper permits, I wonder? Should I inform the Town Council?" Stella threw a cushion at her, which Krissy dodged expertly. Without warning, Krissy dropped a bag of pastries on the floor with a flourish, then perched on the arm of a chair. "Anyway. Thought you lot should know – word's officially spread. You're being called The Storm's Echo."

Stella raised a brow. "What does that even mean?"

"Oh, I don't know," Krissy said, voice syrupy with amusement. "Something about the storm last month, your opening night, and the way everyone's convinced you channel old shipwreck spirits now."

Eloise let out a bark of laughter. "That's ridiculous."

"That's Ashcliffe," Krissy shot back with a wink. "You give them mystery, they'll give you legend. You give them a scandal, they'll turn it into a ballad."

Stella chewed on the edge of her thumbnail, smirking. "Storm's Echo, huh?"

Albert sat up slowly, rubbing his eyes. "Honestly? I've been called worse."

The mood shifted again, not darker, but deeper. They felt the undercurrent now—not just warmth, but inevitability. Whatever they were becoming had already started to echo outside their walls. The Siren creaked in the quiet, like it was listening. Or waiting. The spell of morning comfort slowly gave way to a familiar restlessness. The Siren, with its lazy warmth and the scent of last night's stories still clinging to the cushions, had begun to feel too full of echoes. Stella stretched, her fingertips brushing Albert's, then Eloise's ankle beneath the blanket – quiet acknowledgments exchanged in silence. They needed air, and maybe coffee that hadn't been reheated three times. So they bundled themselves into coats and scarves, laughter still clinging to their shoulders like sea spray, and made their way through the mist-draped streets toward The Chiron Café. The walk was pften wordless, always easy, and punctuated by the occasional inside joke, but as the café's weathered blue awning came into view, so did something heavier – like the tide pulling back, ready to reveal whatever truth waited beneath the sand.

The bell above the Chiron Café's door gave its usual cheerful jangle – half rusted, wholly endearing. Outside, fog pressed close to the windows like a nosy cat, obscuring the salt-laced street beyond. Inside, the clatter of cups and the low hum of conversation provided warmth far deeper than the overworked radiator ever could. Stella slid into the booth beside Albert. Eloise already sat across from them, arms crossed but smiling, and Krissy balanced a tray of oat flat whites like a seasoned acrobat. Krissy set the tray down and flopped beside Eloise. "Right. Time to address the salted elephant in the room."

"Oh God," Stella muttered, reaching for her cup.

Albert leaned back with a grin. "No use trying to hide, Storm's Echo."

"Please don't start calling me that," she groaned.

"But it's so poetic!" Krissy protested, taking a dramatic sip. "Salted Fire, siren's voice, wild night after the opening – Ashcliffe's romantic engine is purring."

Eloise cocked an eyebrow. "They're not wrong, you know. It was kind of cinematic."

Stella flushed, but there was no venom behind the teasing. Just heat, and something that curled a little deeper. She looked between them – all too comfortable poking fun at her, but also holding space for something truer beneath the laughter. Albert leaned forward, fingers tracing the rim of his mug. "There's a story my nan used to tell. About the siren only truly waking when three hearts sync in harmony. Three voices. Three frequencies."

"Oh, come on," Stella said, though her voice had softened.

Eloise chimed in, unusually serious now. "It's not just folklore. Miles Thornton wrote something similar in his private notes. I've been going through his archives."

Albert's head tilted. "I didn't know you were digging into that."

"You're one to talk! I wasn't going to," Eloise admitted. "But something about the way Rhe Siren responded to your show – it didn't feel like coincidence. So I started looking. And I found something interesting."

Stella stilled, attention sharpening. "What sort of something?"

"Miles was obsessed with the idea of harmony," Eloise explained. "Not just musically – spiritually, architecturally. He believed that spaces could be designed to respond to sound. That The Saltwater Siren was built as a conduit – not just for one performer, but for three. A trinity. He called it 'synergistic resonance.'" She pulled a weathered notebook from her bag and flipped it open. "His words: 'Only in the triangulation of desire, memory, and sound can the sea truly answer.'"

Krissy let out a low whistle. "That is creepily specific." Albert's fingers drummed lightly on the table. "You didn't just wake the melody," he said, eyes locked on Stella. "You became it. With us." The words hung in the air, heavier than they should've been. Stella met his gaze, then flicked to Eloise, who was already watching her. Her pulse thrummed – not with embarrassment, but with recognition. Something had clicked into place during the opening night of The Saltwater

Siren. Not just between bodies, but between frequencies – something ancient, yet unfinished. Krissy looked between them. "You know, this is starting to sound less like gossip and more like prophecy."

"I don't want it to be a prophecy," Stella said, voice quiet. "I just want it to be real. Whatever it is."

Albert reached across and brushed her hand, grounding. "Then let's call it what it is – connection.

Doesn't have to be mythic to matter."

"But what if it is?" Eloise's voice was soft, speculative. "What if what we did – what we are doing – is exactly what the Siren was waiting for?"

Krissy laughed under her breath. "So what now? You three form a band, conjure spirits, save the town from a sea-witch?"

"Honestly?" Stella murmured. "Wouldn't even be the weirdest part of my year."

That cracked them all up, tension dissolving into a shared, open laughter. But underneath it all, Stella felt it: the pull of something that had always been there. She thought of that night again – how it hadn't felt messy or complicated. It had felt right. Three voices, rising in rhythm, no one leading, no one swallowed. Albert nudged his mug aside. "So, what else did Miles Thornton believe?"

Eloise flipped another page in the notebook. "That the Siren's acoustics weren't just tuned to a single note. They were tuned to resonance – something that only happens when frequencies match, but not mirror. Complement, not copy. He said it had to be instinctive. Organic. Built from affection and friction in equal measure."

Stella blinked. "That sounds like a metaphor for –"

"Sex," Krissy said cheerfully. "And polyamory. And probably your entire love life right now." Eloise chuckled, but there was warmth in it. "He called it trinal energy. A braid, not a line. Something that binds without trapping."

Stella leaned back, her throat tightening slightly. "And what happens when it fades? If one strand pulls away?"

Albert didn't look away. "Then the melody shifts. But it doesn't have to break."

Eloise nodded. "That's the thing about harmony. It isn't static. It evolves. Moves."

Krissy drained her cup. "God, I love it when our existential crises come with coffee." They all laughed again, but the silence that followed was rich, full of unspoken invitations. Eventually, Stella looked out the window, the mist thinning just enough to show the familiar silhouette of The Saltwater Siren down the hill. Her voice was quiet. "So if this is more than a fling, more than a night or two of epic sexual acrobatics – what does it become?"

Eloise leaned in. "It becomes what we choose."

Albert added, "And what we continue to make – together." Stella looked at them both. There was no pressure in their eyes, no ultimatum. Just presence. Invitation. And a shared frequency, humming quietly under their skin. The fog lifted a little more outside. And with it, clarity began to form – not in answers, but in intention. They weren't chasing the legend. They were living it.

By the time evening fell, the moon hung low and full above the coast, casting a silver-blue sheen across the sand. The tide had receded just enough to expose the stretch of beach where the sea foam curled like breath. The siren's call was softer here, more felt than heard. The three of them moved without speaking, drawn forward by something older than curiosity – something instinctive. Stella carried her guitar like a talisman, her bare feet sinking lightly into the wet sand. Albert and Eloise flanked her, their presence anchoring her in the moment. Wind tugged playfully at their hair, the salt air thick with unsaid things. They'd come here for the ritual – yes – but more than that, to understand what pulsed between them. What it meant. What it could become.

Stella sat first, grounding herself in the earth's chill. The guitar settled on her thigh like it had grown from her, her fingers already finding the chords before she consciously thought to play them. Albert lowered himself beside her, his hand brushing hers as he steadied her wrist – not a correction, just contact. Eloise knelt opposite, watching Stella with a gaze so steady it nearly undid her from her insides out. The melody unfurled slowly, fluid and low like a tide drawing breath. Stella closed her eyes, letting the music move through her body, head tipping back as the song found its shape. The notes weren't just heard, they were felt – vibrations skimming over skin, stirring sand, whispering against the cliff face. A deeper resonance stirred from the sea, as if something out there, either beneath or beyond them, was answering. The echo wasn't just auditory now. It rippled through Stella's bones, syncing with her heartbeat, pulled forward by the nearness of Albert's body and Eloise's silent, magnetic stillness. They weren't just witnesses, they were part of the sound.

Albert's voice, when it came, was low and reverent. "You're the fire in the tide..." He reached out, fingers tracing the line of her forearm before his palm came to rest over her hand, grounding the chord she held. "...and we're the salt that keeps it burning." The air between them shimmered, somewhere between tension and reverence. Eloise leaned forward then, her hand finding Stella's shoulder, firm and certain. "Do you feel that?" she murmured. "It's never echoed like this before. Not until now." They let the final note fade before moving. Stella reached into her satchel and pulled the large shell free – the same one she'd placed here during the last low tide, the one that had hummed with an energy she couldn't name. This time, there was no hesitation. She set it gently on the sand before them, the sea just far enough to allow them a moment.

All three knelt now, forming a triangle around the shell. The wind stilled. Each of them extended a hand, fingers meeting briefly over the curve of the shell's back, and then resting together in quiet contact. Not ceremonial, but intimate. Wordless. Real. Something shifted then – beneath the shell, beneath the sand. A soft hum, barely perceptible, vibrated up through their fingertips and into their chests. Stella gasped, not from fear, but from recognition. This wasn't metaphor.

This was bond. Synergy. The trinity Miles Thornton had written about. The siren didn't rise alone, she rose with. Albert's thumb traced the side of her hand. Eloise's fingers curled slightly around hers. The shell seemed to pulse once more, then stilled. And in the hush that followed, the sea, for just a breath, seemed to sing back.

When they returned, the light inside The Saltwater Siren had dimmed to match the softness of twilight outside. The afterglow of their beach ritual still clung to them – not as energy, but warmth, like the last heat of sun caught in sand. The usual clutter of the main room – blankets, mugs, discarded books – formed a nest of comfort that welcomed them back without question. Stella settled onto the worn velvet couch first, curling her legs beneath her, her damp hair curling at the ends from sea mist. She still smelled like brine and cedarwood. Eloise followed quietly, taking the seat beside her without needing to speak. Albert moved slower, methodical as always, bringing in a steaming mug of tea and setting it in Stella's hands before sitting at her other side. No words at first. Just the sound of the wind against the windows, the gentle creak of The Siren adjusting with the tide.

Albert's hand came to rest on Stella's back, a thumb tracing slow, unconscious circles between her shoulder blades. She didn't tense. Instead, she leaned into it, letting herself be held without having to ask. Eloise reached forward and plucked a strand of seaweed from Stella's hair, her smile teasing, affectionate. "You always bring back souvenirs," Eloise murmured.

Stella gave a soft, half-laugh. "Guess I'm a collector now." They let silence stretch for a while. Everything that needed to be said was still humming between them, like the echo of that low tide melody. "I kept thinking I needed to... prove it," Stella said finally, her voice low but sure. "That if I couldn't explain it, show it, measure it somehow – it wouldn't be real." Albert's hand paused briefly on her back. "And now?" She looked toward the window. The ocean beyond glimmered with the dying sun, its waves gilded and slow. "Now I think...

not everything has to be proven to be true," she said. "Some things just are."

The confession sat in the room like a small, glowing ember. Not dramatic, not grand. But real. Her vulnerability wasn't sharp-edged – it was offered like a bridge. Eloise leaned in slightly, her tone teasing but gentle. "Look at you. Getting all poetic on us. You're going to give Albert a run for his money, at this rate!"

"I'm serious," Stella said, nudging her. "We've been chasing answers, digging through lore and letters and chords, and I think maybe... the answer's been here. In the way we feel. In what happens when we're together."

Albert's gaze was warm, steady. "You don't need to justify anything, Stella. We feel it too. That's always been enough."

The silence that followed was different – saturated with mutual recognition. There was a subtle shift in the air, a thread tightening between Stella, Eloise, and Albert. Stella turned to meet Albert's gaze, and in that moment, everything unsaid between them passed in a breath. His hand moved from her back to her jaw, not rushing, just offering. She tilted her head into his palm. Eloise watched them with something like amusement – yes, that was the top layer of it, but there was also something softer, deeper. She wasn't on the outside of this moment. She was part of its shape. "You two gonna stare at each other all night?" Eloise said, voice lazy and fond.

"Maybe," Stella murmured, smiling faintly. Albert chuckled, but didn't look away. There was no kiss – not yet. But there didn't need to be. The intimacy was in the stillness, the nearness, the quiet. In the way their shoulders touched, how Stella's knee pressed lightly against Eloise's, how Albert's arm curled protectively along the back of the couch.

The last light outside dipped into gold, then rose into a deeper blue. Shadows stretched long across the floorboards. Eventually, Stella let her head fall gently onto Albert's shoulder, her fingers wrapping around the mug, still warm. Eloise leaned into her other side, and together they made a constellation of contact – interconnected, quiet, true. From the window, the ocean glistened like a mirror to the sky. Calm, for now. But alive. Stella spoke again, this time barely above a whisper. "Not everything has to be proven to be true..." Albert shifted just enough to press his lips to her temple. "...just felt," she finished. And the tide, somewhere in the distance, began to rise again.

Eloise was the first to move, shifting just enough to grab the old knit blanket tossed over the armchair. She flicked it open with a lazy grace and draped it across all three of them without ceremony, her fingers brushing Stella's wrist in the process. A silent offering. A closing of the circle. The air in the Siren had cooled with the coming dark. Outside, the wind picked up just enough to stir the chimes by the back door, and they sang low and mournful, like a lullaby from the deep. For a while, no one said anything. They didn't need to. Stella traced the rim of her mug with her thumb, letting the quiet spool out around them like thread. She felt herself sinking – not into sleep, but into something safer. Deeper. A stillness that didn't ask for performance or explanation. Just presence. "I think," she said eventually, "that the Siren isn't a place, or even a myth. I think it's this."

Albert turned his head slightly toward her. "This?"

She nodded. "Us. This feeling. The way we resonate – like chords played in harmony. I used to think the magic was in the melody... but it's in the connection. The blending."

Eloise let out a soft breath that wasn't quite a sigh. "You sound like Miles Thornton more and more each day."

"Maybe he wasn't completely wrong," Stella said. "Just looking in the wrong direction." Albert's fingers were still at the nape of her neck, gentle, almost meditative. "I think he was looking forward. Trying to find what hadn't been seen yet."

"And maybe we're it," Eloise added, quieter now. "The thing he was missing."

They let that idea settle between them. It didn't feel too big any more. It felt like something they could carry together. The tea had long since cooled in Stella's mug, but she kept holding it, fingers wrapped around ceramic like it was an anchor. She shifted slightly to glance at Eloise, who met her gaze with calm, curious eyes. "I'm glad it's you," Stella said simply. Eloise blinked, then smiled. Not sharp or clever this time. Just open. "Me too." Albert's arm tightened subtly around Stella's shoulders. "Me three," he said, with that dry humour of his, which somehow made it more sincere. And there it was again – that current, soft and slow, moving between them like a tide beneath still water. A recognition that this wasn't an accident. It wasn't chaos. It was a choice being made in every quiet, shared breath.

Eloise leaned her head back against the couch cushion and closed her eyes for a moment. "Do you think people will understand? The Town Council kind of people, I mean."

"Maybe not those particular people," Stella admitted. "But I don't think we need them to."

Albert nodded. "Some things aren't meant to be defined. Just lived." Silence returned, this time threaded with a sense of completion. The chapter wasn't over – not really – but the shape of it had settled. Found its balance. Outside, the moon had risen, casting its silver glow across the water and sending fractured light through the window-panes. The Saltwater Siren groaned softly, as if responding to the shifting tide. Stella's eyelids grew heavy, but she didn't want to sleep yet. Not while this moment still held her. "What now?" she asked softly. Eloise opened one eye and considered. "Tomorrow, we can go through Miles Thornton's last notes again. I think I missed something about the triad references – there might be more to it than we realized."

Albert snorted. "Even when we're not trying to prove anything, we're still digging."

"Can't help it," Eloise said, smirking. "It's in our stars."

Stella laughed, low and sleepy. "Okay. But tonight... can we just be here?"

Albert leaned his head against hers. "That's all I want." Eloise nodded, her hand finding Stella's beneath the blanket. Their fingers curled together, warm and sure.

The Siren creaked again, and a breeze swept through the window crack, carrying with it the scent of salt and something older – seaweed, driftwood, and the distant promise of storm and song. Stella let her eyes fall closed, surrounded by warmth, by quiet hearts, by people who saw her not as a legend or a spark – but as something alive and loved. No chords. No spectacle. Just the hush of togetherness and truth. Somewhere, the ocean whispered its approval. And in that whisper, a promise: the melody would come again. But for now, this stillness was enough.

20

CHAPTER TWENTY:
ECHOES FORWARD

Stella's journal, dated one year to the day since the grand reopening. She never intended to share these, but leaves them out anyway:

    Warm light on old wood
Fretboards hum like shorebirds cry
History in tune
    Salt on windowpanes
Driftwood stacked like memory
We built what we kept
    Laughter finds the seams
In cracked barstools, chipped-glass nights
Everything still sings

Downstairs, The Saltwater Siren awakens. Albert flips the lights on in a slow sequence – like bringing a stage to life. The big filament bulbs hum to life with a buttery glow, casting soft shadows over the scratched floorboards. The jukebox clicks in the corner, calibrating itself like an old friend clearing its throat. Krissy sets up her trivia slips at the bar, chewing a pencil with the intensity of a general planning a siege. A young couple giggles over their first drinks, unsure whether they're here for the music or each other. The old mural of the ship and the moon has faded a little more, but someone has stuck tiny pressed flowers along the frame. A quiet kind of reverence. Out front, Eloise arranges her tarot deck by feel, not order. Her fingers are ink-smudged. A group of teenagers peers in through the open door. She nods at them: come in, it's safe here. And upstairs, Stella writes. The journal rests in her lap, the ink still damp on the page. Through the half-open window comes the distant sound of tuning strings, a child's squeal, the clink of glasses. The rhythm of the place. The rhythm she has chosen to live by. Stella closes the book softly and listens. The Siren exhales, then inhales again – timeless, tireless, and entirely alive.

ONE YEAR LATER

The Saltwater Siren glowed like a lantern against the blue dusk. From the old deck, the soft flicker of string lights made the polished driftwood railings look gilded. Laughter spooled out from its open doors, tangled with the warble of a fiddle in mid-rehearsal. Summer rolled through the breeze in slow, honeyed waves – salt, lilac, something cooking somewhere down the street. It smelled like staying. A set of boot soles paused at the threshold. The new performer was young, maybe twenty, if that. Guitar case gripped like a life raft, denim jacket covered in stitched-on patches: comets, cats, queer pride flags faded from washing. They looked up at the arched sign over the door and blinked, just once. "You made it," Stella said. The performer jumped slightly. They hadn't seen her. Stella stood just inside the doorway, silhouetted by the amber-lit interior. Her hair was piled high and imperfect, wisps caught in the night air like kelp in tide. No stage lights, no applause – but she had presence, like a lighthouse knows its own beam.

The performer nodded, lips parted but uncertain. Stella didn't press. She simply stepped forward and held something out. A guitar plectrum. Etched with a tiny moon. "For luck," she said. They took it with reverence. "Thank you."

"Break their hearts a little. That's how you know you've played it right." The performer smiled, and finally stepped inside.

Krissy, inside, was already mid-rant. "I will personally challenge the British Museum to a custody battle over that artifact if someone says the wrong answer." Laughter burst out across the bar, falling in unhurried waves. The trivia slips were piled like confetti along the countertop. Krissy wielded a mechanical pencil like a gavel, her brow furrowed in exaggerated menace. She wore a pinstripe vest and mismatched socks, the latter hoisted over tattooed calves. Trivia Night was her kingdom, and the Siren her unruly court. "What ancient object, supposedly cursed, was donated anonymously to the Smithsonian in 1987?"

"The Hope Diamond!" someone shouted.

"Wrong shiny, wrong continent. But at least you yelled it with confidence. That's worth half a point." Krissy tossed a pretzel into the crowd and it was caught mid-air by a cackling Rita. A pause as Krissy scanned the next card. Her smirk softened. "This one's a little different," she said, quieter. "You get double points if your answer makes me cry." People leaned in. "What's something – or someone – you carry with you, even when they're gone?" The bar fell still. A woman near the back whispered something to her partner and squeezed their hand. A man scribbled fast, then folded his paper with the care of a letter. Krissy didn't rush them. For a moment, The Saltwater Siren didn't need trivia, or music, or even words. Just space to hold things that still mattered. Krissy smiled. "Okay. Moving on – round three, 'Epic Fails in Maritime History.' Let's go." The room exhaled in laughter again.

In the back, near the shelf of battered poetry books and faded hand-printed zines, Eloise sat cross-legged behind her table. Her tarot cloth was galaxy-black with threads of gold stitched like constellations. Incense trailed like sea fog above her cards. A teenager approached, hesitant. Hoodie sleeves tugged over their fingers. Eyes quick and searching. "Can you... tell me something?" they asked. Eloise nodded. "Sit." She dealt three cards without looking down. The

Hanged Man. The Star. The Page of Cups. The teen frowned. "Is that bad?" Eloise tilted her head. "It's not good. It's not bad. It just is. You're in a waiting place. But you've got something blooming in you. It's loud, and scared. You're trying to carry a secret like it won't grow teeth."

The teen's face twitched. "Are you always this weird?"

"Yes," Eloise said calmly. "But I'm also accurate." They didn't argue. Just nodded, slowly. After a minute, they asked, "Did you ever feel like you were wrong? Like, your whole self?"

"I felt like I was too much," Eloise said. "And then I realized too much was exactly the right amount. For the right people." The teen blinked. Then smiled.

Outside on the deck, a first date unfolded with nervous grace. The couple sipped local cider and played with the candle's wax. One wore hiking boots, the other vintage red lipstick. They laughed softly, knees knocking beneath the table. Behind them, children twirled near the jukebox, which spun an old jazz tune remixed with glitchy beats. A girl with purple ribbons in her hair led the charge, her dancing half-play, half-ritual. Inside, an old man hunched at the end of the bar. He sketched musicians in pen on napkins, swapping one for another with quick, expert lines. The fusion band on stage wove cello harmonics with synth loops and stomp-clap percussion. The lead singer – a powerhouse in velvet hotpants – channelled something that sounded at least half holy. "Thanks to Stella for the house style," they murmured into the mic. "She taught us ghosts don't end. They remix." The crowd roared its approval.

The interior of the Siren told its own stories. Photos lined one corner – sepia tones, Polaroids, candid shots. In one, Stella and Albert carried a crate of records together, both laughing. In another, Eloise was a blur in motion, arms full of books. Someone had added fresh annotations in silver ink. Above the coat rack, a chalkboard bore the evening's quote: "Laughter finds the seams / In cracked barstools, chipped-glass nights / Everything still sings." Underneath, someone had written in smaller chalk: Stella's words. Our truth. There were new additions, too. Reclaimed wood benches shaped like waves. A bookshelf that turned when touched, revealing a listening nook behind it. A drink menu scribbled on pressed sea glass. But nothing old was erased. Only built on.

Stella moved through the night like a steady orbit. She didn't linger. She adjusted chairs without fuss. Replaced a candle. Refolded a trivia slip someone had crushed in excitement. Smiled at the old man's sketches. Tapped a finger twice against the shoulder of the lead singer, her way of saying: "you're doing it right." Albert's laugh echoed from upstairs. Eloise's tarot corner murmured with new queries. Stella took it all in like breath. The music rolled on. Someone clinked glasses. A child shrieked in delight. Outside, someone kissed someone else and the world kept going. Stella stepped away. She moved past the bar, through the side hall, up the narrow stairs. No one stopped her. No one needed to. In her upstairs studio, the window was cracked open. The sounds of the Siren came faint but clear – like a song you can hum in your sleep. Stella sat down. Opened a new journal. The ink hadn't touched the page yet, but she smiled anyway. Below, The Siren lived on. Not because of her, but because of all of them. And because she had let go – not of the place, but of needing to hold it alone. She wrote one word: Again. Then she set down her pen and listened.

The floorboards creaked the same way they always had: in sighs and groans, like they too were settling in for the evening. Stella sat cross-legged on a faded velvet cushion, spine tall, pen poised. The journal was open across her lap, a loose handful of its predecessors fanned around her like drifted leaves. The air smelled of sea salt, old wood, and bergamot from a tea Albert must have brewed downstairs. The sun slanted low through the west-facing windows, casting soft ribbons of apricot and amethyst across the studio floor. Dust hung suspended, catching gold like it belonged to it. From the corner, a record spun something soft and wordless – part ambient, part jazz. The melody rolled in and out like breath: not regular, not predictable, but entirely right. Her chalkboard wall stood beside her, a dark tide of scribbled chord ideas and haiku fragments. One corner read: 'C – a wave in-side the body / disappears, returns.' Another line hovered below it, written in white grease pencil: 'Don't force it. Follow.' Stella leaned forward and began to write: 'waves forget nothing / they come back only softened / as if by dreaming.' Her pen paused. She added another, shifting the rhythm: 'four steps from silence / a child hums an ancient tune / no one taught her why'. She tapped the page. Somewhere below, laughter drifted upward from the deck. Someone rang the bell near the bar – the way Krissy signalled a perfect trivia score. The Siren was still singing, Stella just wrote the echoes.

From the far corner of the room, Albert hummed tunelessly. He sat surrounded by coils of cable and open amp guts. His long fingers tightened a tiny screw as he leaned in, squinting at the soldering. A ce-ramic mug of tea steamed beside him, unattended but fragrant – gin-ger, honey, something grounding. "That F was nice," he said, without looking up.

Stella smirked. "Which one?"

"The one in the fifth bar. The breath between the last line of the haiku and the chorus." He plucked a string on the lap steel beside him, holding the note in the air like a held gaze. It resonated, then disap-peared. She nodded. "Too on-the-nose?"

"No," he said. "It feels like a question."

"That's what I was hoping for." He tightened one last bolt, then flicked the amp on. A low thrum answered him. Albert nodded in satisfaction. He reached for the mug, sipped, and stood with a quiet grunt. "Tea?"

"I'm good," Stella said. Instead, he walked over and placed his mug on her windowsill. They didn't speak for a long moment – just stood there, shoulder to shoulder, looking out at the sea. The breeze carried in the faintest notes of the band downstairs. When he finally turned to go, he patted her shoulder. Once. Familiar, wordless. Enough.

Near the bookshelf, Eloise lay curled up beneath a threadbare shawl she'd claimed months ago from The Saltwater Siren's 'Lost &

Found' bin. Her lips parted slightly in sleep, and one hand twitched as if still turning cards. "Pineapple," she murmured. Stella arched an eyebrow. Eloise shifted, then fell still again. Stella crossed the room and gently lifted the shawl, tucking it around her with care. Her fingers lingered on Eloise's hair – soft curls splayed across the cushion like inkblots. A familiar ache bloomed in her chest. Not sadness, not joy. Just the weight of love, quiet and relentless. Stella went back to her journal. This time, the pen moved slower. Less a channel, more a searchlight: 'this is how we stay / not through walls or locks or names / but the breath between'.She flipped the page and wrote in prose: 'I've lost count of the seasons. Not because I wasn't watching, but because they've started to braid together. Last week, a winter coat hung next to a straw hat in the cloakroom. No one batted an eye. The Siren's rhythms don't obey the calendar. They follow music. Memory. The pitch of a returning regular's voice. The footfall of a nervous first-timer. Eloise's deck has seasons of its own, mapped in mystery. Albert measures time in repairs. I do it with chord changes. This year wasn't about achievement. It was about weathering. Mending. Tuning back in.' Stella stopped writing for a moment, paused, listening. The record had finished. A soft hiss filled the air. She let it stay. 'We said goodbye to Emily Thornton in spring. She went out singing. Left her tambourine behind – Albert mounted it on the wall above the bar. We added a string of bells to it. Krissy calls it the 'laugh chime.' Eloise kissed someone. I didn't ask who. She glowed like wet stone in moonlight for days. Albert almost sold the old Les Paul he'd picked up at an estate sale, then restrung it instead. "I just wanted to see if it still had fight," he said. It did. He played it that night. Only for me.' Stella closed the journal. Laid it gently atop the others, then stood and walked to the chalkboard wall. She traced her finger through the dust, rewriting one of the old lines: 'we built what we kept'.

The sky outside was shifting, deepening into indigo and periwinkle. The sea was silver-glass now, soft ripples catching the last light. Lights blinked on along the shoreline like little constellations, human-shaped and close enough to reach. Behind her, the room breathed around her: Stella picked up her guitar. Not to play, just to feel the neck in her hand. Her thumb found the groove worn into the back – years of fretwork traced in skin and sound. She didn't need to go back downstairs. They didn't need her every moment. That was the whole point. They could sing without her. She stepped to the window. Looked out. Below, a child was climbing onto a barstool, grinning wildly as someone pointed them toward the jukebox. A couple slow-danced on the deck with their shoes off. Someone had lit candles in old jam jars. The Siren was lit from within. And she, Stella, was not its owner, its anchor, or even its star. She was just its rhythm-keeper. She smiled, quiet and full, set the guitar down and turned toward the dusk – the journal at her back, the rush of sea in her chest. The beach had emptied, the way a theatre does after the final note. Only the wind remained – combing through dune grass, lifting hair from the back of Stella's neck like a quiet benediction.

She stepped barefoot into the sand. The night was coming soft. No stars yet, but the horizon had begun its slow fade from lavender to ink. Behind her, The Saltwater Siren flickered like a dream someone had almost forgotten to wake from—gold light through old windows, music like breath held and released, the gentle murmur of lives unfolding. Shells cracked faintly underfoot. The tide was high, and rising still. She walked without rush, each step a deliberate unspooling. Her dress fluttered around her knees, light enough to dance when the breeze turned curious. The beach curved out ahead in silver arcs, waves hushing against the shore like they were telling stories to the sand. A freighter moved along the horizon – just one white light, steady and far. Stella paused to watch it, her eyes tracking its path the way she used to track storms on radar as a girl. She used to wonder where those ships went. What they carried. Who waited at the other end.

Now, she simply let it go. No need to chase its cargo or plot its course. It was enough to see it pass. She turned back to the water. Her shadow stretched beside her – long and low, bending slightly with the ripple of the tide. She smiled faintly at the sight of it, this tall and softened version of herself. The woman she had become not all at once, but like sediment building layer by layer. She'd stood here a year or more ago, clutching a bag of sheet music and a cracked dream. The Siren had been shuttered then, its windows boarded and its insides echoing with the ghosts of what-might-have-beens. Now, it glowed like a heartbeat behind her. And she – Stella – was not quite the same as she had been, nor entirely different. She carried her old selves like nesting dolls, smaller still within her, each one watching quietly through her eyes. Stella bent and picked up a shell, turning it in her hand. Smooth and pink-edged, like a blush that had survived the tide. A whole one. Rare. Her fingers closed around it. A line of melody curled through her mind. Just five notes. Nothing dramatic. Just her own, unprovoked, unrehearsed. She didn't hum it, didn't write it down. Just let it echo. She reached the edge of the surf and let the water touch her toes. It was cold, then warm, then cold again. She closed her eyes: breathed in. The tide pulled away. Breathed out: the tide came back.

In that breath, she thought of Albert. His quiet fixes, his cups of tea, his way of hearing music even when she didn't know she was making it. She thought of Eloise – her tarot cards laid out like constellation maps, her dreamy logic, her soft "mmm"s of agreement when the universe aligned. She thought of Emily's tambourine, of Krissy's booming voice over trivia rounds, of laughter ricocheting off stained wood. She thought of a child spinning barefoot by the jukebox. She thought of that performer – not much younger than she had been – stepping onto The Siren's stage for the first time, hands trembling, voice steadying with each note. Stella had given them a plectrum before they went on. Not because they needed it, but because Stella had once needed it herself and there had been nobody there to give it to her. And she thought, then, that maybe legacy isn't what you leave behind. Maybe it's what sings even after you've stopped.

Stella opened her eyes. The sea had darkened to blue steel. The waves gleamed like breathing silver. The wind moved through her ribs like a songbird settling in. She smiled – not the rare, guarded one she gave the world, but the small, secret one she reserved for the moments when she felt fully part of something, not beside it. She took one last step toward the water, letting the sea rush up around her ankles. And then she spoke, not aloud, but clear in her mind, shaped like language, shaped like truth: the tide rose and I rose with it.

Stella felt the cold seep up from beneath, a pleasant shock that sharpened her senses. She didn't turn around immediately, just stood there for a moment, letting the rhythm of the waves wash over her – a constant pulse, ancient and knowing. It wasn't a feeling of completion, not exactly. More like alignment. Like she was finally in tune with the place, not as its keeper or its star, but simply as one of its notes. "You're late," a voice said, low and amused. She turned to see Albert standing at the edge of the sand, his silhouette framed by the last sliver of fading light. He was wearing his usual uniform: faded flannel, well-worn boots, and a smudge of something on his cheek. A mug warmed his hands.

"The tide had other plans," Stella replied, smiling.

He nodded, taking in the scene – the retreating waves, the darkening sky, her stillness. "Always with the tides." He took off his jacket and draped it over a smooth piece of driftwood. "I was just checking on a new part for the old jukebox. Found a bit of dissonance."

"Did you fix it?"

"Of course," he said dryly. "It's a jukebox, not a Stradivarius." He paused, then added quietly, "You seem centred tonight."

Stella considered this. "I think I finally realized there isn't much to centre. Just to listen."

He nodded again, taking a sip of his tea. "That's the trick, isn't it? Listening for what wants to be heard." He gestured toward her journal, still clutched in her hand. "You were writing about echoes."

"They keep coming back, as echoes have a tendency to," Stella said. "Not just memories, but feelings. Like ripples in a pond. You throw a stone, and they spread out, changing shape as they go."

"And sometimes," Albert said, his voice dropping even lower, "they come back stronger than the original."

Stella looked at Albert then, really looked at him, noticing the lines around his eyes, deepened by years of light and shadow. "Do you ever think about where we'd be if we hadn't fixed up The Saltwater Siren?" He didn't answer immediately. He simply stared out to sea for a long moment. "We'd probably still be stuck in the same dusty little town, drinking lukewarm coffee and listening to the rain at The Chiron Cafe."

"Or maybe," Stella said softly, "we'd have been lost already."

He turned then, a small smile playing on his lips. "Maybe we just needed a good dose of salt and moonlight to find our way back to ourselves."

A figure emerged from the shadows – Eloise, her shawl pulled tighter around her, a faint glow emanating from her like she carried a tiny lantern within. "The moon is calling for tarot," she announced, her voice a little raspy. "It wants to know if we'll all be here tomorrow night."

"I suspect we will," Stella said. "We have a quota of spilled drinks to meet, after all."

Eloise nodded sagely. "And a teenager who insists on knowing whether they're destined for a life of travel or of settled domestic bliss." It was these small moments that made The Siren, and Ashcliffe-on-Sea itself, feel like home. "I've been thinking," Stella said to Albert and Eloise, "about this whole 'legacy' thing. People keep asking me if I'm building something lasting."

"You are," Albert said firmly. "You've built a community. A place where people feel seen and heard."

"But is that enough?" she asked. "Will they still be here when I'm gone? Will the music still play?" He put his hand on hers, his touch grounding. "They'll remember you, Stella. And as long as someone remembers, the music keeps playing." He paused. "And besides," he added with a twinkle in his eye, "who else is going to mediate when Krissy, Tom, and Rita start arguing about maritime history?" Stella laughed, and that sound – a little rusty at first, then gaining strength – seemed to fill the space around them.

Later, as she sat at her desk writing in her journal, a shadow fell across it. She looked up to see the young guitarist from earlier standing in the doorway – their face illuminated by the soft light. They held out her plectrum. "Thank you again," they said quietly. "It helped." Stella took the plectrum, turning it over in her fingers. It felt familiar, like an old friend. "Break their hearts a little," she murmured. "That's how you know you've played it right." They smiled – a shy, grateful smile. "I hope so," they said. "I really do." As they stepped back into the night, Stella noticed something – a tiny sprig of lavender tucked behind their ear. She hadn't seen it before, but with it a memory surfaced – sharp and vivid. The day she'd found them busking on the boardwalk, playing a melancholic tune on an old acoustic guitar. They had looked up at her then, eyes full of quiet longing. "You look like you carry a storm inside you," she'd said. "Don't let it drown out the sunlight." She'd known from that first encounter that the music they were playing was made to be shared, and that The Saltwater Siren was the perfect backdrop for it to flourish.

A few moments later, Eloise shuffled over to her desk, carrying a tarot deck wrapped in velvet. "I sense something shifting," she said. "A connection?" She dealt three cards without looking down. The Tower. The Moon. The Sun. "It's about letting go," Eloise said, her gaze fixed on the cards. "But not of everything. Just of what holds you back." She paused. "And someone is waiting for you to recognize them." As she spoke, a faint scent of lavender filled the air. Stella looked up from her desk. Standing by the bar was the young guitarist – and beside them, a woman with purple ribbons in her hair, grinning mischievously at the jukebox. The music shifted subtly, as if acknowledging the new arrival.

Eloise said, smiling knowingly. "A little lost. A little hopeful. And carrying a secret like it's a favourite coat... I wonder who that reminds me of?" Stella gave Eloise a long, warm look as a familiar blush settled across her cheeks. Eloise chuckled.

Downstairs, Albert was wrestling with a recalcitrant speaker. "I think I found the problem," he announced, holding up a tangled mess of wires. "It's been singing out of tune." He grinned and gave her a quick kiss on the cheek. "Just like you." Stella watched him work, feeling a sense of contentment settle over her – not happiness, exactly, but something deeper, more enduring. It was the feeling of knowing that even when the music faded or the lights dimmed, everything would always return to its rhythm. As she closed her journal that night, she noticed a new entry in her reflection - a single word scrawled beneath: 'forward.'

Outside, the first stars began to appear. The sea was dark and vast, but it held a sense of promise – like an invitation to keep exploring, to keep listening, to keep singing along. Stella walked over to the window and opened it wide. The scent of salt and lavender drifted in, mingling with the sounds of The Saltwater Siren – laughter, music, conversation. Community. Stella took a deep breath and smiled. "Again," she whispered, her voice barely audible above the waves. "Again." And as she did, she realized that building a legacy wasn't about creating something permanent. It was about creating echoes – ripples of connection that would continue to resonate long after she was gone. The echoes of laughter and music, of love and loss, of stories shared and secrets kept, these were the things that caught up on the shoreline, just like stardust in the tides. The tide continued to rise, pulling at the sand, carrying away the old and bringing in the new. And as it did, Stella knew that The Saltwater Siren – and everything it represented – would continue to live on, not because of her, but because she had let it go. And that, she realized, was more than enough.

The Siren's Lament

The sea she sheds another tear,
    for your return, my lover dear.
        Nine months have passed and now the squall
of reddened face and lungs scream full.
Come back to me, my love, my heart!
Echoes in the thunder start
as I pace long and hard the floor
your footsteps never reach my door.
As if, my love, you've longed to part...
now cracks surround this siren's heart.
The storm she hurls her voice at me,
she carries words across the sea.
She tells me of your scuppered boat,
how no more will your laughter float.
Come back to me, my love, my heart!
Echoes in the thunder start
as I pace long and hard the floor
your footsteps never reach my door.
As if, my love, you've longed to part...
now lightning strikes this siren's heart.
The sea remembers all she sees,
a lover's promise on the breeze,
a forlorn cry as all turns dim,
another lost one, dwindling.
Come back to me, my love, my heart!
Echoes in the thunder start
as I pace long and hard the floor
your footsteps never reach my door.
As if, my love, you've longed to part...
now thunder beats for this siren's heart.

Rise Above The Siren's Snare!

Storm's comin' fast to shore, listen out!
Hear her singin' round about!
Ashcliffe's song will fill the air,
and rise above the Siren's snare!
The wind she howls a mighty sound,
as waves are cresting all around!
But fear ye not, nor dread the sight,
just harry strong past Ashcliffe's plight!
Storm's comin' fast to shore, listen out!
Hear her singin' round about!
Ashcliffe's song will fill the air,
and rise above the Siren's snare!
She calls them back from deep below,
the sailors lost long ago.
A siren's kiss and then they're gone,
and Ashcliffe's thunder's rollin' on!
Storm's comin' fast to shore, listen out!
Hear her singin' round about!
Ashcliffe's song will fill the air,
and rise above the Siren's snare!
Ashcliffe's Siren, Ashcliffe's Song
Ashcliffe's siren, Ashcliffe's song,
listen well and listen long:
she calls to you, she calls to me,
"Come to me now and set him free!"
Nine months beyond his shallow death
his baby sleeps with whispered breath.
Still, siren calls and calls in vain,
"Come to me now, come back again!"
Ashcliffe's siren, Ashcliffe's song,
listen well and listen long:
she calls to you, she calls to me,
"Come to me now and set him free!"

Kiln Cold

Y ou touched the edges, never deep
   Mapped my skin but not my heat
     Spoke in fires, lit with pride
But never saw what burned inside
   You called my chords a cradle song
Too smooth, too safe, too sweet, too wrong
But lullabies can turn to knives
When sung beneath electric skies

You chased the flame, but feared the slow
The steady pulse, the undertow
Now every note's a bitter gloss
A kiln-cold silence – everything lost

You wanted war inside a frame
Mistook restraint for lack of flame
But there's a freeze that burns the same
A hush so loud it haunts your name
   You wrote the script, then shut the play
Declared me dull, then walked away
But silence has its own decay
And now it's yours to hold – okay?

You lit the fuse, but missed the melt
Dismissed the world I slowly felt
Now every note's a bitter gloss
A kiln-cold silence – everything lost

Stardust in the Tides

I came with hands too tired to hold
The fire I once called mine
   Found echoes in a salt-worn hall
And chords beneath the brine
   The walls remember lullabies
That never found an end
But storms that sing don't break a thing –
They shape the way we mend
   And we were
Stardust in the tides
Wreckage turned to light
You, the moon I circled 'round
You, the spark that caught the sound
In silence we reside –
Stardust in the tides
   You held the wire, you read the stars
You both saw who I'd been
One with quiet, steady hands
One with fire on the wind
   I wasn't built for staying still
But you let me belong
A home not made of roots or walls –
But harmony and song
   'Cause we are
Stardust in the tides
Wreckage turned to light
You, the moon I circled 'round
You, the spark that caught the sound
And we, the truth we hide –
Stardust in the tides
   Not every fire burns to ash
Not every wound must scar
Some storms just shift the shoreline
To show us where we are
   So call me from the water's edge
I'll answer with my song

Not perfect, but still singing
And finally, I belong
    We are
Stardust in the tides
Falling, then we rise
You, the hands I didn't seek
But found me when I couldn't speak
A love that never hides –
Stardust in the tides